Friends Verity, Jane, Prue, Melissa and Lucy are unconventional ladies with scandalous yearnings and big ambitions—to be writers, painters, musicians—but the only safe sanctuary to exercise their talents is in one of their family's turrets!

They have no wish to conform and be drawn into society's marriage mart, unless they can find gentlemen who value and cherish them for who they truly are...and *not* the size of their dowries!

Read Verity's story in
Least Likely to Marry a Duke

Jane's tale in
The Earl's Marriage Bargain

Prue's journey in
A Marquis in Want of a Wife

Lucy's romance in
The Earl's Reluctant Proposal

and

Melissa's happy ending in
A Proposal to Risk Their Friendship

All available now!

Author Note

I never thought that when I met Verity Wingate sitting at the bottom of an archaeological excavation, face-to-face with a very polite and very angry duke, that the encounter would lead to a five-book series. But Verity's friends, Liberated Ladies all in their own ways, demanded to tell their stories, and this is the fifth and final episode.

I hope you enjoy following their sometimes-rocky paths to true love as much as I enjoyed writing them.

LOUISE ALLEN

—

A Proposal to Risk Their Friendship

HARLEQUIN
HISTORICAL

HARLEQUIN®
HISTORICAL™

ISBN-13: 978-1-335-50624-5

A Proposal to Risk Their Friendship

Copyright © 2021 by Melanie Hilton

This edition published by arrangement with Harlequin Books S.A.

For questions and comments about the quality of this book,
please contact us at CustomerService@Harlequin.com.

Harlequin Enterprises ULC
22 Adelaide St. West, 40th Floor
Toronto, Ontario M5H 4E3, Canada
www.Harlequin.com

Printed in U.S.A.

Louise Allen has been immersing herself in history for as long as she can remember, finding that landscapes and places evoke powerful images of the past. Venice, Burgundy and the Greek islands are favorites. Louise lives on the Norfolk coast and spends her spare time gardening, researching family history or traveling. Please visit Louise's website, www.louiseallenregency. com, her blog, www.janeaustenslondon.com, or find her on Twitter @louiseregency and on Facebook.

Books by Louise Allen

Harlequin Historical

Marrying His Cinderella Countess
The Earl's Practical Marriage
A Lady in Need of an Heir
Convenient Christmas Brides
"The Viscount's Yuletide Betrothal"
Contracted as His Countess

Liberated Ladies

Least Likely to Marry a Duke
The Earl's Marriage Bargain
A Marquis in Want of a Wife
The Earl's Reluctant Proposal
A Proposal to Risk Their Friendship

Lords of Disgrace

His Housekeeper's Christmas Wish
His Christmas Countess
The Many Sins of Cris de Feaux
The Unexpected Marriage of Gabriel Stone

Visit the Author Profile page
at Harlequin.com for more titles.

To all my readers, and my fellow authors, who have kept up my spirits during a tough year for all of us—thank you!

Chapter One

London—April 10th, 1816

Lord Henry Cary leant on the balustrade above the lower terrace of Lady Pernell's garden and contemplated the strange whims of London's society hostesses. Not content with holding one of the first balls of the Season, she had decided to throw open the doors on to the gardens, despite a fall of snow that was still lying on the hills around Highgate.

He had recently returned from Vienna, so was not finding the temperature particularly chilly, but then, he was not one of the female guests, clad in flimsy silks and muslins. Very few people were braving the night air, despite braziers set out on the terrace and lanterns dotted all along the pathways to make a relatively modest garden resemble Vauxhall en fête.

But some guests were out and he watched the path five feet below him, feigning a casual interest.

'I'm freezing. You coming in, old chap?' Reggie

Pomfret sent the glowing end of his cigarillo arching across the path and into the shrubbery beyond.

'In a moment. I will see you inside, no doubt.'

And here came his target, strolling towards him on the lower level, as Reggie walked away briskly on the upper. Graf Klaus von Arten was deep in conversation with one of the attachés from the French embassy. Pierre Laverne, if he was not mistaken. How very, very interesting.

It might be that Graf Klaus was exactly what he said he was. Certainly, according to *Almanach de Gotha*, a Thuringian nobleman with that title did exist. But in the absence of any Thuringians to confirm it, who could tell? The man had drifted around at the Congress, amiably present at every social occasion and without any apparent reason for being there.

He had attracted the vague interest of Henry's superiors as an unsolved puzzle, but when he appeared in England that attention sharpened. The Congress was over, the final treaties signed. France, its colonies, client kingdoms and possessions had been organised and distributed in the aftermath of the collapse of Napoleon's empire—and now here was the amiable Count in intimate discussion with a junior French diplomat. It could be nothing, but it might be the first ripple of water over a hidden reef, waiting to hole the freshly constructed structure of treaty and alliance that was holding a new Europe together after years of war.

The Frenchman stopped, bowed abruptly and vanished into the shrubbery that filled the centre of the garden, leaving von Arten to walk on towards the ballroom alone. He slowed, hesitated, and Henry glanced left to see what had attracted his attention. An elegant blond man was strolling along, a young woman on his arm. The Graf speeded up and passed them with a nod, just before they reached Henry's lookout.

Henry almost turned away to follow Reggie, but something about the couple below gave him pause.

'I am cold.' The young woman sounded more than chilled, she sounded thoroughly uncomfortable, her voice a little shrill.

'There is a delightful little summer house just inside the shrubbery,' the man said. 'We can converse in comfort there.'

'But I should not be alone with you. I should go back.' Her voice had an edge of panic now and she pulled back against the very firm grip that the man seemed to have on her arm. 'Ow! You are *hurting* me.'

'Don't be a little goose.' His voice was caressing, teasing, but Henry saw something else in the set of his shoulders, the way he was forcing her towards the darkness of the shrubs.

He put one hand on the balustrade and vaulted over, landing solidly on both feet on the gravel path below.

'What the—?'

As the blond man took a step back, another young woman, tall and dark-haired, emerged from one of the paths through the bushes.

'Oh, there you are, Belinda darling,' she said brightly. 'I thought we had lost you. You must be frozen and the dancing is about to begin again.' She shot Henry a questioning look as she took the other woman's free arm, as though to link it through hers.

'Miss Forrest is with me,' the man said, his smile tight with anger.

'Goodness, that would be silly of her, wouldn't it?' the tall woman said. 'One step into the shrubbery would be *so* bad for dear Belinda's reputation, don't you think, Mr Harlby?'

She gave Miss Forrest's arm a little tug. Harlby stood his ground.

Henry sauntered up, put one arm companionably around the other man's shoulders and beamed at him, the very picture of slightly tipsy amiability. 'Come on, old man, back to the dancing, eh?' His thumb and forefinger closed together at the angle where Harlby's collarbone and shoulder joint met and tightened suddenly.

Harlby gave a gasp of pain and released Miss Forrest. 'You bast—'

The tall woman turned so rapidly they might have choreographed the move. She linked arms with Miss Forrest and set off back towards the ballroom. Her voice, clear and assertive, drifted back. 'Such a good orchestra, don't you think?'

Henry kept his arm where it was and steered Harlby in their wake. 'Got cramp, old man? A stiff brandy will sort you out.' He kept his hand poised, waiting for retaliation, but the other man came meekly enough until half a dozen steps from the glass doors on to the terrace.

Harlby twisted away. 'I'll not forget you, you interfering devil.' He pushed through the door and vanished into the ballroom.

Henry followed. 'I won't forget you either, friend,' he murmured, looking round for Miss Forrest and her rescuer. They were on the far side of the room and the dark woman was talking animatedly to—of all people—the Duke of Aylsham, otherwise known as the Perfect Duke. As Henry watched he smiled at her warmly, bowed to Miss Forrest and led her on to the dance floor.

The rescuer moved along to a group that included two men he didn't recognise and one that he most certainly did—The East End Aristocrat, the Privateer Marquis—otherwise known as the Marquis of Cranford. All three men smiled, glanced to where the Duke was turning Miss Forrest in the midst of a complex country dance, and nodded.

Clever. She was placing the young woman with two powerful men and possibly others. Harlby would think twice before accosting Miss Forrest again. The dark woman had an air of authority and he wondered who she was. The wife of one of the men he did not know? Or Cranford, possibly? He had heard that the scarred Marquis had married recently.

Driven by sheer curiosity, Henry began to move around the edge of the ballroom to intercept her.

There, that should make foolish Miss Forrest secure. Not only would Harlby see that Belinda had friends with influence but, if he tried to spread stories about her wandering off with him, there she was, in full view of everyone, dancing with a duke. Melissa mentally dusted her hands together and set off to look for her friends.

'Ma'am. May I congratulate you on your tactics? I hope the other young lady is not suffering any distress.'

It was the blue-eyed man who had vaulted over the balustrade to help Belinda Forrest. Melissa smiled warmly, instantly inclined to like him. 'No, she will be perfectly all right, I believe. Will would calm any-one's nerves. I must thank you for your help.' It had been rather impressive the way he had acted—athletic, instant and effective.

She studied him frankly. Tall, dark blond with darker brows and lashes, slender but with shoulders that promised strength, and amused blue eyes. Really very decorative and Melissa had an appreciative eye for decorative men.

'Melissa Taverner,' she said, holding out her hand. 'Miss Taverner. So stuffy to have to find someone to introduce us, don't you think?'

'I quite agree—after all, we have already carried out manoeuvres together. Lord Henry Cary at your service, Miss Taverner.'

'You must be the son of the Duke of...of Walton?'

'Son number four,' he admitted, somewhat ruefully.

'Let me guess. Not the army, not the navy. That leaves the church?' He did not look like a clergyman, but it was the most likely occupation for a younger son who wasn't a soldier or sailor and he wore no uniform.

'Goodness, no.' His smile was disarming. 'I would probably bring about another Reformation, if not total theological chaos, if I were to be let loose in a pulpit. No, I am with the diplomatic corps. May I fetch you some refreshments?'

'Thank you, but I am just on my way to join my friends to report on the success of our tactics against Harlby, the slimy little beast.'

'May I call on you? I confess I would be happier if reassured that Harlby does not make a nuisance of himself.'

'Of course. Here, do take one of my new cards.' She found one in her reticule and then, on impulse, she tucked her hand under his elbow and began to walk again. 'Come and meet my friends and be thanked all over again.'

The others were still sitting where she had left them, clustered around a little table in a small alcove. 'Here we are.' She indicated her catch with a wave of her hand. 'Behold my accomplice in the routing of the ghastly Charles. This is Lord Henry Cary who is the fourth son of the Duke of Walton, although I expect you all know that, being so much more exalted than I am. Lord Henry, this is the Duchess of Aylsham, the Marchioness of Cranford, Lady Kendall and Lady Burnham. You can sit there.' She pointed to a free chair between Verity, the Duchess, and Lucy, who was just becoming used to being the Countess of Burnham.

'Your Grace…ladies.' He sat down.

'Lord Henry is a diplomat, as you can tell,' Melissa added, taking her own seat. 'Smooth.'

'Melissa, *honestly*,' Verity chided, sending Lord Henry an apologetic smile.

'Well, he is. He did not even blink when confronted by all of you. And he was positively heroic—jumping down from the top terrace to accost Harlby and then seizing him in some ferociously painful grip when he tried to be unpleasant.'

Lord Henry shrugged. 'The man was making himself obnoxious. You are apparently well aware that he can be a nuisance.'

'Yes,' Lucy said, not looking at Prue. 'He seems to have moved on from seducing young ladies for sport to attempting to find one with money in order to compromise her.'

'In the hope of forcing a marriage, no doubt. Unpleasant.'

'Very. But he will leave Belinda alone now,' Verity said. 'Have you recently returned to London, Lord Henry?'

'Yes, I was in Vienna, at the Congress, and stayed on afterwards as things were winding down. There are always little details to clear up. It is a pleasure to be back in England in time for the start of the Season.' He stood up. 'Delightful to meet you, ladies. I can see my eldest brother and, as I have not encountered him since I arrived in London, I should go and speak with him, if you will excuse me.' He stood up, bowed and made his way through the crowd to where a tall man with very blond hair was just walking off the dance floor.

'Oh, yes, that's Viscount Morfield, the heir,' Verity remarked. 'They are a good-looking family. You have found yourself a very handsome swain, Melissa.'

'Goodness, he's no swain of mine, merely a gallant gentleman. He really was exceedingly effective with the ghastly Charles. You should have heard the little swine yelp and all Lord Henry seemed to do was put his arm around his shoulders. It would have done your heart good, Prue.'

Prudence, now the Marchioness of Cranford, had been seduced by Harlby. She had then escaped disgrace by marrying the widowed Marquis, who needed a mother for his young son. The hastily arranged match had, wonderfully, turned into a romance. Now she darted a look across to where her husband stood talking to his friends. He did not know the identity of her seducer and they all knew that she very much wanted to keep it from him. Nobody wanted the formidable Marquis to have to go into exile for tearing Harlby apart with his bare hands.

'I had hoped he had left London for good,' Prue said with a sigh.

'Anybody with any sense would have been terrified that you had told Ross about him. He must have realised that you haven't, so he feels it is safe to come back,' Jane, the Countess of Kendall, said. 'But he seems to be keeping well clear of you.'

'I suspect he is short of funds. Now he has the whole Season in front of him to find a victim he can force into marriage,' Verity said grimly, 'I find his choice of Belinda Forrest rather worrying, because she is so very wealthy. We are going to have to be on the alert constantly if we are to foil him. It only takes a few minutes and some bad luck and a reputation is ruined.'

Prue grimaced. 'And it will not *be* bad luck because he will *want* to be caught. We need to find him out in a situation where the woman concerned isn't revealed, but what he is becomes general knowledge.'

'Tricky. I have been telling all the mothers and chaperons of my acquaintance to beware of him,' Verity said. 'But there are dozens of likely girls and so many opportunities.'

They sat, sunk in gloom until Melissa signalled to a passing footman. 'We need cheering up. A bottle of champagne and five glasses, if you please.'

'Tell us about your new house,' Prue said, sitting up straight and finding a smile. 'We would all have come to see you yesterday, only Verity couldn't and we all wanted to come together.'

'How is Thomas?' Melissa wasn't particularly interested in babies, but the six-month-old heir to the dukedom was an engaging child.

'He is a very miserable little boy, but much better today than he was yesterday. Nurse says he will be well enough now until the next tooth starts.'

'Come and see me tomorrow, then,' Melissa said. 'You know it is in Half Moon Street, of course. And I told you that Great-Aunt Melly died three months ago and left me a legacy because she was also my godmother? Well, she willed the house to Papa and he had no clear idea of exactly where it was and, of course, being Papa, didn't like to admit it. So, I let him think it was really a very shabby genteel neighbourhood, although respectable, and unlikely to fetch a huge rental.'

She grinned, still amazed at how easy it had been. 'When he had finished huffing and puffing and insisting that *of course* I must not leave home and come and live in London, I pointed out that I would be perfectly safe there if I had a chaperon as companion. And the poor man so hates anyone arguing with him—Mama never does, as you know—that he said yes, just for peace and quiet.'

'He knows that now you have your legacy and you are twenty-four, there was no way he could stop you,' Jane said cynically.

'True.' Melissa couldn't help feeling smug. 'And he knows he has a duty to look after Cousin Almeria after her investments failed, so he didn't raise a murmur about her being my companion. In fact, he thinks it is all his own idea.'

'Something tells me that your Cousin Almeria is either very lazy, or deaf as a post,' said Prue.

'Somewhat preoccupied with her own interests, shall we say,' Melissa said vaguely, her attention on the dance floor. That nice Lord Henry had asked Miss Forrest to dance, which was kind of him. He appeared to be a very good dancer, light on his feet and able to converse at the same time—

'Melissa!'

'What? Sorry, I was just checking that Miss Forrest is all right.'

'We were asking if we could visit before luncheon tomorrow? We will bring some ices and things from Gunter's.'

'That is an excellent idea. And I need advice about redecorating and new furniture. Great-Aunt was a sweetheart, but her taste was firmly in the seventeen nineties.'

Next day the ices and macarons from Gunter's provided an indulgent end to a lengthy luncheon. It was eaten amid a pile of fabric patterns, two furniture warehouse catalogues, the latest copies of the most fashionable magazines and a small snowdrift of notes.

Lucy sprawled on the sofa, licking her fingers in a thoroughly unladylike manner. 'There are masses of ideas, but can you afford it all?'

'I shouldn't think so for a minute,' Melissa said, looking round with satisfaction at her friends at ease in her very own drawing room. 'But I will work through the house in stages. Paint will perform wonders, there is a lot of fabric I may be able to reuse and I can send the worst of the furniture to the auction rooms. It will make space and there might be enough money from that for some new pieces.'

'I really must go home. Look at the time—almost three.' Verity began to look around for her belongings and the others, reluctantly, sat up straighter.

There was a knock at the front door and the sound of Gertrude, Melissa's formidable new maid, marching down the hall.

'Who can that be?' Lucy wondered vaguely. 'Have you left any cards? It is the right time for callers, I suppose.'

'Lord Henry Cary, Miss Taverner.'

Melissa sat bolt upright. 'Good grief. I mean, show him in, Gertrude, and fetch tea, if you please.' She exchanged a look of exaggerated speculation with the others and stood up. 'Lord Henry, good afternoon.'

'Good afternoon, Miss Taverner. I ventured to hope you were receiving.'

'Do take a seat. Tea will be here shortly.' They had eaten all the macarons unfortunately. 'You know my friends, of course.'

'Your Grace…ladies.' He sat in the nearest chair and crossed long legs in elegant biscuit-coloured pantaloons. 'I called to enquire whether there were any…repercussions following last night's incident.'

'No, nothing at all. But I wouldn't expect it,' Melissa said. 'Harlby seems to work by sliding around, not by stirring up a fuss. We have probably put him off Miss

Forrest for good. Ah, the tea. Just put the tray there, Gertrude, thank you.'

'Not for me, dear. I was just going.' Verity stood up and he rose again. 'Pray forgive me, Lord Henry, but I have left my young son too long already.'

'I will walk with you.' Jane was on her feet, too.

'I must be away as well.' Lucy managed a becoming blush. 'I believe Max will be home by now.'

'Not long married,' Melissa heard Prue murmur to Lord Henry as the three of them sat down again. 'You know, I did intend to go to Wilding and Kent for some embroidery wools. I had quite forgotten.' She bounced up again. 'You must excuse me, too, Lord Henry. Melissa, should I let Miss Staines know you have a visitor?'

Melissa sighed. They were all, curse them, tactfully removing themselves because Lord Henry was a gentleman and they thought she would wish to be alone with him. Five minutes' contact with Cousin Almeria must have convinced Prue that she was a completely ineffectual chaperon and worth summoning just for the look of it. 'If you would be so kind,' she said between gritted teeth.

'Goodbye, Lord Henry. Lovely luncheon, Melissa dear.'

Lord Henry stayed on his feet as she went out, leaving the door open behind her. 'I should go.'

Yes, he should. Single young ladies did not entertain gentlemen alone for one moment and that gave her a perfect excuse for sending him on his way and settling down to some work.

She found herself smiling. 'No need, my companion will be down in a moment.'

Chapter Two

Goodness knew why, but Melissa felt certain that the company of this virtual stranger would be more entertaining than working on the first chapter of her new novel and more worthwhile than finishing the report on last night's ball for the *Morning Post*.

He still had his hand on the doorknob when Cousin Almeria wandered in, her spectacles pushed back into her bundled-up hair, a large book in her hands. She blinked at him. 'Lady Cranford said there was a gentleman,' she said vaguely.

'Cousin Almeria, Lord Henry Cary has called. We were just having tea. Lord Henry, Miss Staines.'

'Delighted, I'm sure,' Almeria said. She poured herself a cup of Bohea, drifted over to the table in the window, sat and began to read.

Lord Henry might be an experienced diplomat, but clearly Almeria was outside his experience. He shot her a dubious glance and took his seat again.

'It is quite all right to converse,' Melissa assured him. 'We will not disturb her. My cousin is an expert on moths and she has just received that volume on the subject from a German professor.'

They sat, stirring their tea, the only sound the pages rustling as they were turned and the clink of silver against porcelain.

Why has he called? And why did he not take the opportunity to leave when the others did?

Why did I not leave when I had every reason to? Miss Taverner is clearly not concerned about Harlby. Say something, numbskull.

'Moths? How interesting.'

And what a banal comment, Henry! What is the matter with you?

'Yes,' Miss Taverner said brightly. 'I know nothing about it, but I gather my cousin is about to embark on a study of the moths of Westminster and our little garden will be full of moth traps every night. I expect a large bill for candles.'

'You have lived in London long?'

'One week. I have visited before, naturally. This house belongs to my father, who has only just inherited it, and it really cannot be in a better position for me.'

'Because of the moths?'

'The publishers. Or rather, one publisher: Mr Murray in Albemarle Street. I write, you see, and have every intention of impressing the worth of my new novel upon Mr Murray in person.'

'You are published?' Miss Taverner hardly looked old enough—not twenty-five yet, surely?—to be embarking on a career and living virtually alone in London.

'No serious novels as yet.'

Now, why is she looking positively shifty?

'I have a number of small pieces in the various journals—*Ackermann's Repository*, *La Belle Assemblée* and so on. And I now have a commission from the *Morning Post* to write accounts of various society events—who attended, the ladies' ensembles, that kind of thing.' She smiled. 'That is anonymous, naturally.'

Henry found himself smiling back. 'Naturally. The newspaper offices are all in the City, are they not? Surely you are not contemplating visiting those?'

'Certainly. A veil, a stout umbrella and a reliable hackney carriage driver are all that is needed, I am sure.'

It was simply not done for ladies to venture into the City, unless on their way to see their lawyer or banker, and then only when accompanied by a male relative. But Miss Taverner had stood her ground last night...

'What would you have done if I had not been there and Harlby had brushed you off?' he asked abruptly.

'Why, stayed with them, of course. He could hardly get up to anything, even in the depths of a shrubbery, with one determined spinster sticking to him like a burr and talking at the top of her voice. Either he would have given up and retreated or someone would come and then I would have accused him of accosting us and making lewd suggestions. Or worse.'

She would have done, too.

Henry found he was smiling again at the thought. 'Let me guess: the two of you would be found on the point of swooning, hardly able to articulate the awful fact that Harlby had leapt out of a bush with his falls unbuttoned. If it were not for the distress to Miss Forrest, I could almost wish that had occurred.'

'I know, so do I. It would have made him look both ridiculous and unsavoury.'

'I must apologise for interfering, it seems.'

'It was with the best of intentions and you had no way of knowing that I had the situation under control,' Miss Taverner said magnanimously.

Henry was not quite so certain about that. Who else was going to be wandering about in a chilly shrubbery ready to rush to their aid? Even so, he was enjoying the picture.

'You have family in London?' he asked.

'No. My parents live in Dorset. You are wondering at my living here? I came into an inheritance which enables me to be independent and to follow my ambition to write. My parents do not approve, but they know a lost cause when they encounter one.' She smiled and he found himself smiling back. 'Expecting me to be a respectable young lady sitting meekly at home playing the harp until a suitable suitor happens along is, most definitely, a lost cause.'

'Ridiculous!'

They both turned to look at the companion who was glaring not, as Henry expected, at Miss Taverner, but at her book. 'He is completely mistaken on the food plants of the caterpillar of this species,' she muttered and turned a page.

Henry cleared his throat. 'Er…quite.' Miss Taverner was a puzzle. She was clearly a lady, her friends were married to members of the aristocracy, her home was in a highly respectable area of London and yet here she was, ineffectually chaperoned, talking lightly about being a spinster, not turning a hair at the prospect of indecent exposure and plotting the discomfiture of a rake. He had absolutely no idea what to make of her, other than that she made him want to laugh out loud.

Young gentlemen in the diplomatic service were not encouraged to laugh out loud, he reminded himself. The clock chimed.

'I should go. Thank you for the tea, Miss Taverner. Miss Staines, delighted to make your acquaintance.'

Instead of ringing for the maid, Miss Taverner rose, too, and showed him to the door, then, when they were in the hall, handed him his hat and cane. 'Thank you for calling, Lord Henry. You are my first visitor, other than my friends. Please call again.'

He should not commit himself to that, so he merely remarked, 'I wish you joy of your new home.'

She opened the door and he stepped out into Half Moon Street, feeling rather pleasurably unsettled. The Congress had been invigorating, the female company sophisticated and amusing but, somehow, not quite as intriguing as the self-assured Miss Taverner.

Henry took half a dozen steps down the street, then stopped and, without giving himself time to think about it, turned around and went back.

Miss Taverner opened the door to him. 'Lord Henry? Have you forgotten something?'

'Only to ask if you ever walk in the Park of a morning and, if you do, whether you would welcome company occasionally.'

'I intend to—after all, I have no excuse for not taking exercise when Green Park is literally at the end of the street. And, yes, I would not be averse to company. But I should warn you, I am an early riser. If you are in the Park before breakfast, then we may meet.'

Melissa watched as the elegant figure strolled off towards Piccadilly and the Park beyond, then closed the door and went back into the drawing room.

Almeria looked up from her book. 'Who was that?'

'Lord Henry returning to ask if I ever walked in the Park in the morning.'

'Indeed. An interesting young man, I thought.'

'You were not as engrossed in the book as it appeared.' Melissa told herself that perhaps she had underestimated her cousin.

'I have very selective hearing and I need to listen to enough to be certain that he is going to behave himself. If I appear to be totally engrossed, it might encourage inappropriate behaviour and that is best recognised early, don't you think?' Almeria removed her spectacles from the end of her nose and smiled wryly. 'After all, I am enjoying most comfortable accommodation, well situated in London for the libraries and lectures, and I should at least attempt to fulfil the role for which I am receiving these benefits.'

'Lord Henry is not courting me,' Melissa said. 'I am certain of that.' It was not as though she had any experience of being courted. She had no patience with flirtation and her down-to-earth manner seemed to keep gentlemen at a distance, which was helpful.

'Perhaps he wishes to be friends,' her cousin suggested. 'I have a number of gentlemen friends who share my entomological interests.'

'Have any of them proposed marriage?' Melissa asked, aware she was being inquisitive. Almeria was in her mid-forties and, Melissa supposed, would be considered plain by most people. But her figure was good, if sturdy, her dark hair glossy despite its sprinkling of grey and her smile was charming. But of course, she was an intelligent, educated woman with scientific interests, so would be dismissed as a bluestocking spinster.

'Occasionally one of the widowers has a notion that his life would be more comfortable with a wife and proposes,' her cousin said. 'But they soon recover their senses when I point out that a good housekeeper would be less expensive in the long run.'

Almeria went back to her book and Melissa curled up on the sofa with her notebook. *Do I want a male friend? What for?* Female friends were for confiding in, for sharing experiences and amusements. For comfort and for celebration. They would understand all the problems, the worries, the triumphs, of another woman.

But men were different. Melissa wrinkled her nose at such a self-evident conclusion. Yet, she mused, Verity, Jane, Lucy and Prue appeared to be friends with their husbands, which was certainly not the case with her parents, or with most of the other young ladies she knew who were married.

Interests in common, concern for each other, a shared sense of humour, a basic liking—perhaps that was what it took. Presumably, if one were not married to one's friend, there was the matter of physical attraction to be taken into consideration, but if you did not desire one another and the whole, tiresome, matter of marriage was set aside then, yes, it might be possible to have a male

friend. Lord Henry would certainly provide a different
outlook on matters. She would walk in the Park tomorrow morning and see what happened.

Henry took the stairs two at a time up to the apartment in Ryder Street he shared with his friend and col-
league James Herbert. It was a large lodging over two
floors and they both had their own small sitting rooms,
but they normally gravitated to the big, shabby, front
room overlooking the street on the first floor.

James was, as usual, surrounded by a litter of paper
slips and several foreign dictionaries. There was a blackboard covered in symbols propped up against the wall.

'A new code?' Henry asked. James was a cryptog-
rapher and tended to live in a world of complex calculations that Henry did not even pretend to understand.
He could code and decode messages provided he had
the key, but that was as far as his skills went.

'A variation, I think.' James looked up and a pencil
slipped out of his hair and landed on the page in front
of him. 'And in Russian, just to add to the joy. You have
been down to the office?'

That was in Whitehall, a short walk away. Henry
nodded. 'They haven't decided where to send me next.
Philps is muttering about Constantinople. It would be
just like him to choose a country where I don't speak
the language. He's got a bee in his bonnet about the
Russian intentions towards the Ottoman Empire and
the security of Indian frontiers now the Czar doesn't
have to worry about the French any longer.'

'So, you are a man of leisure at the moment and not
inclined to be learning Turkish,' James said vaguely.

'Aha!' He jumped up, scribbled something on the blackboard and sat down again to stare at it.

'I have to keep an eye on our friend Klaus von Arten. The powers that be cannot make up their minds whether he is friend, foe or just a person of no account who enjoys parties. But I did see him deep in conversation with someone from the French embassy last night which made Philps's nose twitch when I reported it. My orders are to work out what he is up to, if anything.'

'Parties every night for you, then,' James said.

'Mmm. Probably,' Henry said vaguely. He flopped down into one of the two battered old armchairs by the empty fireplace and contemplated the next few days.

'What?' James tossed aside his pencil. 'I cannot concentrate, you are thinking so noisily.'

'Met someone last night. Unusual. I can't quite work her out.'

'A woman? Tell me more. Exciting? Beautiful? Rich? Potentially a mistress or a wife? Has she any rich, beautiful friends?'

'Interesting, intelligent, handsome rather than beautiful. Unconventional. A lady. Her friends are all married. And neither a mistress nor a wife, I suspect. More of a puzzle.'

'Tell me more.'

'I will, when I have worked it out.'

Had she really expected to see him at seven in the morning? Melissa was not sure, but Lord Henry was no phantom, although he looked dark and mysterious with the last faint tendrils of mist hanging about him.

He stood, one shoulder propped against a tree, near the gate opposite Clarges Street.

He straightened as he saw her and his hat was in his hand by the time she reached him, at which point she realised why he appeared so black and white—he was wearing evening dress.

'My lord, have you been up all night?' He was heavy-eyed, but she thought that perhaps they did not know each other well enough yet for that observation to be well received.

'I have.' He replaced his hat, disguising a yawn as he did so. 'One musicale, two balls, a diplomatic reception at the French embassy, a game of cards at White's and another at some ghastly hell in Pickering Place.'

They began to stroll diagonally towards The Queen's House, although neither had named a destination.

Lord Henry frowned. 'Not necessarily in that order, now I think about it. There was supper somewhere as well.'

'Are you drunk, my lord?'

He made a rocking gesture with his right hand. 'So-so... Perfectly sober enough to escort a lady.'

'Doubtless the exercise and fresh air will do you good,' Melissa said, attempting to sound reproving. The severe black and white suited him. Even the shadow of a morning beard and the tired blue eyes added a certain louche glamour to his appearance.

She wondered if she could use him as a model for the charming ne'er-do-well in the serious novel she was planning, although it would be tempting to make him the dashing villain in something more lurid for the Minerva Press. They had already published two of her

Gothic tales, but now that Mr Newman had taken over from the late William Lane she suspected he was trying to move away from the sensational style. It was difficult to know what to do for the best.

Meanwhile she was being cautious about who she told about her sensation novels for fear they would not take her ambitions seriously. She was conscious of being evasive with Lord Henry when she had told him about her writing but, hopefully, he would never need to know.

'You are a soothing companion at this hour of the day,' Lord Henry remarked and, startled, Melissa realised they were almost halfway across the park.

'Is that a polite reproof for my silence, Lord Henry?'

'It is a genuine expression of gratitude,' he said. 'Look, there is a bench. Shall we sit a while?'

'If you like.' Melissa sat, taking the opportunity to look him full in the face as she did so. 'You seem a trifle more awake now, my lord.'

'Henry,' he said as they sat.

'And I suppose that means I should allow you to call me Melissa?'

'May I?' He leaned back and closed his eyes. 'I had the thought yesterday that we might be friends.'

'Did you indeed? Strangely, so did I.'

'It must be the case, don't you think, as I have dared to close my eyes in your presence and you have not struck me with that very handsome umbrella for my impertinence?'

'We hardly know each other.'

'Friends at first sight.' He opened slightly bloodshot blue eyes and smiled at her.

'They do say there is such a thing as love at first

sight,' she said dubiously, 'but I do not know about friendship.'

'I always know immediately whether I am comfortable with a person, don't you?'

'I know whether I trust them and, yes, whether I am comfortable with them. But it is not easy for a man and a woman to be friends, I suspect.'

'Possibly because of the expectations of others,' Henry suggested. 'I realise I might give your suitors the wrong impression—I shall have to be discreet and not drive them away.'

'The sight of you creeping about being discreet would be enough to raise the direst suspicions about our relationship,' Melissa protested and laughed when he did. 'Besides, I have no suitors and do not want any. I intend to remain unmarried.'

'Why?' Henry sat up straighter, frowned, then took off his hat as though that would make it easier to study her.

'Why are *you* not married?' she countered. 'You are older than I am.' Twenty-seven or eight, she would guess, to her twenty-four.

'I have no title or estates to inherit, so producing an heir is not an issue. I am a fourth son so, unless one assumes a major disaster, I am never going to inherit. My position requires me to travel a great deal,' Henry recited. He had closed his eyes again.

Melissa gave him a gentle poke in the ribs. 'Wake up and we will walk some more.'

When he had got to his feet she linked her arm through his as they strolled. It felt surprisingly comfortable and right. 'I thought ambassadors were expected to be married.'

Henry snorted. 'I am far from that rank.'

'At the moment.'

'At the moment I am more use flirting in a respectable manner with other people's wives and gathering what information I can.'

'Respectable? Really? Are there no fatally glamorous female spies that you are expected to seduce?'

Chapter Three

Melissa's question produced another snort from Henry. 'Fatally attractive female spies? That is the fantasy of all young men in the diplomatic corps. I haven't met one yet. Now, tell me why you intend to remain unwed.'

'Women are oppressed,' Melissa said seriously. 'We are subject to our fathers and then our husbands, we have no control of our own property or our actions. The only escape is by not marrying or, if one has to, becoming a widow, which does seem rather drastic.'

Henry grinned. 'Exceptionally drastic. Are the happy marriages of your friends not an encouragement? They appear to be four very contented ladies.'

'They are four exceptionally lucky ones. It is such a risk and, even when a man turns out not to be a bully or to live a dissolute life, or be a gambler, there is the risk they will be resentful of their wives' intelligence and achievements. I love my father and mother dearly, but Papa is an absolute domestic tyrant and Mama, who I would swear is by far the more intelligent, agrees with everything he says. Her constant motto is *Your father knows best*. And that is the case even when it is patently clear he does not!'

'And yet here you are, living independently in London.'

'I baffle Papa. I refuse to do as he says and, in the end, he just gave up the argument to secure some peace. If I am out of sight, he can pretend he is an indulgent father and this is all with his full agreement, instead of a merciful relief from the brangling. If our neighbours and friends enquire about me, he can say that I am in London under the wing of my very exalted friends.'

She made herself smile as she said it because keeping a smile on your lips made the words sound light and cheerful. Of *course* she should not pine for parental approval: if she had been a son she would be out in the world already, earning her living, being independent. Being a source of pride.

Her father's baffled cry of 'I don't understand the girl! It is not as though she is plain. She could catch a husband easily enough' echoed in her memory, stiffening her resolve. She had value beyond being a wife, she told herself yet again. Verity, Jane, Prue and Lucy had had the miraculous good fortune of finding men who fell in love with them regardless of their minds, their intellects and their talents, but she was not going to sit around waiting for the same miracle to occur for her. She had read Mary Wollstonecraft's book and this was the nineteenth century, the world was changing, women's lives were going to change with it and she was determined to do her best to help achieve that.

'Difficult,' Henry remarked.

There was nothing much to be said to that and it

was time to change the subject. 'The Duke, your father, must be proud of you being selected as part of our delegation at the Congress.' Henry was relaxed and confident and she suspected that amiable manner held a very sharp brain.

He shrugged. 'I am the fourth son. When my father encounters me, I can see him working out which one I am. I'm not Morfield—he is the heir, so the old man sees him every day. I'm not George, because then I'd be in uniform, and the same goes for Ernest, which means I must be… *"Ah, yes. Henry. Been abroad, have you, my boy?"*' His voice deepened into gruff bonhomie. *'"Excellent, excellent. Where was it now? Lisbon?"'*

'Oh.' How…flattering. At least her parents knew who she was. 'What about your mother?'

'In Paris.' He pitched his voice higher. *'"Thank God, darling. Decent modistes at last! However did we manage while That Man was Emperor?"'* Melissa felt him shrug. 'I suspect a dashing *comte* closer to my age is entertaining her. She usually manages to find one.'

'And your brothers George and Ernest are both in the army?'

'George is a cavalry colonel—very dashing fellow, all scarlet and gold and a big sabre. Ernest is a captain in the navy. He's commanding a frigate on the West Indies station. Both of them are sulking because we're at peace now and they are hoping for a nice war again with prospects for promotion.'

He grimaced. 'I may be maligning them, to be fair. Morfield—that's Frederick—is a good solid type. He strides about the ancestral acres with a shotgun under his arm, says profound things about forestry and sheep and doesn't trouble his brain too much about anything else.'

Henry made it sound amusing, but Melissa recognised someone making a jest out of a lack of family support and closeness—after all, she did it herself all the time.

'Many men in your position would simply enjoy the status of being a duke's son and become social gadflies,' she said, taking care to sound matter-of-fact and not overly sympathetic. 'You are doing something worthwhile with your life.'

Henry shrugged again. 'I hope so. The work is interesting, I must admit.' They were almost at the boundary of the park. 'Where to now?'

'Home for breakfast for me and bed for you,' Melissa said briskly, turning on her heel.

Henry wheeled round, obedient to the tug on his arm. 'Lord, yes.'

'Do you have to write a report before you fall on to the mattress?'

'What do you mean?' She felt his attention sharpen.

'Your itinerary last night sounds like that of a man looking for someone. Did you find him?'

Henry made a sound that might have been appreciation of her insight, or merely a faint moan caused by a developing hangover. He hesitated just a fraction too long before saying, 'Very observant. I was looking for an old friend—I have been out of London for so long, one loses touch.'

Melissa did not believe that for a moment. If he was hiding his real purpose last night, then, presumably, it was because he was working. How intriguing. She tried silence, but Henry was too experienced to fall into the trap of blurting out something to fill the gap. 'Are you a spy?'

'I assume you do not mean for some foreign power?' he enquired evenly.

'No, of course not. I wouldn't be here with you if I thought that.'

'I observe,' he said after a moment. 'All diplomats do. Some visitors to this country are worth keeping an eye on, that is all.'

'We are at peace,' Melissa said tentatively.

'For now.' She heard the smile in his voice as he added, 'To be more accurate, we are not actually firing lead at anyone.'

'But we might be fighting a war in which we do not know who the enemy is?'

'Exactly. It sometimes takes a while to impress that on new recruits to the service. A pity we do not employ women.'

'Do you not? Are you saying there are no female agents? No diplomats' wives and daughters or maidservants with sharp ears and inquisitive eyes?'

'Are we back to the fatally seductive female spies again?'

'I should think they might be more use—or at least less obvious—if they were ordinary,' she said, much struck by the idea. 'I could help.'

'Thank you. But I do not require assistance to locate an old friend.'

Botheration. He had not fallen into the trap that she had thought so neat and said who he had been searching for.

'We are back to the gate,' Melissa pointed out, careful not to allow her chagrin to show.

'I will walk you to your door.'

'There is no need.'

'You came out without a maid. What kind of gentleman would you think me if I left you to walk home alone?'

'A weary one with rather too much brandy inside him?'

Henry laughed. 'You are as refreshing as a bucket of cold water over the head, Melissa.' He continued at her side, tossing a penny to the crossing sweeper as they negotiated Piccadilly. 'Walk with me tomorrow at a more civilised hour?'

She considered it as they turned into Half Moon Street. His behaviour was certainly not that of either a suitor—and why on earth would he be?—or a seducer. That, too, seemed improbable. She enjoyed his company and, it would appear, he liked hers. Lord Henry, it seemed, was a friend.

My goodness, it would appear that I am an independent female with a male friend! How gratifying.

'That would be very pleasant,' she replied demurely as they arrived at her doorstep. 'Where were you thinking of going?'

'It is Saturday tomorrow and, by some miracle, given the recent rain, it looks as though the weather will stay fair.' Henry held out his hand when she removed the front door key from her reticule, then opened the door for her. 'Kensington Palace gardens will be open. Provided we are respectably dressed, carry no large parcels and are without unruly dogs in attendance, we may join the throng and promenade like fashionable folk.'

'That sounds delightful,' Melissa said politely, rather spoiling the effect by adding, 'and think of the notes I will be able to make on fashionable costumes. The *Morning Post* will be exceedingly happy.'

'Shall I collect you at two?'

She agreed and Henry walked briskly away, long overdue for a strong sup of coffee and his bed, Melissa thought as she closed the door behind her.

The welcome aroma of coffee was wafting towards her from the kitchen and she ran upstairs to remove her bonnet and pelisse and tidy her hair. The thought of breakfast was suddenly exceedingly alluring, but it did not prevent her picking up a notebook and pencil before going down to the dining room. If she would be prom-enading in a fashionable lounge the next day, then she must have something suitable to wear and make some progress with her work. A list was necessary.

She found Gertrude ordering the nervous little kitchen maid about as the child dumped a laden tray on the table where Cousin Almeria was already seated, a pile of journals by her elbow.

'Do not bang it down, you will spill things, besides disturbing our ladies' tranquillity,' Gertrude directed in an undertone. 'Good morning, Miss Taverner. Here is your coffee and toast. Your tea, Miss Staines. Bacon and eggs will be up directly. Quick, Prissy, down to tell Cook that we are ready for the hot food.'

'A pleasant walk, dear?' Almeria enquired, folding a journal crisply and weighing it down with the butter dish. 'The first post is by your plate.'

'Very pleasant. I met Lord Henry. He appears to have been up all night.'

'One can only admire his stamina,' Almeria said vaguely, pouring tea with one eye on the open page.

'Indeed.' There would be no more conversation from Almeria. Melissa added cream to her coffee, buttered a slice of toast and smiled at Prissy as she solemnly carried in the platter of bacon and eggs.

Her list grew as she ate.

Borrow walking dress from Verity

Of all her friends she was the one who would have the most fashionable outfit that would suit Melissa's colouring.

Finish fashion reports

And earn some money, she added mentally.

Continue outline of novel for Mr Murray

Not that the publisher knew he was to be targeted with her masterpiece.

She must finish her reports first, then go and borrow the clothes from Verity after luncheon. That would leave her the rest of the afternoon clear to work. A sensible plan and not procrastinating in the slightest…

At midday Melissa read through her final piece as she sat down to vegetable soup and cold chicken alone,

Almeria having gone to investigate a collection of moths from western Africa at the British Museum.

> *Now that the severe weather of the early spring has passed, the fashionables may be seen about in promenade costumes of lighter hues, in earnest hope of an amelioration of the damp and chills.*
>
> *A charming bonnet of Dunstable chip straw was observed only yesterday, the ribbons of ribbed silk to match the pelisse of Russian Blue, a most effective combination when worn with the Caledonia cloak, its front embroidered with flowers in chenille floss.*
>
> *A fetching example of this style was observed at the Marchande de Modes of Charlotte Street, Bedford Square.*

She had promised the proprietor that she would mention the emporium.

And if that is not worth at least a spencer or a pair of gloves, I don't know what is.

And now she could take a hackney carriage, drop off her article at the newspaper offices—she could perfectly well send it by messenger, but the small pleasure in trespassing into the male preserve of the City was worth the cost of the fare—and then return via Verity's house in Grosvenor Square.

'I do swear that if waistlines rise any higher they will be up to the collarbone,' Melissa grumbled as she forced her bosom into the space available in the bodice of the gown Verity's maid found for her.

'It's the French mode, Miss Taverner,' the woman said as she secured a hook. 'At least with a day dress there isn't the problem about the neckline.'

'Rogers means she has great difficulty ensuring I do not pop out of mine,' the Duchess explained. She had come in to collapse on the *chaise* in her dressing room, complaining that she was quite worn out by the energy of Thomas, her son. 'Surely waistlines will drop soon?'

'Not before next year, I'd say, Your Grace.' Rogers stepped back to survey Melissa. 'Very nice, Miss Taverner. Like my lady, you have the height to carry off the gathering in the skirt and the ruffles on the cuffs. Here is the spencer.' She held it up to display lines of dark green cording running across the bosom and ornate dark green tops to the sleeves. 'The latest from Mrs Bell. She calls it her British Walking Dress.'

'What is British about it?' They all studied the garment.

'Goodness knows,' Verity concluded. 'Now you must borrow the bonnet I bought yesterday. It will be perfect.'

'Ooh.' Melissa reached for it. 'That is so stylish.' The hat was green with an upturned brim that dipped down in a swoop on the left. The straight sides of the crown were swathed in a simple cream net adorned with a sprig of artificial roses and it was tied with a cream silk ribbon. 'How can you bear to lend it?'

'I am prepared to make any sacrifice for my friends,' Verity said piously. 'And it will dazzle Lord Henry.'

'Oh, *Verity*!' Melissa thrust the hat back into the abigail's hands. 'I told you it is not like that with him. This is because I need to look absolutely in the mode because the Broad Walk is such a fashionable lounge. I could not promenade there looking a dowd.' She took back the hat and put it on her head. 'This is delicious. Where did you find it? I must visit and buy myself something—I cannot keep borrowing from you.'

'You expect to have many occasions during the day-time when you'll need the latest modes, do you?' Verity asked slyly. 'I know you have some very charming gowns for evening, but, forgive me, I thought you intended working at home a great deal.'

'I do. But I have come to the conclusion that it is not good to spend all day, every day, hunched over my writing desk. Some…er…*rational* exercise is necessary and I have no desire to appear shabby genteel.'

That was all perfectly true. Melissa had invested in some evening gowns from dressmakers that her friends recommended as not extravagantly priced, but her day dresses and outer garments were much simpler and of sufficiently hard-wearing quality to stand several refurbishments in the course of their lives. Now she could not but help feel they were lacking in a certain something in terms of style.

'Of course, dear. That seems very sensible.' There was a smile lurking around Verity's mouth, however firmly she compressed her lips.

Melissa resisted the temptation to lob the powder puff from the dressing table at her and was too cautious to make any defensive remarks and appear to have something to hide. Her friend, a personable gentleman, had suggested an outing of pleasure in a fashionable area. Naturally it would be rude to appear looking anything but her best, she assured herself.

'I will bring it all back on Monday,' she said as Rogers helped her take off the outfit. 'I am so grateful, Verity. Do you attend Lady Frithsden's soirée this evening?'

'Yes, and Jane will be there also. The others are going to the new play at Drury Lane.'

They talked of their plans for the next few days and the worrying lack of any information about what Charles Harlby might be up to. Verity made no further reference to Lord Henry.

'I think Harlby has gone out of town for a while to lick his wounds,' Melissa said as she pushed hatpins into her own bonnet and prepared to leave. 'It bodes ill for any country heiress he might chance upon, I fear. But we cannot be everywhere. I will see you this evening.'

'We will collect you,' Verity said, getting up to kiss her goodbye, 'and drop off the walking dress and bonnet.'

'Bless you. That means I can walk home.'

It was perhaps half a mile, perhaps less, from Grosvenor Square to Half Moon Street. Melissa was still finding her way about the streets around her new home, but she thought that the best route would be to Berkeley Square, then along Charles Street, turn left down Queen Street, left again into Curzon Street and then almost immediately right into her own road.

It was as though an inept cabinetmaker with no idea how to match woodgrain had laid sections of timber down at cross purposes, she thought ten minutes later, realising she had missed Queen Street. None of the blocks of streets seemed to flow into each other in a logical manner—it was enough to confuse even someone with the best sense of direction.

Still, if she kept going and took the next left… Yes,

looking down Chesterfield Street she could see a wide thoroughfare at the end—surely that was Curzon Street? It was. Two minutes later she was able to turn left and stopped for a moment to admire the large mansion set back from the street on her left, then looked around, committing this new area to memory.

Opposite was a small church or, more probably, a chapel of ease, one of the many that had sprung up in newly developed areas of the West End, as Verity had explained when Melissa had asked about places of worship.

She was ready to walk on when two men emerged from the chapel porch, with heads together, deep in conversation. One looked like a shabby clergyman— even from across the street Melissa could see his black coat was greenish, his stockings sagged and his clerical bands flopped limply. He would not have merited more than a glance, if it were not for the fact he was deep in conversation with Charles Harlby.

Chapter Four

Melissa stepped back sharply behind a cart that stood at the kerb while its driver unloaded some crates. She had no desire to be seen by Harlby, especially when she was quite unaccompanied. The man worked smoothly and secretly, relying on deception and his charm—when he chose to use it. How he would react, in public, to a woman who had frustrated and humiliated him she had no idea and had no desire to discover.

The men shook hands and, from the way the clergyman slid something into his pocket, money was exchanged.

Now, that was interesting. What on earth had Harlby to do with a churchman and why should he be paying one? The carter removed another crate and he seemed to have several more. He was behaving like a man with all the time in the world so she was well hidden for the moment.

Harlby sauntered off towards Hyde Park swinging his cane, his hat at an angle. From his jaunty step he was pleased with his encounter. When she glanced back the clergyman had vanished and she recalled that Shepherd Market lay just to the east of where she was. She would not be able to follow him through its little alleyways and, anyway, she doubted that doing so would answer her questions.

On impulse Melissa crossed the road and entered the chapel. An elderly man in a black cassock was sweeping between the pews in a desultory kind of way—a verger, she guessed.

He straightened when he saw her hesitating. 'Yes, ma'am? May I help you?'

'The clergyman who just left… I thought I recognised him.' No response, just a pursing of the man's lips. 'Or perhaps not. Do you know his name?'

The verger propped the broom against a pew and walked towards her. 'I might call it to mind. Not that he's a clergyman, as you'd know if you did recognise him, miss.'

Melissa fished in her reticule and came out with a coin. 'I am holding you up in your work. Perhaps I could give you this to put in the appropriate offerings box.'

'Thank you kindly, miss.' Dusty fingers left smudges on her gloves and she was thankful she was wearing them. The coin vanished into some pocket in his robe. 'That was Horace Cartwright. The Reverend Horace Cartwright as was, before the Archbishop took his licence away. Must have been five years ago. No, more than that—almost ten, now I think about it. Time does fly.'

'You mean, he has been defrocked? He is no longer a priest?'

'Ah, now that's where folk get it wrong.' The verger

seemed smug about his superior knowledge. 'Them Romans and so forth, they unfrock 'em when they are wrong 'uns. But here, Church of England, they get their licence removed. Means they can't administer the sacraments, nor preach neither.'

'So, if Mr Cartwright were to marry a couple, it would not be valid?'

'That's right, miss. No more than if you or I were to do it.'

'I see. Thank you. Good day.'

Melissa went on her way, deep in thought. If Harlby tricked someone into a false marriage, then what good would it do him? Surely the friends and family of the deceived woman would scrutinise every aspect of the ceremony and the church courts would declare it invalid. And if all the beastly man was doing was attempting to get some innocent into bed, then, surely, this was a complex way to go about it?

She was still puzzling when she arrived home a few minutes later. Perhaps Jane or Verity could answer the riddle.

Melissa was still brooding the next morning. The soirée had been no help at all. Jane had stayed at home with a sore throat, Verity had been distracted by the need to support her husband in persuading a political opponent to vote for some proposed legislation and the entire party had been overheated, overcrowded and too noisy for prolonged conversation.

She glared at the sheet of paper covered in notes for her new novel and wished that any of them excited her. What she wanted to do was write the story that was bubbling away in her mind—it had a swashbuckling hero with blue eyes, a dark-haired heroine, a sneering villain and… And was not a serious novel of social observation and cutting wit that Mr Murray could publish in three volumes of elegant tooled calfskin to restrained critical acclaim.

On the other hand, she should probably write it and get it out of her head. She knew she could sell it, she would enjoy crafting it and she hoped her readers would love it.

Melissa crumpled up the notes, lobbed them neatly into the wastepaper basket, reached for a fresh sheet and wrote across the top:

The Rogue Lord of Castle Darke

Chapter One

'You look very pleased with life,' Henry observed as he helped her up into the hackney carriage. 'And that is a most fetching bonnet, if I may say so. Is that the reason for the smile?'

Melissa remembered her manners. 'No, just something that went well this morning, but mainly because I am being taken on an expedition of pleasure by a friend who is so influential that the rain that was threatening has blown away.'

'None of my doing, I'm afraid.' Henry was looking exceedingly smart in biscuit-coloured pantaloons, well-made Hessian boots, a swallow-tailed coat in deep blue and a tall hat with a rakish curl to the brim. 'I have absolutely no credit with the weather gods. Tell me about your successful morning.'

'I decided to write something I would enjoy, rather than something more serious, and it is going like a dream.'

'Will Mr Murray like it?'

'It isn't for him,' she confessed, deciding to take the plunge and trust him a little. 'It is very Gothic and romantic and perfectly improbable. I am enjoying it immensely.'

'May I read it?'

'I shouldn't think you would enjoy it.' Melissa eyed him dubiously.

'Try me,' Henry said, with a smile that sent an odd shiver through her. Most peculiar—it must be apprehension at the thought of his critical remarks.

She glanced out of the window and saw they had halted at the Hyde Park turnpike. Then they were through and trotting down Knightsbridge towards Kensington, past large houses behind high walls and scattered market gardens to the left, the brick wall of Hyde Park on the right.

'Do we enter through the Palace gates?'

'Yes, then we skirt the formal garden to the south and join the end of the Broad Walk where we will stroll elegantly up and down and you may have your bonnet admired.'

'I have a confession to make,' Melissa said ten minutes later as they skirted the formal beds that were looking depressed and soggy after the cold, wet spring. 'This is not my bonnet, I borrowed it.'

'That shows considerable cunning,' Henry remarked. 'You save the cost of the hat and yet you find one that suits you admirably.'

'How very good you are at compliments! It must come with being a diplomat. I was somewhat nervous about not matching the standards of elegance of the other promenaders in the royal gardens. Or your own for that matter.'

'I think we stand up very well to comparison.' They had reached the south-eastern end of the Broad Walk and joined the mass of people already walking up and down. 'This is a crush.'

'The first dry Saturday for some weeks, I suppose. Oh! I do like the Palace. It looks quite domestic, not at all what I had imagined.'

'That's the Dutch influence of King William. He came from a nation that is a great believer in respectable domestic comfort,' Henry said. 'Here is the Basin.'

Right in front of the Palace was a great pond, like a rectangle with curves inside the corners, set in a wide gravelled area with formal, geometrical paths leading off towards the Serpentine and Hyde Park.

The crowd was particularly thick there, with people staring at the Palace, children rushing up and down screaming at the ducks and some languid fashionables posing artistically against the various statues.

'I should be making notes,' Melissa said, 'but I can hardly stand here and do so.'

'There are benches further along,' Henry said, weaving a path through a group that appeared to be worthy citizens from the City in their best clothes, the effect somewhat spoilt by the fact they could hardly stop gawking at some of the more outrageous fashions.

'Here.' He produced a handkerchief and flicked the seat clean.

'Why, thank you, kind sir.'

'I am, naturally, the perfect gentleman,' Henry said gravely, sitting down next to her. 'Now, what are we looking for? Notables we can identify so you can include their names and what they are wearing?'

'Absolutely. And anyone in particularly novel or *outré* outfits.'

They spent half an hour with Henry spotting and dictating while Melissa scribbled. 'Lady Fanshawe in a walking dress of oxblood red, cut in the latest Russian style with French influences in the detailing accompanied by... Oh, dear, *not* Lord Fanshawe, but a very pretty young gentleman in exceedingly tight Inexpressibles. They may explain his expression, of course. Oh, and his tailcoat is cut with an exaggerated wasp waist and silver buttons.'

'I can't put that! And how do you know her outfit is in the Russian style?' She peered at the couple in question. 'And I cannot call that oxblood, that is too gruesome. Deep garnet, it will have to be.' She took another look. 'I see what you mean about the young man. Goodness, where *is* a lady supposed to look these days? Above the top waistcoat button, I suppose. How ever does he get them on?'

Henry crossed his own elegantly trousered legs. Melissa glanced to the side—yes, very tight and excellent for showing off well-muscled thighs, but fortunately for her blushes not quite as indecent as Lady Fanshawe's escort's garments.

'I imagine those are knitted,' he said, narrowing his eyes against the light. 'And straps under the feet to prevent any sagging or wrinkling and, of course, he must then stay on his feet to prevent any bagging at the knees.'

'Hmm.' Melissa made some carefully tactful notes about Lady Fanshaw's outfit. 'Oh, do look at that hat—isn't it gorgeous?'

Obligingly, Henry followed the direction of her nod. 'The feathers are rather—' He ducked his head suddenly and bent over as though he had dropped something. 'Has the tall, dark man with the yellow waistcoat, walking with the shorter one with a cane and a bright blue coat, gone past yet?'

'What? Who? Oh, yes, they are just passing now.' Melissa lowered her voice and bent, too, as though helping him search. 'Who is it?' she asked.

Henry straightened up cautiously. Von Arten was safely past, deep in conversation with Pierre Laverne, the same Frenchman from the embassy that he had been with on the night Henry had met Melissa. They certainly showed no apprehension about being seen together and he suspected that he would have hardly thought anything of it now if the Frenchman had not slipped away into the shrubbery so secretively that night.

Beside him Melissa was positively quivering with interest.

'Can you keep a secret?' he asked. 'A serious one,

government business, not to be shared with anyone, including your friends.'

'Yes,' she said, earnestly. 'I promise.'

Henry got to his feet. 'I ought to follow those two. Yellow Waistcoat is a man calling himself the Graf Klaus von Arten. He may well be, in truth, but we aren't certain. He was around a great deal during the Congress, for no apparent reason.'

'I heard it was a great social occasion as well as a political one.' Melissa walked beside him as he cut across the gravel around the pond.

'That may be all it was, of course. But now he is in London and this is the second time I have seen him with the blue-coated gentleman, Pierre Laverne, who is a minor functionary at the French embassy. The first was at Lady Pernell's ball where they were behaving surreptitiously.'

'They aren't now,' Melissa observed. 'But there is such a crowd and people are conversing everywhere you look, so perhaps they do not feel conspicuous here.' She slid her hand into the crook of his elbow. 'Are we following them?'

We. Hell, he should not be following possible spies with a lady in tow.

'No, of course not. I didn't think.' He slowed as they reached the edge of the Basin. Von Arten and his companion were already making towards the central walk that led away towards the boundary with Hyde Park.

'Why not? Oh! Because of me? What nonsense, Henry. I will make admirable cover. If they glance around, they will see a couple out for a stroll. What could be more innocent?'

She was right. It was broad daylight, there were other people around, even in the further reaches of the grounds, and, whatever those two were up to, they were not going to attack someone they thought might observe them in the Palace gardens.

The broad swathes of grass that lay between the wide, radiating paths had been planted up with small groves of trees, young yet, but giving some cover. 'We will walk down here.' He indicated the pathway leading off at an angle from the main one that von Arten had taken. 'We can observe them in the gaps between the trees, even though we can't get close enough to overhear them.'

'What do you suspect they are about?' Melissa asked.

'Don't know, that is the trouble. Now we are at peace, all the nations that have been distracted by Napoleon have the opportunity to sit down and consider what they want. Have they gained all the prizes they hoped for? What still rankles? Who has done better than they have and what are the prospects for the next twenty years?'

'I can see that,' she said, with a firm nod of that dashing little hat. 'They are not going to be content to sit around singing hymns of harmony and mutual love, not if they think there is an advantage to be gained.' She was silent for a moment. 'I imagine there is a feeling that Britain might get too big for her boots in this new world.'

'Precisely,' Henry said, impressed. The great political hostesses, the wives of some men of influence and those from the powerful families in the City understood the situation, but to most single girls from gentry families the practical issues of world politics must be a complete mystery. He was not surprised, somehow, that Melissa grasped it. With her refusal to behave like a well-bred single female waiting to be scooped up in marriage he would wager that she read the newspapers from cover to cover.

He found he liked discussing things with her. Male colleagues, however amiable, tended to be competitive, squashing ideas, jostling to have their own heard. Melissa, he sensed, would join in creatively with examining a theory.

'So, we do not know for whom von Arten is working,' she said now. He smiled now at the *'we'*. 'But presumably he is setting up the Frenchman—but as a spy on us or within his own embassy? Finding out who he works for is very important, I imagine.'

'Absolutely,' Henry agreed. 'Knowing who our enemies are in this new world is key— Curses, I've taken my eyes off them and they've stopped.'

The two had their backs to them, but even as they watched, the men began to move again.

'And they are turning back this way. Quick, in here.' Melissa grabbed his hand and ran into a little summer house that looked out towards the water.

He flattened himself against an internal wall and peered, hat in hand, around the edge. The building, he guessed, was supposed to be a little Roman temple with its three arched openings on to small, shallow, chambers behind. They had dived into one of the two flanking rooms.

'Have they seen us?'

'I don't think so, they are still deep in conversation. But they are heading this way.' He looked around for cover or a back way out but, although there was a door that must lead into the central space, and a simple wooden bench at the back—much besplattered by pigeons—there was no other exit except the front arch. There was nowhere within to hide.

Footsteps crunched on the gravel path and Henry risked another look. 'They are coming in here.'

Melissa already had the connecting door to the central room open and they slipped through and closed it just as the two men's voices became audible. She went across and tried the door into the far room. 'Locked or jammed,' she whispered.

They were stuck. Leaving would make them completely visible on the semicircle of gravel in front of the little temple and, not knowing exactly where the two men were standing or facing, Henry did not want to risk sliding out of the far side of the arch. It was not that he thought there was any danger that von Arten would become violent, but he or Laverne might well recognise him. If that happened, they would simply go to ground, stop associating and he would be left without any clue as to what they were discussing.

He put his ear to the door, but could make out no words, only that they were speaking in French. Then one of them said, quite clearly, *'Pah! Ce banc est sale.'*

The bench is filthy...

Then, in von Arten's slightly accented French, *'L'autre pièce.'*

'They are coming in here,' Henry whispered urgently. If they could time it right, they might be able to slip out of the front as the other door opened.

Then Melissa pulled off her hat and propelled herself

at him. Henry reeled back, the bench caught him behind his knees and she was sprawled half on him, her lips pressed to his. His mind caught up one beat behind his body as his arms went around her, gathering her close, and he heard a muffled exclamation.

'Les amoureux!' Someone laughed and he heard the door close.

It was a brilliant piece of quick thinking and had effectively routed the two conspirators. He could let go now.

Chapter Five

He could let go and Melissa would lift her head and those warm, soft lips would no longer be clinging to his and that slim, curving body would no longer be pressed against him and…and this kiss would end. And he did not want that.

Nor, it seemed, did Melissa. It was an inexperienced kiss, he could tell, even with all the blood in his brain draining downwards. Her mouth remained closed, her hands stayed where they had landed on his shoulders, but she made a little purring sound deep in her throat and every primitive male instinct leapt to attention and demanded that he turn that purr into a moan, a gasp, a cry.

Henry sat up. Where he got the willpower from he had no idea, but there they were suddenly, side by side on the bench, rumpled, somewhat breathless and, in his case, most inconveniently aroused. He jumped up, made a business of straightening his coat with his back to her, then retrieved his hat and held it strategically as he brushed it down.

'That was very quick thinking,' he said when his brain allowed speech.

'I hope it was convincing,' Melissa said, frowning as she tugged her bodice straight. 'I have absolutely no practical experience of that kind of thing. Luckily this bench is not as filthy as the other one.'

'Of course not. I mean, of course you would not have practical experience.' *Stop gibbering, man.* 'I think you may be certain that they suspected nothing,' he said, rather more calmly.

'It was the only thing I could think of to stop them seeing your face,' she went on, looking round. She located her own hat, picked it up and blew dust from it. 'I think there is no permanent damage, thank goodness.'

Not to the hat, at any rate. What was the matter with him? He had been kissed by lovers of great experience and skill. One innocent pressing her lips to his as part of a charade could hardly weigh against those encounters. It was because he had been tense already, on edge, that was all it was. Melissa was a friend, not a lover. An innocent, not a woman of the world.

A friend. We have something special—do not ruin this.

His body was at least under some kind of control now. He could safely put his hat to the purpose for which it was intended, his breathing was steady and his expression, he sincerely hoped, gave away nothing of his inner turmoil.

'Have they gone, do you think?' Melissa asked, giving the veiling on her hat one last tweak.

Henry looked out cautiously, then checked around the sides of the building. 'They are walking away towards the Palace, somewhat briskly. I do not think there is any point in trying to catch them up.'

'No, I suppose not.' She put her hat back on and tied the ribbons in a rather lopsided bow.

Without thinking, Henry went across and retied it. How had he not noticed her scent before? Roses with a trace of something faintly warm and herbal. 'Rosemary?' He realised he had said it out loud.

Melissa looked perplexed, then laughed. 'Oh, my hair rinse. That tickles.'

'What? Oh, sorry.' His fingers were still on the bow, touching the smooth skin under her chin. He removed his hand as casually as he could. 'It is safe to follow now, I think.'

A lot safer than staying here. Melissa is a friend, he reminded himself as he followed her out of the summer house. *She trusts you, as a friend, not to be reacting like this to her, not to be thinking about her scent, the feel of her. Her mouth.*

'What is wrong?' Melissa asked, tucking her hand into Henry's crooked arm. She felt him give himself a little shake.

'Nothing. Just something I am feeling rather guilty about.'

For some reason that did not make her want to tease the cause out of him: he seemed genuinely concerned about it. 'Is it very serious that you have lost the opportunity to listen to them? Will your superior be annoyed with you?'

'It was pure chance we happened on them,' he said. 'I will report it, of course, but I do not think anyone could expect me to eavesdrop successfully in the middle of open parkland. No, it is just something personal.'

'Perhaps you make too much of it. It seems to me that you are a very honourable person, Henry.'

'Thank you.'

It did not sound as though that had been a helpful remark, so it was probably past time to change the subject. Her friends accused her of tackling issues head-on, without tact or finesse sometimes. Somehow, with this man, it seemed important to be more sensitive.

'I have a puzzle that perhaps you can advise me about.'

'Of course.' The flat tone had vanished from his voice. 'Tell me.'

'I saw that awful man Charles Harlby yesterday. He was coming out of the chapel on Curzon Street and he was talking to a shabby person dressed like a clergyman. It was not casual—they had their heads together and I think Harlby gave him money when they parted. They did not see me and when they had gone, I went in and asked the verger who the priest was. And he said the man's name is Horace Cartwright and he was no longer a clergyman because the Archbishop had removed his licence about ten years ago.'

'Defrocked him? Or is it unfrocked?'

'Neither, not in the Church of England apparently. But having his licence revoked has the same effect— he cannot perform any of the sacraments, nor may he preach.'

'So, what was Harlby doing with him?'

'Exactly. And why should Harlby be giving Cartwright money? I cannot imagine what he wants with a false clergyman because, if he is set on finding an heiress, surely he needs to be legally married to her?'

'Yes,' Henry said thoughtfully. 'And no heiress is likely to have guardians or trustees who are so careless as to agree to Harlby marrying their charge. Even if they did, a legitimate clergyman would perform the ceremony. But, wait, I have it! Imagine for a moment that you are an innocent and highly respectable virgin.'

Melissa tried to suppress the laughter, but it escaped anyway. Henry had gone scarlet and his usual easy manner appeared to have completely deserted him.

'Oh, hell—I didn't mean… Of course you *are* a highly respectable—'

'Henry, I think the hole is quite deep enough. You may stop digging. I know what you mean.' She got her giggles under control. 'You refer to a sheltered girl of impeccable morals who has no experience of rakes and libertines and no idea of their dangers.'

'Precisely.' He removed a large handkerchief from a pocket in his tails and made an exaggerated show of mopping his brow. 'Now, imagine that Harlby has wormed his way into your affections, but he warns you that, because of their prejudice, your guardians will not permit the marriage.'

'He would probably admit to a wild youth, or some dreadful error he committed as a young man,' she said, imagining his tactics. 'But he is now deeply repentant and affectingly penitent. He would imply that it is only my virtue, purity and saint-like trust that has compelled his reformation.'

'That's it exactly. He works on you until you feel guilty for feeling the slightest doubts about him. He explains that to be together, and to force the hands of your prejudiced guardians, you must elope.'

Melissa gave a little jig of excitement. 'That is just how I would put it in a novel. This is fun, working it out with someone else. At least, it would be if it were not real and serious. Now I see his plan. I am so virtuous that I will agree to elope, but I insist that we must be married first. He promises to arrange everything, including a licence and a priest who is sympathetic to true love.'

'The mock marriage is performed,' Henry said, picking up the story. 'There are enough churches standing empty during the day in London to make that easy enough if you bribe the verger. Brandish an imposing piece of parchment with seals to act as the licence, ask a couple of passers-by to be witnesses, produce some aged ledger as the register and there you are. Apparently married.'

'And by the time any pursuit catches up with them the poor girl has been bedded, may already be with child—and there was no inconvenient screaming and protest in inns along the way, just a happy bride on her wedding night,' Melissa concluded. 'I suppose the guardians would have no option but to make the best of it and get them legally married.'

'They might risk it, take her away, hope there is no child and trust that her wealth means she is still marriageable.'

'Like a shop-soiled gown, brushed down and sold again. It makes me very grateful I have no wealth, just a comfortable competence.'

'And it makes me grateful I am not a woman,' said

Henry with a shiver she felt through his arm. 'I never really thought about it before. Obviously, such behaviour is dishonourable, cruel, despicable. But I hadn't considered it from the point of view of the woman's feelings.'

'Our lovely afternoon's outing is proving to be rather depressing,' Melissa said sadly.

'Cheer up,' Henry said. He seemed to have recovered his spirits while hers had sunk. 'We have realised what Harlby's plan is; now we can set about countering it. We need to identify the woman concerned and warn her. I did think for a minute of finding the disgraced priest and warning him off, but then Harlby will only find another one.'

'Yes.' Melissa told herself to be more positive, but she hated not seeing a clear way ahead. She liked a plan. Henry had gone quiet again so she nudged him. 'What is it? You look as though you are brooding.'

'You hate Harlby and you know what he is about. How is that? He hasn't— Oh, hell, there is no nice way to edge around this—he has not hurt you, has he, Melissa?'

'No! I know of someone that he did deceive, last Season. That was when he was not fortune hunting, just enjoying himself. And the person concerned was by no means some ignorant little miss. She really believed in his sincerity. When we found out—my friends, whom you have met, and I—we realised how dangerous he was and determined to do something about him.'

'Good. On both counts. Obviously because you are unscathed and I don't have to kill the bastard, which tends to cause the devil of a fuss, but also because someone is trying to do something about him.'

She gulped. 'You wouldn't kill him, would you?'

'Obviously, I would have to challenge him,' Henry said, impatient.

'Goodness,' Melissa said faintly. 'I would rather you didn't. Challenge anyone on my behalf, I mean. Really. I would worry about you having to go into exile.'

Henry looked down at her and smiled. 'I appreciate your confidence that I would win.'

Her nudge this time was more like a jab in the ribs. 'Stop it. Whatever happened, you would be full of righteousness over being honourable and brave and I would be feeling guilty.'

'I've never considered that,' he admitted, tucking her hand more securely under his arm.

'Men don't,' Melissa grumbled as they reached the Broad Walk again. It was beginning to cloud over and the crowds had diminished. 'I can't see von Arten or the Frenchman.'

'They will be long gone. I will report what we saw. It is definitely suspicious behaviour and I expect they will put someone on to Laverne to dig out some background. It would be good to find out where von Arten is living, although how, other than by encountering him and then following, I don't know.'

'I do,' Melissa said. 'He was at Lady Pernell's ball. Unless he sneaked in uninvited he must have received an invitation. We can go and ask her secretary.'

'Genius. Shall we go now?'

When the hackney carriage deposited them on the corner of Cavendish Square Henry looked around appreciatively. 'I hadn't really thought about it before, but Lady P. has done well to find somewhere with such a large garden so centrally.'

'It is the largest on the Square, I believe, and in daylight isn't quite as impressive as it appears in the darkness. Jane—Lady Kendall—was telling me about it. She is taking an interest in remodelling her own London grounds,' Melissa said, as Henry knocked.

The butler accepted their cards with a bow but regretted that neither Her Ladyship nor His Lordship were at home.

'That's quite all right, I was simply hoping to have a word with Her Ladyship's secretary, if he is available,' Melissa said.

'Certainly, Miss Taverner. If you and His Lordship would care to wait in here.'

They were left for only a few minutes in the opulent drawing room, a fortunate circumstance in Melissa's opinion.

'I am beginning to feel seasick,' she murmured. 'Why is it necessary to decorate every available surface in sea-green, do you think? And all that swooping plasterwork and drapes.'

A thin young man came in, bowed and stood awaiting their pleasure with an air, she thought, of a lapdog that expects more kicks than titbits. 'I am Watts. Portman said you wished to see me, Miss Taverner?'

'It is simply the matter of the address of one of the guests at Lady Pernell's ball on Wednesday, Mr Watts. I promised Graf von Arten an invitation to my friend Lady Kendall's soirée and I have completely misplaced his card. So careless of me.'

'Yes, of course I can find it for you, if you would

excuse me for a moment. Would you care for refreshments while you wait?'

'Thank you, no.'

They sat and looked out of the window to where the clouds were gathering and threatening rain, and Melissa was just contemplating whether she would need to borrow an umbrella when Mr Watts returned.

'I do apologise for the delay. Graf von Arten was an acquaintance of Lord Pernell, so I have had to ask his secretary for the details. They met at His Lordship's club, I believe. Here you are.' He handed a folded piece of paper to Melissa. 'May I be of any further service, Miss Taverner?'

'No, thank you, although perhaps one of the footmen could hail a hackney carriage for us. I believe it has begun to rain.'

They made polite conversation about the dreadful spring weather until the footman, somewhat damp, returned to hold an umbrella over Melissa as she went down to the carriage. She was pleased to see that Henry tipped him.

'Where to, guvnor?'

'Wait one moment.' He took the address from Melissa and gave it to the driver.

'He has access to a club, it seems,' Melissa observed as they moved off.

'Probably as someone's guest. He's a sociable devil is von Arten,' Henry said. 'I thought we'd have a look at where he's living in Golden Square—I'm not very familiar with the address.'

'Respectable enough, I think, but surrounded by some very dubious areas. It is almost in Soho.' She frowned in thought. 'The Regent's librarian lives there, although goodness knows who told me that. But it was Jane who said that there are any number of émigrés there and quite a few foreign artists and musicians. And there's a Catholic chapel near there as well, I think. A German one.'

'Interesting. What a very convenient area to *accidentally* bump into agents of a foreign power.'

The vehicle stopped and the driver leaned over at a perilous angle to shout, 'Where now, guvnor?'

Henry dropped the window glass. 'Drive round the square, would you, and then drive past the Catholic chapel. I believe there's one near here.'

'Aye, guvnor. Our Lady, they call it. Warwick Street.' The horse plodded on slowly. Clearly the man thought they were rather unusual sightseers.

'A cosmopolitan neighbourhood,' Melissa said, peering through the rather smudged glass. 'These houses were fine once, but it looks as though they are divided up for lodgings now.'

The carriage turned right and then right again and they saw the brick façade of the chapel.

'Must have been built under the patronage of an ambassador,' Henry said. 'They are entitled to have their own chapels and the public can worship there. Makes life much easier for Roman Catholics in London than it is for those outside.' He leaned out again. 'Stop here for a moment.'

He jumped out, went across, studied the simple notice board outside the chapel and, as he came back, Melissa heard him give the man the Half Moon Street address.

He climbed in again and sat back looking thoughtful. 'I don't suppose your principles would permit your attending a Roman Catholic service, would they?' he asked after a minute.

'You mean go to that chapel? Tomorrow? Oh, yes, I have no qualms about that. I had better find a veil, don't you think? But what about you? If von Arten is there, he might recognise you.'

'Not looking as I will be, I hope. Can you borrow a dress from your maid? And a bonnet and cloak? We want to look like humble shopkeepers, or servants, I think.'

'It will be an adventure.' This was even better than imagining intrigue and writing about it, and there was something about sharing the experience with Henry that added a fizz of excitement. 'Will you do something for me?'

'Certainly, if I can.'

'Escort me this evening.'

'Delighted, ma'am,' Henry said with a courtly bow that looked ridiculous in the cramped space.

'Excellent,' she said, mimicking his bow, which made him grin. 'Jane, Verity, Lucy, Prue and I are splitting up to cover as many social events as possible in the hunt for Harlby's heiress, but I cannot go by myself, so that is four groups. If you accompany me, we will make another couple and we will be able to attend more functions. I will send notes to the others and tell them about the clergyman and your theory and we can adjust the list of who is going where.'

'I wish I had met you sooner,' Henry lamented.

'Imagine how much better my social life would have been.'

'Idiot,' she said, thinking, *and mine would have been so much more fun.*

Chapter Six

'Is it raining?' James asked. He looked up blearily from a sheet of paper covered in scrawled calculations as Henry came in.

'No. Threatening to, though.' Henry tossed hat and gloves on to the battered sofa and strolled across to look over his shoulder. 'How is it going?'

'Badly,' James grumbled. 'I thought it was in Russian, but it isn't. How was your day?'

'Lounged around at Brooks's, read the papers and had some luncheon, then I escorted Miss Taverner to Kensington Palace gardens and we had an adventure.'

'Tell all,' James demanded, swivelling round so he could look at Henry, who had flopped into an armchair.

'I saw our friend von Arten with his French acquaintance, Laverne.'

'Which means it was no chance meeting, that first time you saw them. They are connected.'

'Definitely. Miss Taverner and I had a narrow escape playing hide-and-seek with them in some Classical summer house in the park.'

'Queen Caroline's Temple,' James said, nodding in recognition. 'I sketched it last summer and sent measurements to Father. I thought it would look rather good in his grounds as an eye-catcher.'

'And Miss Taverner found out where von Arten is lodging,' Henry continued, ignoring James's architectural digression. 'Golden Square. And given that there is a Roman Catholic chapel nearby we thought we would attend a service tomorrow and see if we can spot another "chance" meeting.'

'Our Lady of the Assumption and St Gregory. The Bavarian Embassy chapel originally,' James said. 'Rebuilt after the Gordon Riots. Can't recall who the architect was, but—'

'Never mind the architect. I wonder if von Arten's a Bavarian, which makes it fairly certain he's Roman Catholic. Although Arten is in Thuringia... Not that that's particularly relevant so far as I can see.' Henry mused for a bit. 'Would he have an interest in stirring up the Irish question?'

'Stop maundering and tell me about Miss Taverner. *Interesting, intelligent, handsome*, you said. What more have you discovered about her?' James clasped ink-stained fingers over his heart. 'Don't tell me you are in *lo-o-ove*.' He dragged out the word and batted his eyelashes.

'No, I am not.' Henry hurled a cushion at him. He wasn't at all sure what he was—more than a bit in lust, certainly, but he was hanging on to the idea of friendship with grim determination. He liked Melissa—she was amusing company, she took an intelligent, supportive, interest, she had guts and was quick thinking:

everything one looked for in a friend, in fact. He was not going to spoil that because one playacting kiss had caused his heart to thump and his toes to curl.

'Melissa's a friend. She's helping me with von Arten and I'm assisting her with a problem she and her friends have.'

'Tell all. Can I play, too?'

'It isn't a game.' He thought over what Melissa had told him. There was nothing confidential, he thought. In fact, the more the word went around about Harlby, the better. 'I don't suppose you know a man named Charles Harlby?' he asked.

'Why shouldn't I? Used to play cards with him regularly last Season. Quite good company—wouldn't trust him with my sister or the family silver, though. He vanished over the summer, nothing odd about that, and he was back in October. Saw him around, asked where he was playing now and he said he's given it up. Bored, he said. I wondered if he was in dun territory and most of the houses won't have him until he has paid his debts.'

'That would fit. The suspicion is that he's hanging out for an heiress and intends catching one by foul means, given that no one with any sense would let him have one by fair. Miss Taverner saw him in deep conversation with an unfrocked clergyman and suspects a sham marriage to force the hand of the girl's trustees.'

'You know who he has in his sights?'

'No, and that's the problem. Miss Taverner and her friends are virtually patrolling the balls and parties trying to identify his victim so they can warn her off. That's where I'm going tonight. Apparently, Miss Taverner will come up with a list of social gatherings that are our share.'

'Uninvited, old chap?'

'Her best friend is the Duchess of Aylsham. Invitations are not a problem.'

'I'll take a wander round the clubs and the hells tonight,' James offered. 'Gossip about how I've not seen Harlby lately, see what I can pick up. I'll keep an eye open for our dear Graf at the same time. If I find him, I'll try luring him into deep play and bad brandy.'

'Excellent idea.' Henry got to his feet reluctantly—the armchair had soft cushions and all the comfort of long use. 'I had best see if I've enough clean linen for tonight.'

'I've had some laundry back, you can borrow a shirt—but keep your hands off my neckcloths,' his friend called after him.

Instead of sending a note with a list of allocated events to attend, Jane turned up in person. 'Here you are. Now, tell me all about this Lord Henry of yours,' she demanded, plumping down on the sofa. 'Verity and I are positively agog.'

'You met him.' Melissa scanned the list, mentally sorting them into order.

'We saw him, we exchanged a few words. We know he is capable of vaulting parapets and gallant enough to go to the aid of a lady, that he has rather a fine profile and a pair of charming blue eyes. What we do not know is why he is willing to squire you about to half a dozen engagements at a moment's notice.'

'Henry is a friend. I told him I wanted help with

Harlby. In return I am helping him with something to-morrow. Jane, have you ever been to a Roman Catholic service?'

'A mass?' Jane blinked at her. 'Goodness, no. Never say Lord Henry is a Roman Catholic? It would cause all kinds of problems if you married him. And think of the children—they couldn't go to university or hold any government position or—'

'No, he is not. And of course I am not going to marry him, so it wouldn't matter if he was,' Melissa said sharply.

'But you are going to a Roman Catholic service?'

'Yes, I am, tomorrow morning, disguised as a lady's maid. Don't look like that—I'm sure they are all perfectly decent people.'

'I suppose they must be, I never really thought about it, to be honest, although Papa is absolutely red-hot on the Irish Question and completely against Roman Catholics having any rights. He says it would lead to us all being guillotined in our beds. To hear him you would think Charles Stuart was still about to invade at any moment. But why does Lord Henry want to go to mass?' Jane asked, still dubious.

'He is investigating someone, but I cannot say any more because it is confidential, diplomatic business.'

'My dear, you *are* having an exciting time of it since you came to London! Spies, our campaign against Harlby *and* a gorgeous man.'

'Henry is a friend, nothing more, nothing less. I find that a very relaxing relationship—and I have to say, he teases me a great deal less than my female friends,' Melissa said firmly.

She waved the list at Jane to get her attention off Henry. 'Now, I think the logical order for these five is to drop in on Mrs Filby's musicale and escape before anyone is seated. Then Lady Radcliffe's reception for the Portuguese ambassador, Lady Tottingham's house-warming, the Danecastles' ball and finish at the Paulings' masquerade in time for the unmasking at two in the morning. The addresses look to be fairly close together.'

'They are.' Jane stopped teasing and came to look over her shoulder. 'Verity and I spent ages trying to work out the best combinations and routes—and just when we had, along came your note. Not that we were complaining, because it means five more gatherings that we couldn't have managed before. You've got the diplomatic reception, which I rather coveted because I have never been to one.'

'Henry should enjoy that, I hope, unless he is very bored with embassy people.' And there were two balls, which she was looking forward to. From what she had seen that evening they had met, Henry was a very good dancer, and Melissa loved to dance.

'Are you certain that he sees this relationship in quite the way that you do?' Jane asked.

'How else would he see it? He is no rake—his behaviour and conversation are beyond reproach—and he is definitely not courting me.' She shrugged. 'I am not at all eligible for a duke's son and anyway, I've made it clear that I am not intending to marry.'

'If you say so, darling.' Jane drew on her gloves. 'I must be off. I expect we will wave at each other from our carriages as our paths criss-cross this evening.'

Melissa wrote out the list again for Henry, rang for Gertrude and asked to have it delivered immediately, then she ran upstairs and began the difficult task of deciding on an outfit. It was not as though flitting from one gathering to another was unusual, or regarded as ill-mannered, but even so, finding something that would not look positively overdressed for a musicale, yet would be suitable for a ball, required some thought. And she must not forget a mask and domino for the masquerade.

Henry knocked promptly at eight. 'I have borrowed one of the St James's Palace carriages,' he said when he came in. For a moment she thought he was going to kiss her cheek, then he seemed to check the movement.

'From the Palace? Is that allowed?' He certainly looked very much like someone who had just stepped down from a royal vehicle, in a black suit with a sapphire pin in his neckcloth and the gold watch chain with its fobs across his pale blue waistcoat the only ornamentation.

'It is one of the small ones with the crest covered,' he said with a shrug. 'We are attending a diplomatic reception, after all.' He stood back and swept her with his gaze. 'Besides, I could hardly escort you around London in a hackney carriage, not with you looking like that.'

Melissa felt herself blush, just a little. She had to admit to being rather pleased with her efforts and had even managed to take a nap for an hour. She had decided on a cream silk ball dress with gold floss at the hem and with gold thread woven into the little puff sleeves. A brand-new pair of kid gloves almost reached the hem of the sleeves, an aquamarine necklace, bracelet and earrings were a fortuitous choice, echoing Henry's sapphire, and a spray of artificial miniature golden roses in her hair was a finishing touch.

'Thank you. I have a domino and mask, so now we have our own carriage I can leave them there until I need them.'

'Then shall we go?' Henry offered his arm and they swept down her two modest front steps in style.

The musicale was largely attended by a sedate crowd of middle-aged persons. 'I thought it as improbable that Harlby would be here,' Melissa whispered once they had completed a circuit of the room. 'There is hardly a young lady to be seen.'

They waited until the audience began to go through to the ballroom where the chamber quintet was tuning up and then made their escape.

The reception for the Ambassador was equally devoid of susceptible young heiresses, but the guests were livelier, the Portuguese entourage were cheerful and sociable and Melissa found that an hour flew by.

Henry appeared to know a great many people and Melissa was soon in the midst of a number of flirtatious dark-eyed young men. She normally despised flirtation, but now, after two glasses of champagne, she found she was enjoying it very much. Too much, probably, she told herself severely. She should do some work.

'I met a Graf von Arten the other day. Is he a diplomat, do you know?' she asked the man who had just handed her a glass of champagne.

The young man, some kind of military attaché, shook his head. 'I have never encountered this person, but he may be, of course. Now, tell me, may I hope that you will be at our Embassy ball next week? I would be most honoured if you—'

'So sorry to interrupt, must go. We will be late, I fear.' Henry descended and swept her off. 'What were you doing, dallying with João Sequeira? The man is incorrigible.'

'I like that!' She gulped her champagne and handed the glass to a passing footman. 'You abandon me to all those very handsome young men and then come back and accuse me of flirting. That is exceedingly unfair when, for all I know, you were making eyes at the Ambassador's daughters in the next room.'

'He has three sons who are not at all my type. They all have moustaches,' Henry said, retrieving their cloaks in the hallway. 'I was asking a few questions about our German friend, but no one knows him. And no sign of Harlby either.'

'Too much competition there,' Melissa said, as they settled into the carriage. 'All those gorgeous men. He wouldn't stand a chance.'

'You make me feel decidedly inadequate,' Henry grumbled.

'Don't sulk and fish for compliments. They are all shorter than you are,' she said consolingly and patted his hand. 'Now for Lady Tottingham's smart new house. She has just had it restyled from attics to basement and, Verity assures me, she is an exceedingly generous hostess. We may well find Harlby there.'

Lady Tottingham, the wife of one of the wealthiest men in London—'her father made his fortune in

India,' Jane had confided—greeted them effusively, urged them to refresh themselves with champagne and invited them to tour the house as they wished. 'I am so delighted with the results that I want to share them with all my friends,' she announced, beaming.

'As her acquaintance appears to number half of society, I just hope her carpets stand up to the strain,' Henry murmured as they accepted brimming glasses and strolled through to the main drawing room.

'It is very fine,' Melissa whispered back. 'I had expected vulgarity because, you have to admit, she is somewhat...forthcoming, but now I am wishing I could take notes. Not that I could afford to shop wherever it is she does, but I love the colours and how things are arranged.'

They drifted from room to room, her hand tucked comfortably in the crook of his elbow, stopping to chat to acquaintances, more of whom were Henry's than Melissa's, which she enjoyed. They were different from the people she had met through her friends—two artists, a Dutch diamond merchant and a rather louche young man who made eyes at Henry for a moment, much to her surprise.

'Idiot,' Henry remarked when he strolled off. 'One of these days Wilson is going to get into trouble, but he is so exaggerated it is almost a defence in itself.'

That was an interesting encounter. Melissa stored it away to consider later, to add to some theoretical knowledge she had acquired. She was certainly discovering more about the world at Henry's side than she had with even her very liberated and open-minded friends.

'The upper floors are also open for inspection, my

lord, ma'am,' a footman informed them when they arrived at the foot of the sweeping double staircase.

'Shall we?' But Henry was already turning to mount the stairs. 'Imagine having this in the house—one would have to learn to sweep down it in style, even to go to breakfast.'

'Surely you grew up in houses far grander than this?' Dukes must own mansions, surely?

'Walton House has a severe seventeenth-century stone staircase which puts one in mind of clanking down in armour rather than sweeping. Of the others there's a Tudor one with fantastical beasts and several rather grand ones, I will admit. But no double sweeps.'

Discussing staircases had made her forget where they were, exactly, but three steps into the first, empty, room had Henry stopping dead in his tracks. 'We should not be here,' he said, beginning to back out.

Melissa resisted. 'Why not? Oh, do look at the way the window curtains have been done. I could copy that.'

'It is a bedchamber,' Henry said.

'Yes,' she agreed, turning to face him. 'But the door is wide open and other people will come in any moment, I am sure. Now, I really do not like that wallpaper. Too fussy. Henry?'

He was looking decidedly uncomfortable. 'You should not be in a room with a bed and a man.'

'But it is *you*. I feel quite safe with you, Henry.' But his discomfort was beginning to affect her and the bed did seem to loom, rather. A lot of slippery dark blue silk covered it and she had a sudden vision of naked white bodies sliding over it. Goodness, but that made her feel quite...

'If you are feeling uncomfortable, then of course we'll leave,' she said briskly, hoping her face was not as pink as she feared it might be.

She was sure she heard a sigh of relief and he was certainly avoiding looking at the bed. 'Come on, we will go downstairs again.' She linked arms with him and turned to the door, just as a choked sob halted them both. *'Shh...'*

A door opened on the other side of the corridor, but further towards the back of the house and the speaker— or sobber—must have stepped out, because her voice became audible. 'I just do not know. Oh, if only I had more courage.'

There was an inaudible rumble of male speech from inside the room.

'Of course I trust you. You know I have faith, my love. Oh, I am such a coward. Give me strength, Charles.'

Henry said something sharp under his breath and stepped back, half closing the door. 'Charles...?' he whispered.

Melissa squinted through the crack at the door jamb. 'It must be.' She held her breath as a young woman ran past towards the stairs. After a moment Charles Harlby came into sight and strolled after her.

They had found what they were looking for: Harlby's next victim.

Chapter Seven

Henry closed the door and leaned back against it. 'Did you see the smirk on Harlby's face? The bas—swine. We can't follow yet or he'll see us. Was the young lady someone you know?'

'Letitia Houghton.' Melissa propped herself up against the door, shoulder to shoulder with him. 'I do not know her personally, but I recognise her. She inherited everything her father left when he died last year, and he was an East India Company director, so I imagine he was exceedingly wealthy. I suppose that is how she comes to be a guest of Lady Tottingham.'

'What do you want to do now?'

'I will visit her, warn her. It sounds as though she is still holding out and is full of doubts, thank goodness,' Melissa said. 'I think it was Lucy who was telling me about her, so she will know where she lives for certain, but I believe she resides with an aunt and uncle in Brook Street.' She tilted her head sideways to rest against his shoulder. 'I cannot imagine that she would contemplate eloping on a Sunday, not a girl so full of scruples and, I am sure, well brought up, so I will visit on Monday morning. It is such a relief to discover her, but I dread how Letitia will react when I tell her about him. She will be so upset.'

'But nothing like as distressed as she would be to find out just what she had married—or thought she had married,' Henry said. She felt him shift and his cheek rest against her hair. 'We had better wait, give him a chance to leave.'

Their hands touched and fingers intertwined companionably. 'This is nice,' Melissa said. 'Soothing. You give me confidence that we can deal with Harlby. You are a very comforting friend, Henry.'

His fingers tightened around hers. 'I haven't done anything.'

'You listen. You are here. You have ideas.'

'Ideas. Yes.' They were so close that she heard him swallow.

'And, even though I do not believe that ladies should be shrinking violets and rely on men, I cannot deny that I appreciate your strength.' He was silent and Melissa realised that she was feeling decidedly strange. Warm and agitated in a way that had nothing to do with what they had just observed. In fact, very like she had after they had kissed in that little temple in the Palace gardens.

She wanted to turn towards Henry, wrap her arms around him, be held. It was the effect of that strength, of the solidity of him; his shoulders and the muscles she sensed beneath them, she told herself. She needed some support to face her confrontation with Miss Houghton, that must be what this was.

And, of course, one could not go hugging gentlemen in someone else's bedchamber when anyone might walk in at any moment.

'I expect it is safe to emerge now,' she said and released his hand.

'Yes,' Henry said. He sounded a trifle hoarse.

'Are you coming down with a rheum?'

'No, just a frog in my throat.' He coughed, straightened his neckcloth and turned abruptly to open the door. 'Voices on the stairs, someone is coming up.'

They whisked out of the door and, by the time a group of chattering ladies reached the landing, Melissa was studying a marble group outside the bedchamber and Henry appeared around the far corner, as though he had been somewhere else entirely.

She glanced covertly at him as they went downstairs, but the strange tension seemed to have left him. It was very unreasonable, she told herself, to expect men to feel no nerves about potentially awkward situations. Perhaps she had contributed to it by telling him that she relied on his strength. Clearly there was a lot to learn about having a man as a friend.

Henry paused halfway down the stairs and studied the throng in the hallway. There was no sign of Harlby, but Miss Houghton was standing beside a matron with a formidable bosom, and an even more assertive turban, who appeared to be taking leave of their hostess.

'I think we are safe to make our escape,' he said to Melissa, who seemed surprisingly quiet. He wished she was keeping up her usual flow of comment, speculation and conjecture, because then he would not have to think about how he had felt up there in that damned bedchamber.

She had leaned against the door next to him, touching all down his side, warm and fragrant—and as trusting as she would have been with a brother, her fingers twined with his. And he had felt anything but brotherly. All he could think about was that big bed with its glossy silken coverlet and of Melissa, sprawled, laughing up at him, on the silk.

Had he no self-control? He wasn't some ravening beast who could not overcome his appetites. He was not some cynical seducer like Harlby. He got through day-to-day without the slightest inclination towards debauching virgins, yet here he was, fantasising about doing just that with someone who wanted only to be his friend. He should be ashamed of himself.

They were outside on the pavement. 'Did we say goodbye to Lady Tottingham?' he asked as Melissa waved at their driver, who straightened on his seat and urged the horses into motion towards them.

'I did. You reached the foot of the stairs looking as though you were fifty miles away or had a sudden profound thought. I half expected you to cry *Eureka!* Or does one need a bath to leap out of to do that? Anyway, I thanked her nicely and admired her house. Now, off to Lady Danecaster's ball.'

They had given the driver the list of their destinations before they started, so Henry handed Melissa up into the carriage and climbed in after her. 'We've found Harlby and identified his target. Do you still want to continue?'

'Oh.' In the dim interior he could not make out her expression clearly, but Melissa sounded disappointed. 'I thought— But, no, of course not, if you are bored or tired.'

'Neither.' *Merely in need of a cold bath.* 'I just wanted to make sure you were not.'

'We don't have to go on to the masquerade,' Melissa said. 'I find them rather tiresome because dominos are always too hot and masks are scratchy. But I would very much like to dance.'

'Then we shall.' A crowded ballroom was quite different from a bedchamber, after all. Or the inside of a closed carriage, come to that. Henry told himself that the Danecasters' house was only just around the corner.

Melissa was talking again, considering her approach to Miss Houghton, arguing with herself over the best way to go about breaking the bad news to her and wondering if it wouldn't be better to have one of her married friends do it. Would that be cowardly? Or prudent?

Henry said yes or no and made what were hopefully intelligent noises while his imagination ran through images of ice fields, snow, the temperature of the Peerless Pool in April and any other chilly thoughts he could conjure up.

'Henry?'

'What? Ah, we have arrived. Sorry. I was just thinking that I need—' *A mistress, that's what I need.* 'A glass of champagne.'

As she descended from the carriage, Melissa gave him what he could only describe as A Look. 'You are in a very strange mood tonight, Henry. Now, let us have some champagne and then I expect two dances with you. And do not pretend that you do not dance, because I saw you the night we first met.'

'Yes, ma'am,' he said and found a smile as they entered, shed their cloaks and joined the other guests climbing the staircase towards the ballroom.

'That was delightful,' Melissa said. She sank on to one of the gilt chairs that ringed the ballroom and fanned herself energetically after a particularly vigorous set of country dances. 'But exhausting.'

Henry gestured to a footman and secured two more glasses of champagne. He had begun to lose count of how many he had drunk, which was not something any prudent diplomat ever did. It could not have been so very many, because Melissa was matching him and she appeared perfectly coherent and steady on her feet.

'Now,' she said, studying her dance card. 'Do you waltz? Yes, of course you must. If we sit this set out to recover, then the following dance is a waltz and you can show me how they do it in Austria, which is where it comes from, isn't it?'

'There or Germany, I believe,' Henry said. 'Although the folk dances are similar right across the middle of Europe.' He was prepared to hold forth on the origins of the waltz for an hour if that meant he did not have to dance it with Melissa.

'That's interesting,' she said politely as she wrote *Henry* in firm black letters against the next but one dance.

He was doomed. Henry wondered whether the buffet was serving ice cream. 'Have you been approved to dance it by one of the Patronesses of Almack's?' he asked hopefully.

'Goodness, yes. Such a stuffy rule, although there are at least two of them here tonight, so I suppose I would have behaved myself if I hadn't been approved. Verity secured me vouchers as soon as I arrived in London, dragged me there on my first Wednesday and smiled relentlessly at Lady Cowper until she allowed me to waltz.'

'Oh, good,' Henry said.

'Now, what is the plan for tomorrow?'

He seized the welcome distraction from thoughts of Melissa's waist under his hand. 'Mass is at half past nine, so I will collect you at nine. It might well be a complete wild goose chase, but if they are there together I would like to sit as close as possible behind to see if anything is passed between them, or even if we can hear what they say.'

'If we get there earlier, arrive at nine at the latest,' she suggested, 'we can lurk at the back and then, when they come in, slip in behind them.'

'An excellent idea. Have you managed to find a suitable dress and bonnet?'

'Gertrude will lend me her best Sunday clothes. I protested that second-best would do, but she would not hear of it. There is a light brown dress and shawl and a simple straw bonnet with a brown ribbon. I have a veil and some cream gloves with a few darns, which I thought were a nice touch.'

'You appear to have a natural talent for intrigue,' he teased.

Melissa did not smile. 'You are trusting me to help and to do this properly,' she said, very serious.

Henry felt a pang of something he could not identify. Certainly not lust. Affection, perhaps.

'You will be perfect,' he assured her and they watched the dancers and, in Melissa's case, smiled at the procession of gentlemen asking for dances. With the exception of the next waltz she accepted all offers.

'We can't dance together again,' she said, nudging him in the ribs with a sharp elbow. 'Not if we are going to waltz. I cannot afford to be thought fast. You should go and find some partners or you'll be whatever a male wallflower is.'

'Unpopular with the ladies,' he said with a grin. 'Very well, I will seek out some female wallflowers after this set.'

The dancers came off the floor, the string band did some rapid tuning and then they were on their feet and taking their places. He took her hand and she laid the other on his shoulder and smiled at him as he placed his palm as lightly as possible at her waist, thanking heaven for gloves.

Then the music began and they started to dance. 'Oh, the tempo is rather fast!' Melissa said as they whirled around the end of the dance floor.

'This isn't Almack's,' Henry said with a grin, suddenly realising that he was enjoying himself and was perfectly capable of dancing with his friend in hold without dissolving into a puddle of inappropriate lust. Clearly the answer was to avoid bedchambers and to fill one's head with the requirements of the dance. Melissa gave a squeak as he executed an adventurous move, spinning her under his raised arm, then promenading down the room.

'Are you all right?' he asked, but she was laughing and matching him move for move and he realised how right this felt and how happy he was that he felt easy with her again.

They climbed wearily into the carriage at one in the morning, footsore, slightly tipsy and still laughing.

'I could have stayed longer,' Melissa said.

'We must be sober and serious in the morning,' Henry reminded her. 'And on the alert.'

They reached Half Moon Street in minutes and he climbed down and took her latch key from her. There was a lamp glowing in the hallway and a voice from upstairs called, 'Just coming, Miss Taverner!'

'I *told* her not to wait up.' Melissa sighed. 'Thank you for a lovely evening, Henry. I will be awake and alert at eight o'clock, never fear.'

She went up on tiptoe to kiss him on the cheek, just as he turned his head and her lips brushed his, a fleeting sweet warmth, then she was inside and he heard the bolts being slid home.

'Ryder Street.' Henry got back into the vehicle and brooded for the few minutes it took to reach his lodgings. He climbed the stairs to the dimly lit sitting room, sloshed brandy from the sideboard into a glass and sank into his favourite chair.

'Good God, you scared the life out of me.' James sat bolt upright in the opposite seat, making Henry start. 'What the devil's wrong with you? I haven't heard a sigh like that since my father saw the estimate for re-roofing the Grange.'

Henry licked spilt brandy from the back of his hand. 'Woman trouble,' he said.

'Oh, hard luck, old man. What is it? Expects to marry you, refuses to marry you or informs you that a little surprise is on its way?'

'None of those, thankfully. You recall I told you I had acquired a female friend?'

'Yes. Thought you were all about in your cockloft, but I was too kind to say so.'

'I find I desire her.'

'Well, go to it. If she's a lady, marry her, if she'll have you. If she's another type of female altogether, come to an arrangement, offer *carte blanche*.'

'She is a lady, she does not want to marry anyone and we are supposed to be *friends*,' Henry said. 'I like being her friend,' he added. 'She's amusing, intelligent and she's got spirit.'

'All young ladies wish to marry,' James said. 'She's teasing you, trying to pique your interest.'

'No, it isn't that. I truly believe she means it.'

'In that case you'll either have to stop seeing her, which I can see might be difficult to manage without insulting her, or you will have to control your baser instincts.' James appeared to find that thought wildly amusing.

'Thank you so much for your exceedingly helpful advice.' Henry tossed back the brandy and got to his feet. 'I'm for my bed.' He was not so foolish as to tell James he was off to church early in the morning and with the lady in question.

'You could try changing her mind about marriage,' James said, the teasing note gone from his voice. 'Try courting her.'

Henry stopped in the doorway. 'I have no plans to marry,' he said without turning around.

'Plans? Hah!' James said. 'Where women are concerned plans go out of the window. I suppose I had better try to get some sleep, too. That infernal code is driving me to distraction.'

Henry climbed the final flight of stairs to his room. Marriage? What was the point? He was a younger son with neither title nor estates to leave to an heir. He had a career that could take him anywhere at any time and the freedom to enjoy himself.

Added to which, he had no very clear idea of how a successful marriage might work, he thought as he stripped off and splashed lukewarm water vaguely in the direction of his face. His own parents appeared together at formal functions and, on the evidence of four sons, had occasionally found themselves in the same bed together. Otherwise they might live on separate continents for all the time they appeared to spend together.

Besides any of that, Melissa was set against marriage, so the entire question was moot and if he hadn't had that unwise glass of brandy he wouldn't be even contemplating James's ridiculous suggestion now.

Ridiculous. He hauled up the covers and closed his eyes.

Chapter Eight

'Henry, that is quite brilliant.' Melissa walked all around the figure who had alighted from the hackney carriage outside her front door at eight in the morning.

He was slightly stooped, had a pair of wire-rimmed spectacles on his nose and his chin was darkened by a night's growth of whiskers. 'The suit is one that my landlord found for me. It was left behind by a former tenant who was a writer at the East India Company offices. I sat on the neckcloth before tying it and the boots are old ones that haven't been polished in an age. I just dusted them. I think the effect is just on the respectable side of shabby.'

'Exactly that. You look like a clerk from a counting house. What have you done to your hair?' She peered at what she could see of his normally dark blond crop.

'A liberal application of grease and a hat that is just slightly too large for me. I think we match very well.'

As the carriage clattered off down the Sunday-quiet street Melissa said, 'If someone asks us our names, what are we going to say?'

'Maria and Peter Higgins,' Henry said promptly.

'And are we brother and sister or a married couple? I brought Grandmama's wedding ring, in case.'

'Brother and sister,' Henry said decisively. 'With you veiled, any lack of resemblance does not matter.'

'Excellent. That means I do not have to be your obedient shadow,' she said.

'You really do not have a very high opinion of the married state, do you?' Henry asked. He was polishing the lenses of his spectacles, which she assumed were plain glass.

'Unless it is a mutual love match, it seems to be a highly risky undertaking to me. Of course,' she said casually, studying a darn in her gloves, 'I could take a lover.'

Henry dropped his spectacles, one lens fell out and they both fell to their knees, scrabbling around on the dirty floor.

'Here it is.' She handed it back and they both sat again. 'That has not done a great deal for our appearance of respectability.'

'Taking a lover would do even less for yours,' Henry retorted. He fixed the lens back and polished it furiously. 'Have you taken leave of your senses?'

'I do not see why you are so hypocritical about it. Men take lovers all the time. Are you telling me that you are a—?'

'No, I am not.' He was snapping at her now. 'But the risks are appalling for a woman. For a lady. Loss of reputation, the risk of disease, of pregnancy.'

'I assume men run the same risks.'

'Not usually loss of reputation. Disease can be

guarded against if you know what you are doing and pregnancy can generally be avoided. And if there is, by some accident, a baby, then a decent man will ensure both mother and child are looked after properly. But it is the woman who takes the risk that the man will behave as he should. And what if this theoretical lover turns to blackmail?'

'I—' She had not thought of blackmail. Hadn't really thought any of it through, other than to form the opinion that this was yet another example of men getting what they wanted and women doing without.

Melissa brooded on what Henry had said. It sounded sensible. Not that she was going to tell him she agreed with him, not yet.

'I shall have to choose with great care, I can see that,' she said thoughtfully, fully intending to pour oil on the flames, just to see how he reacted. 'It cannot be much more hazardous than choosing a husband, after all? What if a spouse is diseased or violent?'

'You are taking a lover over my dead body,' Henry retorted. 'Now, put down your veil. We have arrived.'

Over his... She had not intended to make him so angry, only to tease. Penitent, Melissa arranged her veil and then followed Henry out, waiting meekly on the pavement while he paid the driver. She had no desire to provoke him into forgetting the part he must play.

The church was still mostly empty and they slipped into a pew right at the back to watch and wait. Melissa looked around, glad of the concealing veil to cover her curiosity. She liked the smell of incense and the colours, although a few of the brightly painted saints and martyrs were exhibiting the evidence of their deaths in too gruesome a manner to make her feel entirely at ease.

The church began to fill slowly at first, then with increasing numbers.

'They aren't coming,' Henry whispered. 'Do you want to leave?'

'I'd like to stay now we are here, it is interesting. Oh, look—that's von Arten, isn't it?'

'Yes. And that's Laverne behind him.'

They watched as the Graf took his place on a pew tucked away at the side. A moment later the Frenchman joined him. Henry got up, murmuring apologies as he squeezed past an elderly lady, then led the way down the side aisle to the empty pew right behind the two men. He bent over, covered his face with his hand as though in deep prayer and Melissa stared fixedly at her own hands, straining to hear what they were saying.

It was not a great deal, although fortunately they were speaking French and not German and, never having heard either of them speak before, she had no idea which man said what. She caught, *'La compagnie'*, then a long gap where she could make out nothing. Then *'Il veut plus d'argent.'*

It was said angrily, but the other man replied in soothing tones, *'Ça vaut le coup.'*

Melissa slid her notebook out of her reticule and noted the few scraps down.

The company...
He wants more money...
It is worth it...

Then there was movement, the congregation rose and the two men fell silent.

The service continued and she tried to copy what the other women she could see were doing, remaining in her seat, as did Henry, while the sacrament was taken. The Frenchman in front of them went up to the altar and, for a moment, she thought, *Hypocrite.* But, of course, he thought he was doing his patriotic duty, just as she and Henry were. She kept her head bent as he returned and the service continued.

As the congregation began to gather their possessions together and stand up, von Arten turned to the Frenchman and she saw him speak. *'Donnez-moi les papiers, maintenant.'*

The other man hesitated, then nodded and stood to follow von Arten out of the pew. He was fumbling inside the breast of his coat and she saw him take out a folded document.

Right under our noses!

Melissa stood, edged towards the aisle and then, just as the Frenchman handed the papers to von Arten, she stumbled, gave a little cry of alarm and crashed into him. They both ended up on the floor and she felt the folded document jab into her ribs.

'Oh! That *hurts.*' She struggled into a half-sitting position, flailing out at the Frenchman as he tried to help her—or perhaps simply seize the papers. Henry was on his knees beside her and she felt his hand slide under, take the papers, flatten them out, and she flapped about even more.

For a few seconds there was chaos as helpful ladies hurried to assist her, von Arten was pushed aside by

sharp female elbows and showered with indignant pro-
tests as he got in the way.

Beside her, Henry, his accent more East End than
Mayfair, snapped at Laverne, "Ere, you keep your
hands off my sister, mate.'

Finally she was on her feet, veil still in place, Henry
supporting her. They brushed aside the offers of help,
smelling salts, a glass of water, and made their way out,
not looking to see what the two conspirators were doing.

'Did you see anything?'

'Wait until we are in the hackney.' Henry hailed one,
lost it to a plump matron with three children in tow and
secured another. 'Smithfield,' he called up to the driver.

'Are you hurt?' he asked as they collapsed inside.

'No, not at all. Why Smithfield?'

'I'll tell him to change in a moment once we're out of
sight and earshot.' They rounded a corner and he lowered the window and called up, 'Make that Half Moon
Street, if you please.'

He gave the number and there was a remark, thankfully unintelligible, from the driver and he closed the
window. 'What did you hear? That was brilliantly quick
thinking and very good acting. Even I thought you really had tripped at first.'

Melissa showed him her notebook. 'Were you able
to see the papers?'

'Just a glimpse, but enough to know it concerns the
East India Company and there were some initials—
J.P.R.—on the last sheet. That is distinctive enough to
identify the writer, I imagine.' He sat back. 'I'll pass that
on and someone will take action, identify who J.P.R.
is and deal with him. Out of my hands now so I can go

back to enjoying my holiday before they decide where to send me next.'

'Do you think either of them recognised you?' Melissa worried.

'No, I doubt it. I didn't look von Arten in the face and Laverne doesn't know me personally. Thank you for all your assistance. I will drop you off, then go on to Whitehall and report.' He smiled at her, looking so strange with his shabby clothes and spectacles that she laughed out loud.

'How will you spend the rest of the day?' Henry asked. He removed the glasses and stuck them in a pocket. 'Catching up on your writing?'

'Yes,' she said, with rather less enthusiasm than he was clearly expecting. 'I was in a muddle, Henry. I thought I would write something that would appeal to Mr Murray—a witty and incisive comedy of manners, perhaps. But I cannot seem to enjoy it. So I have begun to write another of my romantic adventures. It must be our cloak-and-dagger experiences that are unsettling me.'

'I'm sorry about that.' Henry frowned. 'The last thing I want to do is distract you from your work.'

'It isn't that at all. I think I must wait to get the right inspiration and, meanwhile, I can write what I enjoy. Oh, and, Henry, I did hear what you said about taking a lover. I was only teasing you.'

He shook his head at her. 'You'll be the death of me, Melissa. I had visions of having to patrol outside your house with a shotgun to fend off unsuitable types.'

'There are suitable ones, then?' she asked, smiling to show him she was teasing again.

'None,' he said with emphasis as the carriage slowed. 'We are back.'

'Don't get down,' Melissa said, turning to kiss his cheek. She hopped down before he could move and called up, 'Take the gentleman on to Whitehall, please.'

Henry leaned out of the window. 'I'll come with you tomorrow and wait outside, unless you are going with your friends.'

'Thank you,' she said with relief. 'I thought too many of us would perhaps make her more resistant to reason. But knowing you are there will stop me turning tail and running!'

Henry was a dear, she thought as she closed the front door. He was a real friend and he made her feel safe while managing to let her be involved in situations which might be difficult, even dangerous. That, she suspected, was rare for a man.

Yes, he was a dear man, but he still gave her that unsettling sensation deep inside, that frisson of excitement and…hunger. And the way he had reacted when she had half seriously talked of taking a lover had been almost thrilling, as though he was acting out of jealousy. When, of course, he was simply making commonsense objections.

Cousin Almeria emerged from the back of the hallway as Melissa took off her bonnet. She had a small box in her hands, the top covered in a cloth. 'Ah, there you are.' She blinked. 'That is rather a plain gown, is it not? Surely I have not missed the news that suitable attire for Sundays must be so dowdy.'

'I have been on a small adventure with Lord Henry

and this is my disguise. I will change in a moment. Were you looking for me?'

'No, other than to wonder what time you would be in for luncheon. I believe I will not have time to examine last night's catch of moths until this afternoon.' She nodded towards the box she carried. She placed it carefully on the hall table. 'They will be safe and cool there.'

Gertrude came downstairs and took the bonnet and shawl.

'I am sorry there is dust on the skirt,' Melissa apologised as they mounted the stairs. 'I tripped over in the church. We will have luncheon just as soon as I have changed, Almeria,' she called down. 'Could you tell Cook?'

'And how is Lord Henry?' her cousin enquired over cold roast beef and a salad of lettuce and herbs. 'Such a pleasant gentleman. Your parents will be delighted.'

'He is merely a friend,' Melissa said mildly, aware of the dangers of protesting too much. Although there was nothing *mere* about Henry. She thought of his shoulders and of the form-moulding breeches and shivered a little.

'Pleased by the connection, I mean. I am certain you are much too level-headed to fancy yourself in love, not when you have set your future course so firmly in place.'

Melissa gave her cousin a long look from under her lashes. Almeria was, surely, too sensible to leap to conclusions and too unconventional herself to assume that Melissa was merely being coy when she said she was not searching for a husband.

'Exactly,' she said, realising she had left her answer

rather too long and then—completely irrationally, because what did Cousin Almeria know of matters of the heart?—blurted out, 'Only, I am afraid I am becoming rather too fond of him.'

Oh, what a silly, inadequate word fond *is.*

'You are in love with him?'

'Goodness, no.'

'You desire him?' Almeria might have been referring to the breeding habits of the hawk moth for all the discomfiture she showed.

'I think so. And I like him a great deal. But that is not love, is it?'

'I have no idea. You do not appear to be pining.' Her cousin cast an expressive look at Melissa's empty plate. 'Have you any urge to write poetry about him?'

'Certainly not. What an idea. It is just that he makes me feel that it is right to be with him. He seems to understand me and like me.' She frowned.

'That is unusual in a man, I must say. Well, my diagnosis, for what it is worth, is that you like him as a friend and he likes you—which is always attractive. You desire him physically, which hardly seems strange when you are both young and healthy and he is a rather fine specimen.' She took a mouthful of roast beef, chewed thoughtfully, swallowed and added, 'Acting upon those feelings might, however, be unwise.'

'Yes, of course.' Hadn't she and Henry discussed just how unwise such things would be only that morning? Or, rather, he had expressed himself forcefully on the subject and she had agreed with him. Only…if one were to take the risk, surely Henry, so alert to the dangers, so concerned for her welfare, would be the perfect man? 'Of course,' she repeated with more emphasis. 'It would be most imprudent.'

'The absence of the pleasures of conjugal relations and the resulting children are the two greatest sacrifices a woman makes for living an independent life,' Almeria said. 'Each person must make the decision for themselves as to whether it is worth it.'

'And you think it is?' Melissa asked bluntly.

'For myself, yes. I have no maternal instinct and, I am certain, I would be feeling regrets by now if I had. As for the other, well, brisk exercise and intellectual stimulation are the answer, I find.'

Melissa thought of Henry's mouth on hers, of the feel of his body, lean and hard under her hands, of the way she felt when they danced, and found she was not so convinced about Almeria's remedy as her cousin appeared to be. Brisk physical excise—of a specific kind—with Henry and discussion afterwards, now that *did* seem appealing, but she was coming to regret her curiosity about the process of human coition and the determination with which she had pursued it. She knew too much in theory and now her writer's imagination was filling in the blanks with inconvenient enthusiasm.

She finished her meal and excused herself. Perhaps someone else's problems would take her mind off her own. She settled at her desk to write to her four friends, a brief note to each, describing what she and Henry had discovered and what she intended to do about it.

I propose calling by myself tomorrow morning, if one of you will send me her address—I believe Lucy said she knew it.

*I do not know what the effect on Miss Hough-
ton might be of several of us descending on her
with such delicate and disturbing news. If I cannot
convince her of the danger, then I think we will
have to approach her guardians, and in that case
at least two of you, titled married women, should
carry more weight than one spinster.*

*I will write again as soon as I have anything
to report.*
Melissa

She sat and thought for a while about how she should
tell Letitia Houghton that she was the victim of a cruel
fortune hunter. Try to be kind and soften the message?
But how? No, she decided after much agonising, state
the facts and hope to be believed.

With relief she pulled the few pages already completed of *The Rogue Lord of Castle Darke* towards
her, dipped her pen in the ink and began to make the
changes that were bubbling away in her imagination. A
hero who was kind, intelligent and tough and the pos-
sessor of a pair of mesmerising blue eyes. A heroine
who was independent and who acted at his side, not in
his shadow, and a villain... Now, who would that be?
What were these two working to overcome? What was
the secret of Castle Darke?

Chapter Nine

Henry was at the door at ten the next morning. 'I thought any earlier would be unacceptable for calling,' he said. 'I borrowed a town coach again because I thought it would create a good impression.'

'What a good idea,' Melissa agreed. 'Although any time in the morning is unconventional between complete strangers. I only hope they will receive me.'

She sat next to Henry and tried to fix her mind on the painful interview ahead of her, not on the dreams that had disturbed her sleep. She was not at all sure that she could look Henry in the face without turning crimson because they had been detailed, vivid and quite, quite shocking. And, she had to confess to herself, had done nothing to reduce her desire to find out exactly what it would be like in real life and with the man beside her.

'I had a message from Lucy. The aunt and uncle are the Graingers and I was correct, it is Brook Street.' She showed him Lucy's note and he gave instructions to the driver for the very short journey.

* * *

'Good luck,' Henry said as the groom opened the door for her outside the smart town house. 'I'll keep well out of sight.'

The groom knocked for her, a good loud rattle, but the place was empty when the door opened to reveal a butler who, even by the standards of London butlers, was stony-faced.

'The family is not at home, madam,' he said before she could get a word out.

'Do you mean that they are not receiving or are not in residence?'

The man looked thoroughly affronted.

'It is a matter of considerable urgency. My card.'

He took it and glanced at it. 'As I said—'

'Is there some problem?' Henry appeared beside her. 'My card.'

'My lord.' The tone was slightly more conciliatory.

'We have a matter of importance to discuss with—'

'Mr Grainger. I am sure he does not wish his business aired on the street.'

'The family are out of town. They will return tomorrow. I am certain that those of their acquaintance they wish to be aware of their whereabouts, already know of it. I suggest you call again tomorrow. My lord.'

'Damn,' Henry said, when they had beaten a strategic retreat to the carriage. 'We try again tomorrow. What would you like to do now?'

For some reason the question flustered Melissa. She wanted to be with Henry, but at the same time she felt uneasy about the amount of time they were spending together. Yet she could not say why. She had assisted him, he was helping her, he appeared to enjoy her company and she certainly enjoyed his. Was she more imbued with the ridiculous conventions and taboos about female behaviour than she had thought? That was equally unsettling to contemplate.

'Thank you, Henry,' she said, as calmly as she could. 'I think I had best return home and write, much as I would enjoy your company.'

'Of course.' She could not tell whether he was relieved, disappointed or merely politely indifferent.

Being friends with a man was far more complicated than she had imagined it would be.

When Melissa knocked on Tuesday morning the door was answered by the butler again. He seemed to her to loom more than he had the previous day and his position entirely blocked her view into the hallway.

'Good morning, Miss Taverner.' The early hour was also clearly displeasing him. 'My mistress is not at home to visitors. I suggest that you write—' He was interrupted by a faint shriek from the interior.

'She has left a note! Oh, foolish, foolish girl!'

The butler twitched and Melissa took her chance, ducked under his arm and into the house. 'Take me to Mrs Grainger immediately. I know what has happened.' As she spoke she walked far enough down the hall that he could not push her out of the door again without using brute force.

There was sobbing coming from the room to her right.

'Announce me now, or I will simply walk in,' she threatened.

The butler opened the door and the level of sobs increased. 'A Miss Taverner has called. She says she knows what has happened to Miss Houghton, madam.'

'Show her in, Bateson! What are you waiting for?' a man demanded.

'Miss Taverner, madam.'

A buxom woman in a bed robe of pink silk was slumped on a sofa and Melissa recognised her as Miss Houghton's chaperon from Lady Tottingham's house warming. She clutched a handkerchief while a maid by her side waved a smelling bottle about ineffectually. A burly man with imposing side whiskers and a high complexion had apparently just stopped marching up and down the room.

'Where is she?' he demanded. 'What have you done with her?'

'Nothing. I believe Miss Houghton has eloped with a man called Charles Harlby who has convinced her that he intends marriage.'

'How do you know this?' Mr Grainger demanded over the renewed wails from his wife.

'Harlby seduced someone I know. Recently I saw him in what seemed to be negotiation with an unlicensed clergyman and on Saturday night I overheard him in conversation with Miss Houghton. What was said convinced me that I should call and tell you what I know of him.'

'Hah! I am not some country innocent to be gulled, Miss Taverner, or whatever your name is. You are in league with this Harlby and intend to blackmail us.'

'Would you believe the Duchess of Aylsham, Mr

Grainger? She, too, knows of Harlby's character and history. She has not accompanied me because we wanted to be as discreet as possible, but I can send for her, if that is what it takes to convince you of the truth of this.'

All bluster drained away as he subsided on to the sofa next to his wife and waved a hand at a chair. 'Sit down, Miss Taverner. Where will he have taken her?'

'I have no idea,' she confessed. 'When did she leave?'

'She went out for a walk before breakfast with her maid. The girl returned without her at eight, told us that Letitia had instructed her to come back for a different shawl and then almost half an hour later came back with it saying that Letitia was no longer where she left her. Then she brought us a note she found in Letitia's room. But that simply says she has gone to be with her true love, we are not to worry and that she will write.'

'Not to worry!' sobbed Mrs Grainger.

'May I speak to the maid?'

Mr Grainger tugged the bell pull and summoned the maid, Eliza, who seemed subdued and nervous.

'Where did you leave Miss Houghton?'

'She said she wanted to walk in Hyde Park, then she said she was cold and sent me back for the shawl. We were past Grosvenor Square, Miss. Almost at Park Street.'

Park Street... Park Street. That is familiar.

'I have an idea that I must investigate. I will either return within the hour or send a message.' Melissa stood up and let herself out into the hall, making the butler, who had been listening at the door, jump.

* * *

Henry was reading the *Morning Post*, but cast it aside when she scrambled into the coach.

'She's gone and, if her maid is to be trusted, was last seen in Upper Brook Street near the junction with Park Street. Is there a church or a chapel near there? A quiet one?'

'There's one of the newish chapels in Park Street, at the junction with Green Street, I think. I can't imagine that would be exactly bustling at this hour.' Henry leaned out of the window and called up to the driver, then ducked back inside. 'What happened?'

Melissa gave him a summary as they trotted through the busy morning streets. 'I cannot make up my mind whether the maid is part of this but, whether she is or not, Letitia is now without any protection at all. How quickly can a marriage ceremony be performed?'

'They'd need half an hour, I'd say,' Henry said. 'They'd have to go through some pretence of signing a register, for example—I cannot believe the girl does not know that is necessary. If he scrambles the thing too fast, then she would, surely, become suspicious.'

They arrived at the chapel, a solid brick-built structure. Henry jumped out, reached up and swung Melissa down and they entered together, at a run. The building was empty.

'Confound it.' Henry stood at the top of the steps, looking up and down the street. 'Were we wrong or are we too late?'

Melissa looked, too, then saw, just to the side of the chapel steps, a flower seller sitting on an upturned box, her basket of rather sad little nosegays set out in front of her.

'Good morning.' She fished in her reticule and found some coins. 'Two, please.' The transaction completed, she asked, 'Have we just missed a wedding, do you know?'

The woman looked up at her and smiled, revealing a gap in her front teeth. She must be in her forties, Melissa guessed, although her face was lined with hardship and her clothes tattered, so she was not certain.

'Aye, you have that, miss. Not much of one, though—no guests. I like a wedding with guests...it's good for business. He bought her flowers from me, then asked me to be a witness. "Lord love yer," I said to him. "I can't write me name." And he said I could make my mark. So I did. Me and some old boy who was toddling past. Plain little thing, the girl, I thought. Still, no accounting for tastes.'

'No,' Melissa agreed. 'Which way did they go when they left?'

'Up towards Tyburn—an hour ago, must be.' The woman gestured to the north. 'Post-chaise and four, it was. *Someone's got money to burn*, I thought to meself. *Hiring a yellow bounder and four horses.* Mean so and so, he were, though. Gave me a trooper, that's all.'

Henry had come over and was listening intently. 'Half a crown? You are right, that's downright miserly. Here's a couple of bull's eyes for your trouble.'

The two crowns vanished into a grubby hand. 'I thank you kindly. A proper gent you are.'

'We could catch them—if we only knew where they were going,' Melissa said, frustrated.

'I think I might hazard a guess. I looked into Harlby's family last night. His parents are dead and the only property I can locate that he owns is what seems like a small manor near Kenilworth. If he was headed towards Tyburn, then the chances are he'll take the Edgware Road, then head for Watford and Buckingham. That's the direct road and he'll have no reason to suspect anyone is on his tail.'

'We must go back and tell her aunt and uncle.'

'No time. But I can't just commandeer this coach.' Henry stood, lower lip caught between his teeth as he thought, then turned to the driver. 'Fred, take us to the livery stables at Paddington, fast as you can, then go back to the address in Brook Street and deliver a note.' He bundled Melissa unceremoniously into the vehicle and slammed the door as it lurched into rapid motion.

'Have you got paper and pencil? Good. Write a note for the Graingers. With any luck we'll catch our pair before nightfall.'

'Money?' Melissa asked as she began to compose a message that was as brief as possible while still containing all the facts.

Henry patted the breast of his coat. 'I came with a good supply of bank notes. I learned fairly early on that when one is involved in any kind of, shall we say, mysterious goings-on, a ready supply of cash is essential.'

'Oh, goodness, I forgot to ask about the Graf and the Frenchman. Is there anything you are allowed to tell me?'

'It proved most interesting, and everyone is very pleased with me,' Henry said, looking rather endearingly smug. 'The initials on that paper, combined with the East India Company references, were enough to identify the writer, who, as it turns out, is exceedingly short of funds. And our French friend Laverne is, apparently, half-Russian. The powers that be are most interested. None of that can be repeated to anyone, of course.'

'Of course, I promise. How very intriguing, and rather disillusioning when one considers what a good ally the Czar was against Napoleon.'

He glanced out of the window. 'We're here. Do you suffer from sickness in fast-moving vehicles?'

'Not so far as I am aware,' Melissa said as she handed the note to the driver. 'Please deliver it as soon as possible.' She turned back to Henry, who was talking to a bandy-legged man. 'Frankly, I have not had the opportunity to find out. Oh.' She looked at the vehicle to which the grooms were harnessing a pair of edgy chestnuts. It appeared to consist of nothing but a small seat suspended on straps and springs between large rear wheels and smaller front ones. It looked too fragile to move. 'Am I about to find out? That is a phaeton.'

'You are. And this is a crane-necked phaeton, to be exact. Are you still game for the chase or shall I find you a hackney carriage to return home?'

'Of course I am game,' Melissa said crossly, 'if I can work out how to get up into the thing.'

Henry simply picked her up with both hands on her waist and lifted her over the front wheel until she could stand on the step and then scramble on to the seat. The contraption rocked wildly.

I will not whimper. Or scream. Faint, possibly...

Henry joined her, which stabilised the seat somewhat.

'Let them go.'

'Oh, good,' she said faintly as they turned out of the livery stable yard and back on to the Edgware Road, heading north. 'You *can* drive this thing.'

'Apparently, yes.' Henry sounded a trifle distant. 'Never have before, but it is definitely the fastest vehicle available.'

'Never?' she asked faintly.

'I have driven low-perch phaetons, curricles and gigs.' He gave her a fleeting glance and she caught the flash of white teeth. He was enjoying himself. 'I'm sure we will be perfectly safe just as long as I do not try to turn corners.'

Melissa did not rise to the bait. She'd had time to watch how steady his left hand was on the reins, how his right hand kept the whip clear of the horses, and she could see how the fresh pair were settling under his control. Henry might not have driven one of these spindly little contraptions before, but he clearly knew how to handle spirited horses. Her grip eased on the narrow rail beside her and she let herself settle on the seat.

'That's better,' Henry said. 'I can feel you relaxing. You are a most encouraging companion on an adventure, Melissa.'

'We do appear to be having them, don't we? Passionate embraces in summer houses, disguises in church, foiling spies and now chasing fugitives.'

'Do you think you should put your veil down, by the way?'

'Oh, goodness, I had forgotten it.' Melissa pulled it down to cover her face. 'I should have given the driver a note for Cousin Almeria as well. She doesn't fuss, but if I am out late tonight without having come home first, she may be alarmed.'

'I'll find someone to take a message in Kilburn,' Henry said. 'We're almost there and I want to stop and enquire if anyone has seen them. Goodness knows how many post-chaises pass there each day, but one with a team instead of the usual pair might attract notice. Can you scribble a note as we go?'

Despite the steadily rising ground it was a matter of minutes before they reached The Bell Inn with the Wells pleasure gardens and spring behind it. Henry whistled to a pot boy, who came to hold the horses, thrust the reins and whip into Melissa's hands and jumped down with her note. He was back almost immediately, tossed a coin to the lad and grinned at Melissa as she handed back the reins and whip with some emphasis.

'Nobody noticed a chaise and four, but they gave me a wafer to seal the note and a groom is taking it now.'

'It is like being in the country,' Melissa said, looking around as they drove on.

'There are rather charming tea gardens at the Wells—I'll take you one day when we aren't having adventures.'

'I insist on adventures as a condition of our friendship,' Melissa said, and felt Henry go still beside her.

'I hope this one does not prove too extreme an escapade,' he said. 'I am confident of catching up with them by late afternoon and you are veiled, but what if we find ourselves returning home in the early hours?'

'That is no more than would be the case if we had been to a ball and stayed very late. I have come home at three before now.'

'Even so.' There was no humour in his voice now. 'If the worse comes to the worst and we are out all night, clearly I will have compromised you and—'

'And if you say one more word I will push you off your seat and leave you in the road. Don't talk such nonsense.' Something akin to panic mixed with embarrassment flooded through her. Henry would marry her? But she didn't want to be married and certainly not to a man who felt he had to offer for her. Of course she wanted Henry, but not marriage. Not that. Did she?

'There is no need for anything so extreme,' he said mildly. 'If you would like to drive, you only have to say so.'

She turned, mouth open to deliver an irritable retort, and saw he was smiling. 'You are impossible,' she said instead, and smiled back. He would forget all that nonsense about compromising her just as soon as they caught up with Harlby.

'Now, let me work this out. They are driving a team, so I imagine they will manage at least ten miles before they need a change, which means, if I am not mistaken, Stanmore.'

'You have all the roads in your head?' she asked, amazed.

'No, I've got a map in my pocket. Which, I must confess, is not amazing foresight on my part, but the result of not taking it out after the last time I wore this coat last week and needed to look at the roads to Dover. In the end I didn't need it and have just remembered it. Can you take it out? Inside the right breast pocket.'

It involved twisting round on the seat and sliding her fingers between coat and waistcoat. He was warm and the sensation of the silk lining of the coat on the back of her hand and the slight roughness of the waist-coat fabric on her palm made her feel unaccountably hot, despite the breeze caused by their rapid pace. She could feel his heartbeat against her wrist and the need for him to keep his arms close to his sides made the space very tight.

The map was folded up into some kind of case and she worked the whole thing out by wriggling it.

'That tickles.'

'I can't help it. Look out!'

A dog ran barking into the road, the near side horse shied and the whole phaeton shuddered as Henry fought to steady it.

Melissa found herself plastered to his chest, one hand jammed under the coat, the other clutching at his lapel as his right arm came round to steady her.

'I've got it,' she gasped as Henry said, 'I've got you.'

After a moment she added, 'You can let me go now.'

She struggled back into her seat, batted at her veil until it was hanging straight again, eased the map from its case and tried to fold it to show the section they were on. 'What did you say?'

'Nothing. I was counting in Russian.' Henry's ears had gone red.

'Why?'

'I need the practice. I…er…snatch every opportunity.'

That, Melissa concluded, was an untruth. He was distracting himself from something and then she realised what it was. She still felt a trifle hot and bothered after being so firmly pressed to him, and so did he. Was that

a compliment? Or would any man become a trifle...
agitated if a woman did what she had just done?

This situation was, she was coming to realise, rather
more awkward than simply a matter of when she got
home that night. She was alone with a man, heading
away from London and respectability, and she desired
him and he, apparently, desired her.

*What if we were eloping? How would I feel then? Ex-
cited, a little scared...eager. I would be running away
with the man I loved.*

Chapter Ten

Melissa's thoughts jolted to a halt. She was not in love, they were not eloping, this was not an exciting romantic tale to be woven into another 'horrid' novel. This was real life and she had to deal with it. She had chosen to eliminate marriage from her future, Melissa reminded herself. That meant eliminating physical relations with a man, because, however much she might have fantasied about it, Henry had been right—taking a lover was too dangerous. Even if the worst was a smirched reputation, that would make every other aspect of her existence more difficult, if not impossible.

Therefore she must subdue these feelings, just as Henry was doing, and concentrate on the real world and the urgent matter in hand: the rescue of Miss Houghton. Melissa studied the map. 'Stanmore next. Then Bushey, Watford, Tring, Aylesbury. After that it looks as though there is a choice of two main routes.'

'We won't need to worry about that,' Henry said confidently. 'We'll catch them long before. Remember, Harlby still wants Letitia to think they are legally married. He won't want to upset her or make her suspicious by setting a frantic pace.'

'Like this one,' Melissa said, making a clutch for her bonnet as they turned a corner and the wind caught it under the brim. That meant losing her hold on the rail. Bonnet jammed inelegantly back, she tightened her hold again.

'We'll check at each inn from now on until Stanmore and change horses there ourselves. Which town is about ten miles on after that?'

Melissa found the scale in the margin of the map, used her thumb as a rough measure and tried to place it on the map. 'King's—*ugh!*—Langley, I think. I just bit my tongue.'

'Sorry.' Henry's eyes were fixed on the road ahead. 'Bad bit of road, this.'

He treats me as though I was a man, Melissa thought with a glow of pride. *He doesn't think I am such a poor thing that he must coddle and protect me.*

She wasn't feeling quite so positive about not being coddled when they pulled up at The Abercorn Arms in Stanmore. Fleeting stops at almost a dozen establishments had produced no news of a post-chaise with a team and the road had not greatly improved until just before the turnpike gate in Edgware.

Henry pulled into the yard and called for a change. 'Have you had a post-chaise with a team change horses today?' he asked the groom who led out a pair for his approval. 'Yes, those will do. These are from the Paddington livery stables.'

The new horses were hardly a good match—one

black, one bay—but Melissa decided Henry was looking for qualities other than looks.

'Aye, sir.' The groom shifted the straw he was chew-
ing from one side of his mouth to the other and whistled
for two lads to unhitch the chestnuts. 'Newlyweds on
board, or so the boys said.'

Postilions, she knew, were *boys* whatever their age.

'How long ago?' Henry dug in his pocket and coins
jingled in his hand.

'Not two hours, I'd say.' The man cut them a sharp
look. 'They'd been travelling fast, but not flat out, if
you know what I mean. The team was lathered, but not
distressed-like.' He caught the coin Henry spun him
and added, 'We couldn't give them such good goers
this time, we've been busy today.'

Another coin followed. 'The young lady went inside,
but she wasn't long and she seemed happy enough.'

Henry didn't fall into the trap of trying to explain
their interest, although the man clearly suspected they
were in pursuit of an eloping couple. He paid for the
change and then they were off again.

'These are better than the last two,' he said after a
few minutes and then they were silent, watching the
road ahead, counting off the milestones.

King's Langley brought no news of Harlby and Letitia but another good pair between the shafts. Finally,
wearily, Henry reined in outside The White Hart in
Aylesbury, almost five hours after they had left London.

'Five o'clock,' Melissa said rather blankly as the
church clock chimed.

'They are making better progress than I expected,' Henry admitted. 'I'm sorry.'

'Whatever for?' she said briskly. The man had been driving without a break and it was a miracle that he was still upright and alert beside her. 'Clearly they have been lucky with their postilions and horses and no accidents have befallen them. We know they haven't stopped to eat and perhaps they will now they have put a good distance behind them.'

As if to underline her point her stomach gave a loud and embarrassing gurgle.

'We should stop and eat here,' Henry said and she wondered whether she should agree, if only to make sure he kept his energy up. 'I'll organise the change and ask for news of them first.'

'What about those postilions?' Melissa said, nodding towards a couple of wiry young men who were slumped on a mounting block draining tankards. 'They look as though they have just come in.'

The grooms were already unharnessing their pair as Henry jumped down. 'Coming?'

'Yes.' It was a precarious balancing act to climb down to the step and then be lifted over the wheel, but this was the second time and she knew where to put her feet.

The inn was bustling, but she scanned the public rooms and checked with a maid for anyone answering the couple's description in a private room, before locating the privy.

When she emerged Henry was waiting by the phaeton. 'Those were their postilions and they say that the next couple were told to head to Buckingham. Harlby let Letitia have a cup of tea and some biscuits, but wouldn't wait for dinner. He said they could take it when they arrived at The Lord Cobham's Arms. We've got them.'

'Thank goodness.' The news gave her energy and she almost sprang up to the seat with Henry giving her a boost.

'It is almost another two hours to Buckingham unless we catch them first,' he warned.

'Just as long as we do catch them before he can get her into bed,' Melissa said grimly.

An hour later Henry drew the horses to a halt in front of The Bell on Winslow's market square. 'This would be their last change before Buckingham,' he said. 'Ours, too.'

He sounds so tired, although he is hiding it well, Melissa thought as Henry sent the horses into the tight turn to the stable yard. *I wish I could drive this thing.*

Then she gasped, 'Look!'

'Hell,' Henry said, with no apology.

In front of them was a post-chaise, the shafts empty and two postilions leaning against it while they gossiped with the grooms.

'Two postilions, four horses. We've got them.'

A groom stopped chatting and came to take the horses. 'A change, sir?'

'That depends whether our friends are staying to dine or not.' Henry gestured towards the other vehicle. 'We had expected to meet with them in Buckingham.'

'Fair-haired gentleman and his wife?' the man said.

'The lady said she was tired, so the gent said they'd rack up here.'

'I don't think it will suit us to stay, but we'll eat before we go on, so I'll want a fresh pair in, say, an hour.'

They went into the inn in silence. Henry was clenching and unclenching his fists, Melissa saw. Did he expect Harlby to turn violent? She was mentally reviewing how she was going to break the news to Miss Houghton that she was not married and the man she had fled with was a lying, ruthless fortune hunter.

The landlord showed no reluctance in telling them which private parlour their friends Mr and Mrs Harlby had taken.

'Arrogant devil,' Henry muttered as they made their way along the corridor leading off well away from the public rooms. 'He has not even troubled to use a false name.'

'That might have made Letitia uneasy,' Melissa said, her mind half on how many handkerchiefs she had in her reticule.

'True.' Henry did not trouble to knock. He pushed the door open and they walked in on a scene of domestic harmony.

Miss Houghton was spooning peas on to her plate and Harlby had the carving knife poised over a roast fowl. 'White meat or— Who the devil? *You*,' he added in tones of loathing as he recognised them.

Miss Houghton gave a faint squeak. 'Miss Taverner?'

'Letitia, we have come to take you home. This man has deceived you,' Melissa said, keeping a wary eye on the carving knife.

'We are married! Charles is my husband.'

'It was a sham marriage and the clergyman has been disgraced and had his licence revoked. He cannot legally marry anyone.'

'I don't believe you!' She was on her feet, the shy little innocent replaced by a bristling fury poised to defend her man. 'It is blind prejudice. Charles has made mistakes in the past, but he is a reformed man. He *loves* me.'

'He is a liar, a seducer, a blackmailer,' Melissa retorted. 'He is certainly in love—with your fortune.'

'Put the knife down, Harlby,' Henry said. 'There are ladies present—we do not want anyone getting hurt.'

'That witch is no lady,' Harlby snarled, making a sweeping gesture towards Melissa that had her stepping back. 'Letty, my love, she has a grudge against me because I refused her advances.'

'You lying bastard.' Henry chopped his hand down hard on the other man's wrist. The knife spun away into a corner as Harlby swung a clenched fist and Henry went for his throat.

Melissa would have put a year's allowance on Henry, she could see no more sharp weapons and, thankfully, neither appeared to have a pistol. She turned back to Letitia. 'He seduced a friend of mine, just for sport. Now he is almost penniless and desperate. He needs your money and he needs to be married to you to get it.'

'Then what you say is nonsense, lies. If he *needs* to be married to me, then he would have no reason to plot a false ceremony.'

Letitia, it seemed, was not unintelligent, simply innocent.

'Your trustees would never give permission, any more

than you would have gone with him unwed,' Melissa said patiently, trying to ignore the cursing and thumping behind her. 'But now? You will have been alone with him—he would have bedded you tonight, perhaps left you with child. What can they do but agree?'

Letitia went white. 'I do not believe you. He told me what people would say, how no one would give him a second chance. But true love has redeemed him. My love.'

'Oh, for goodness sake!' Melissa cried as Harlby crashed into her from behind. She went down under him, got a painful elbow in the stomach as he struggled to get up and saw Henry standing over them both.

'Get off her, you pile of—'

What he was about to say was cut off as he dropped like a felled tree on top of Harlby, flattening Melissa under the weight of two full-grown, well-muscled men.

Gasping for breath, she saw Letitia, the solid wooden bread board in her hands. There was a smear of blood on it. She dropped the board and seized Henry by the shoulder, rolling him off Harlby to fall limply to the floor. There was a thud and the table shook.

'Charles!'

'It is all right, my darling.' Harlby scrambled to his feet, elbows and knees in painful contact with Melissa as he did so. 'Bitch,' he hissed, bending down over her. The last thing she was conscious of as she struggled to hit out at him was a blow to the side of her face.

Everything went black.

Everything hurt, especially his head. Lord, but that must have been one hell of a drinking bout last night.

Henry opened one eye and found he was nose-down in a coarse Turkey carpet that smelt…well used. Something heavy and angular was on top of him. With a convulsive heave he sat up and two oak chairs crashed to the floor.

His head was going to drop off at any moment, but through the pain he recognised it for what it was: not a monumental hangover, but the result of a blow.

Where the hell? Who?

His eyes didn't seem to be working perfectly. He rubbed at them and his hand came away covered in dried blood. He reached out the other to push himself to his feet and encountered a foot. A slim, female foot.

Melissa.

'Melissa?' He got on to his knees and lurched across to her side. 'Melissa, darling, wake up.' She was breathing, thank God, but there was a nasty bruise coming up on her left cheek and the beginnings of a black eye.

'What did you call me?' She opened her eyes, muttered something unladylike and shut them again.

'I don't know,' he said, impatient. 'What hurts?'

'Everything. Harlby fell on me, winded me, stood all over me getting up and then hit me.' Her eyes flew open. 'Letitia struck you with the breadboard. There's blood on your face. Henry—'

'I'm all right.' To prove it he got up and almost fell flat on his face. Sick, dizzy, seeing double. He knew enough not to take those signs seriously. Where the hell were the servants? There must have been one hell of a racket. He lurched towards the bell rope, tugged it and reeled back to stop Melissa getting up. 'Wait for some help.'

The first maid who arrived recoiled with a shriek and backed out. Then the landlord appeared.

'What the devil's happened?'

'The couple who were in here attacked us. Where are they now?'

'Gawd. Looked such a nice pair, too. They've gone, sir. Half an hour since. They said you wanted to stay on and finish the dinner and that you'd pay the reckoning when you left, but not to disturb you until you rang.' He stood surveying the wreckage of the room. 'I'll call the Constable, sir.'

'Never mind the Constable, they're long gone. I need a room for myself and—and my wife.' There was a faint gasp from where Melissa lay at his feet. 'And the doctor. The best one you have hereabouts. And some men to carry my wife upstairs in a chair. She's in no state to walk.'

'Neither are you, sir,' the innkeeper said. 'Meggie! Run for Dr Hardcastle, quick as you can, girl. Billy! Get Edward and Sam. Dorothy? Oh, there you are, girl. Stop gawping. Up to the best bedchamber and run a warming pan between the sheets, then fetch hot water. We'll have you both comfortable in a trice, sir, don't you fret.'

Comfortable? He doubted it. He had a concussion and Melissa probably had, too. Neither of them should fall into a deep sleep, so they needed someone to keep an eye on them, wake them at intervals. And he didn't trust anyone else to look after Melissa.

Although he had made a pretty poor showing at looking after her so far, Henry thought bitterly, as he dragged himself up the stairs in the wake of Melissa, enthroned on a chair that probably weighed more than she did.

'They've stolen our bags as well,' he told the landlord as he reached the landing. At least his brain was working well enough to spot that discrepancy in his story. 'They were carrying them in their post-chaise while we rode in the phaeton.'

'A nasty pair,' the landlord said. 'Just goes to show how looks do deceive. I'd have said she wouldn't say boo to a goose and he was very smooth. Very smooth indeed. I'll have the wife look out what your lady will need and if you don't mind one of my nightshirts and my spare razor, I'm happy to lend them.'

'Thank you, Mr—' Henry said.

'Neal, sir. Joseph Neal.'

By some miracle it hadn't occurred to Harlby to go through his pockets and remove the roll of banknotes Henry was carrying. They'd be properly in the midden if he had.

He staggered into the bedchamber and collapsed in an armchair by the fire while, behind his back, the maids and Mrs Neal undressed Melissa and got her into bed. He could hear her protest that she was quite all right but, thankfully, she was not so dazed that she was denying being married to him.

Melissa darling, he had called her. He remembered now that his head was clearing. She had been startled, as well she might be. But somehow she had become very special to him.

He was saved from exploring that thought any further by the arrival of the doctor. He pronounced nothing broken, but warned them of concussion, handed over salves and various potions and departed, several guineas to the good.

'Alone at last,' Henry said, suppressing a wince as he stood up to study Melissa.

'Exactly,' she said, traces of familiar tartness in her tone. 'Given the state we are both in I acquit you of lecherous intent, but why, exactly, are we in the same room, with one bed and, apparently, married?'

'We've both been hit hard on the head. I don't trust a pack of complete strangers to keep an eye on you.' He went behind the screen and changed into the landlord's voluminous nightshirt, ignoring the nightcap, complete with jaunty tassel, that had accompanied it.

Melissa gave a snort of amusement when he emerged. 'Don't tell me that is what you normally wear to bed. And your pocket watch?'

'I normally wear nothing,' he retorted and had the satisfaction of seeing her eyes widen. 'I'll put on the nightcap as well if you don't concentrate on what is important. Now, it is essential that neither of us goes into a deep sleep. I propose that we take it in turns to stay awake, rousing the other after an hour. If one of us won't waken, then the doctor must be called immediately.' He pulled the chair to the side of the bed and sat down.

'No, you don't. Get into bed as well, otherwise you'll never get any rest at all. You must be stiff after all that driving and this is a soft mattress.'

Henry couldn't deny it and he knew he'd be more use in the morning if he wasn't creaking around like an old man. It was a big bed and he supposed that he wouldn't be much closer to Melissa than he was at the moment. When that bedchamber door closed, leaving them alone in here, they had crossed the boundary between fast behaviour into downright scandal. But no one knew, he told himself. He just had to make certain it stayed that way.

'Very well.' He climbed stiffly in on the far side, almost moaning aloud as the blissful softness of a deep feather mattress embraced him. The watch in his hand ticked gently. 'Go to sleep now. I'll wake you in half an hour.' It was difficult to find a smile, looking at the spreading bruise on her face, but he managed something when he thought of what he was going to do to Charles Harlby when he caught up with him.

Melissa gave him a lopsided smile in return, closed her eyes and, within seconds, was asleep. He wanted to let her rest, sleep the night away, but he knew it was dangerous. Not that he was very certain the doctor could do anything if she drifted off into unconsciousness. He pushed the negative thoughts to the back of his mind and reached out to touch her cheek. Warm, but not feverish.

With a sigh, Melissa turned her head, nestling against his fingers. His hand was not exactly trapped, yet he found he couldn't pull away. It might wake her, of course, but that was not the reason, Henry knew. The feeling of that soft, warm skin against his aching hand, cramped from long hours holding the reins, was like a kiss. The tick of the watch in his other hand was soporific; he felt his eyes beginning to close and pushed himself upright, careful not to disturb Melissa. Time to think what to do the next day, assuming she was well enough to travel. Time to consider what he was going to do with Harlby when they found him.

Chapter Eleven

'Hmmph…' Something was blowing in her ear. What a draughty bedchamber. It seemed she had only closed her eyes moments before and now… There it was again. Irritably Melissa tugged the covers higher.

'Oh, no, you don't. Come on, open your eyes, let me look at them.'

She came fully awake and found herself almost nose to nose with Henry, who was gazing deep into her eyes.

'They seem all right.' He moved and the light from a candle made her blink. Then he moved back and looked again. 'The pupils of your eyes get bigger and smaller depending in the light. I believe there is a problem if they are very tiny, or very wide, and do not change.' He frowned. 'Your heartbeat seems somewhat rapid.'

'That may be because you are virtually lying on top of me and you are quite heavy,' Melissa pointed out. The pulse of her blood was not the only one that was disturbing her.

'Sorry.' Henry shifted back fast enough to send one of his pillows thumping to the floor. 'Here is the watch. Can you see it in the light or shall I move the candle?'

'It is perfect, thank you.' Melissa sat up against the pillows and took the watch. Just past twelve. It was going to be a long night, she thought as Henry settled himself down.

It was a large bed, but somehow the mattress seemed bent on pushing them both towards the middle and, although Henry was lying several inches away from her, she could feel his body heat, curiously both comforting and disturbing at the same time.

Her face throbbed, but she did not want to disturb him by reaching for the salve that the doctor had left.

She looked at the watch. Five minutes had passed. It was strange how one man could manage to occupy so much of the bed when he was not sprawling. In fact, he was rather tidily on his side, elbows tucked in. Perhaps it was just the shadows that made him seem so much closer.

He had called her *darling*. She could recall it quite clearly now that her dizziness had cleared. What had he meant by it? Nothing, she supposed. It was just something he had said in the heat of the moment. She should disregard it.

Ten minutes. Her eyelids drooped. Melissa pinched herself, wriggled further up against the pillows and sought for something to keep her awake. She began a mental list.

Send another express note to Cousin Almeria
Send a note to Verity in case I require a story to cover my absence
Send the maid out as early as possible to purchase a toothbrush and a hairbrush

*Change Grandmama's wedding ring over from
my right hand to my left hand*

Henry muttered something in his sleep and she
reached out a hand to stroke it gently over his hair.
'Shh. Sleep now, I'm here.' He settled again.

No one has ever called me darling before.

When she got her hands on that foolish chit Letitia
Houghton she was going to give her a piece of her mind.
The flat of her hand was tempting. The wretched girl
could have cracked Henry's skull, killed him.

As for Harlby, she had an uneasy feeling that Henry
would not be content with strong words or a punch to
the jaw. This situation had *duel* written all over it and
she was not going to risk Henry getting killed, or having to flee the country, because she had a bruised face.
But something had to be done about the man: he was
a public danger with the added complication that they
could not make his sins public, not without risking repu-
tations that would be far more easily damaged than his
would be if his actions became known.

*Too difficult to think about now, with my head ach-
ing and my face hurting.*

She curled up on her side and watched Henry, cata-
loguing the features on what she could see of his face.
A little sickle-shaped scar at the corner of his mouth.
A dusting of freckles, so faint that if he had not been
pale with pain and exhaustion they would not be notice-
able. Dark, thick eyelashes—it was so unfair that men
so often had better lashes than women.

Somewhere deep inside the inn a clock struck the

hour, startling her. She looked at the watch. Fifty-five minutes gone.

Henry needed to shave and she guessed he would normally do so twice a day. Would he let her watch the mysterious male ritual in the morning?

There. Time to wake him. He had blown in her ear, let him see how he liked it! She leaned over, pursed her lips and sent a steady stream of breath into the curls of his ear, resisting the urge to trace them with her fingertip.

Henry's reactions were faster than hers had been. He opened his eyes at the first puff of air and lay still as she waved the candle flame in front of his face.

'They are reacting as they should,' she assured him. 'Do you have a headache?'

'Only when I move,' he said, cautiously levering himself up against the pillows and taking the watch from her. 'How is your face?' His fingers trailed gently down over the bruise and he winced in sympathy.

'It probably looks worse than it feels,' Melissa assured him, secretly convinced that it was the other way around.

'I do not believe that for a moment. Go to sleep now.'

They finally both fell asleep at five o'clock, only to be woken at seven by the bustle of a stagecoach arriving below their window.

Melissa hauled the covers up over her ears just as Henry did the same thing. 'Good morning,' he said, eyes half-closed.

'Good morning. How are you? What hurts?'

There was a contemplative silence, then he said, 'My

feet are perfectly fine. So are my knees. And there is not as much as a twinge in my left ear. Otherwise everything aches, throbs or has seized up like an unoiled axle.'

'You are not driving anything, anywhere, today,' Melissa said firmly.

'I doubt I'm capable of managing a donkey cart,' Henry said with disarming frankness. 'I intend hiring a post-chaise and four.'

'Back to London?'

'No, towards Kenilworth.'

'Won't they be there by now? We are too late.'

'They had not finished their dinner. Letitia is upset and, perhaps, just a little suspicious now after what you said, however vigorously she fought us off. She will certainly be tired. What I would do if I were in Harlby's shoes, would be to go on to Buckingham, which is no distance at all, have dinner and retire for the night. They left us decidedly the worse for wear and unlikely to follow. It would be a risk, but Harlby's type thrive on risk.'

'We might catch them, but she will be ruined,' Melissa said. 'He will have taken her to bed—'

'Again, in Harlby's position I do not think I would press that. He has no need to—after all, he has her, she is completely compromised and no rake worth his salt is going to try to make love to a woman who is tired, on edge and beginning to be suspicious. She has, after all, just seen him hit another woman.'

'I agree. He would be a fool to try. Not in an inn, at any case,' Melissa said thoughtfully. 'Far too public if she becomes angry or distressed. So there is hope if we can catch them before he reaches his own home. And ruined or not, we need to get her away from him, because I cannot believe he will be kind to her, even if he achieves a legal marriage.'

Henry reached for the watch. 'I told the girl to wake us with hot water at half past seven. We have twenty more minutes to sleep.'

How it happened Melissa had no idea—she could certainly acquit a soundly slumbering Henry of encroaching behaviour—but when the maid knocked they were both deeply asleep again and in each other's arms.

'Oh!' Melissa woke, flustered, but the maid showed no sign of embarrassment at the sight of a supposedly married couple entangled in the middle of the bed, and set the ewer of hot water down, bobbed a curtsy and went out again.

'Henry, wake up.'

Wake up and let go of me!

He had one, surprisingly heavy, arm across her stomach and he was lying with his head on her shoulder.

'Mmm…?' His nose was firmly buried in the angle of her neck and he began to nuzzle into the exposed skin where the over-large flannel nightgown had gaped. 'You taste good.'

'Henry.'

'Oh, my God.' He rolled away so rapidly that he fell out of bed, landing out of her sight with a thump and a curse. 'Sorry, sorry, sorry. I was asleep. I didn't mean—'

It took her a moment to reply, because the realisation that she wished he had meant it, that he had been awake and knew who he was with, washed over her like a wave. 'I know you didn't.' Melissa tried to sound as matter-of-fact as she could. 'Did you hurt yourself?'

A tousled head appeared over the edge of the bed. 'No more than I deserve. Go on, use the water while it is hot.'

She washed rapidly and scrambled into her clothes behind the screen, remembered to move her ring and did her best with her hair. When she emerged Henry was studying the road map.

'I'll go and order breakfast and find some writing things. I need to write to Cousin Almeria and I'll let Verity know what is happening: we may need her help. I'm going to send someone out to buy a hairbrush and so forth. Do you need anything?'

'Toothbrush, please. Can you ask the landlord to send up his razor?'

It all felt remarkably domestic, Melissa thought as she made her way downstairs. They both seemed to be working hard at pretending nothing embarrassing had happened, that they had not spent the night together and woken entwined. That Henry's lips had not been tasting her skin.

Henry came down as one maid scurried back with the shopping and another brought a lavish breakfast into the private parlour they had inherited from Harlby and Letitia.

'The landlord has obviously decided that we are going to be a very profitable pair of guests,' he said with a grin, before downing a cup of coffee and attacking a plateful of bacon, egg, black pudding and toast.

Melissa found she was equally hungry, although eating was painful. She'd been lucky, she supposed, not to lose a tooth.

'What have you told your cousin?' Henry asked when the first pangs of hunger had been assuaged.

'That we are still in pursuit of the eloping couple, nothing more.' Melissa watched Henry as he helped himself to more bacon. He seemed surprisingly calm about the fact that he found himself chasing halfway across the country in pursuit of a young woman who meant nothing to him, had been hit over the head by her, put to considerable expense and physical exertion and was still facing at least a day more of the same.

Although without the blows to the head, I hope.

'She is very sensible about this kind of thing,' she added.

'Good grief.' Henry paused in the act of pouring more coffee. 'How do you know?'

'Theoretically. From discussions we have had.'

'Your parents, however, would be considerably less understanding.'

'We do not need to worry about them,' Melissa said confidently. 'They will never know anything about it.'

'Should I ever be blessed with daughters,' Henry remarked, buttering a slice of toast, 'I imagine I will be white-haired with worry before they are twenty.'

'I am different,' Melissa said. 'I am sure any daughters that you have will be perfectly conventional young ladies.'

Mystifyingly, Henry gave her a look that could only be described as disbelieving.

They picked up the trail of the fugitives in Buckingham, as Henry had predicted. Mr and Mrs Harlby had spent the night at Lord Cobham's Arms in Buckingham and had left at nine o'clock, still in their post-chaise with four horses.

'It will be costing Harlby a great deal of money,' Henry said as they rattled out of the inn yard in their own vehicle.

'And so must this be.' Melissa turned to him as he sat back in the corner of the post-chaise. 'I didn't think, I am so sorry. You must let me pay you back when we are in London again.'

Henry started to shake his head, then clearly thought better of it. 'It isn't your responsibility to pay, any more than it is mine, and I can afford it rather more than you can, I suspect.'

'You are only involved because I dragged you into it.'

'Quid pro quo for your assistance with my problem,' Henry said. 'Besides, I am enjoying myself.'

'Forced to drive all day, hit on the head, landed with goodness knows what expenses—how can you be enjoying that?'

'I enjoyed driving a phaeton and I am enjoying your company. And now I am going to get some sleep and I suggest you do likewise. I told the postilions to stop at the usual posthouse in Brackley so we can check to see where Harlby is changing.'

Henry closed his eyes and relaxed as well as he could in the fast-moving vehicle. At least the springs were good and his aching head was not being thumped against the upholstery with every pothole.

He was not tired, he found. Perhaps months of late nights in Vienna had reduced his need for sleep, because it was certainly not that Melissa's company was particularly soothing, not now he had got over the effects of the blow to the head and the long day's driving.

It had been easy, right up to the point when the maid had come in and he had woken up, clear-headed and aroused, to find himself snuggled up cosily with Melissa. His friend. His unmarried friend. His respectable, unmarried friend who clearly had no idea just what a pickle they were in now or what the effects were on a healthy adult male of waking up in bed wrapped around a warm female.

It was one thing to set off expecting to deliver her home at dawn as though they had been to some ball or masquerade. It was quite another to take her home after perhaps two or three nights away. He might trust himself to do nothing out of line—even if it meant hurling himself out of bed to be certain—but if they were seen there was only one thing for it.

And I find myself on the verge of compromising one of the few ladies who would not be delighted to find herself married to the son of a duke. Come to that, delightful as she is, in her own very particular way, she would be a disaster as a diplomat's wife.

He gave his imagination full rein—Melissa informing some senior diplomatic wife that marriage was a prison for women and that spinsterhood and lovers were the ideal. Melissa making an ambassador the villain of the shocking and bestselling novel. Melissa rushing to the rescue of some young lady in distress in the middle of some rigorously formal engagement…

It is not amusing, he reproved himself, aware that his lips were twitching into a smile. But, serious as this all was, he couldn't help feeling that he and Melissa would somehow find a way out of this.

He was still dozing through a series of daydreams featuring Melissa in various ludicrous diplomatic situations when the post-chaise drew up at The Crown in Brackley.

Their quarry had changed there and the distribution of a few coins among the ostlers and off-duty postilions produced the intelligence that the lady stayed inside the carriage and the gentleman had a face like thunder and was a right sting-bum into the bargain.

'What on *earth* does that mean?' Melissa asked when he faithfully recounted what had been said.

'Mean and tight-fisted. Harlby can't have tipped them much, if at all.'

'What a wonderful expression.'

Trust Melissa, he thought, as she made a note.

'But that's good news, isn't it? He must be running short of money.'

'I hope so. Banbury's the next likely place for a change. He cannot make it to Kenilworth without one more stop because it is over twenty miles to Warwick and at least another five after that.'

'How far are we behind them now?'

'An hour—that's the good news. Apparently one of the wheelers cast a shoe five miles out of Brackley, then picked up a stone that cut the frog of the hoof badly and that slowed them right down.' He grinned. 'I've promised our boys a very good tip if they can catch them before he reaches his house. His postilions, if they've had the rough edge of his tongue over the lamed horse and seen how badly he tips, will not be throwing their hearts and souls into making the best speed.'

Her answering smile was lopsided and he felt the anger welling up again as he looked at the purpling bruise.

'Don't scowl at me, Henry.'

'I'm scowling at that bruise. Is it very painful?'

'Bad enough to have me thinking of pincers and hot irons when I imagine catching up with Harlby,' she said.

'You may leave him to me.'

'You will not call him out, Henry,' Melissa said sharply, all the amusement gone from her voice.

'I most certainly will! He has abducted and deceived one young lady and viciously assaulted another in my care. What do you expect me to do with him? Shake hands?'

'Hit him. Or horsewhip him, anything but risk getting killed or killing him. Henry, promise me that you won't fight a duel with Harlby.'

'I will do no such thing.' Henry felt himself going cold at the thought. 'It is the only honourable thing to do.'

'Really?' Melissa sat bolt upright, her face around the bruise white, her expression furious.' Suddenly they were having an argument. A row. 'You could get yourself killed or maimed—'

'Thank you for your confidence in my abilities!'

'You aren't perfect, nobody is. Accidents happen. Or you kill him and have to flee the country—have you thought of *that*, my lord?'

'It alters nothing. It is the—'

'Honourable thing, yes, I heard you the first time.'

There was no need to shout, they were so close in the little, swaying carriage, but they both were now. 'What about my honour?'

'That is what we are talking about, woman!'

'Don't you *woman* me. It is your honour that concerns you, not mine. How do you think I will feel if you end up dead, or losing a limb, or exiled on the Continent, your career in tatters, and it is all my fault?'

Henry opened his mouth, closed it again and took a deep breath. 'One of us is going to have to give way on this,' he said, rather more moderately.

'Honour demands that gentlemen duel,' Melissa said. He nodded. 'Would you describe Harlby as a gentleman? I would not. What would you do if a sneak thief hit me? Or a drunken porter in the street?'

'I'd teach him a lesson he would never forget and then drag him in front of a magistrate.'

'Then do the same thing, omitting the Justice for the sake of Letitia's reputation. I have every confidence that you can make him wish he had never set eyes on any of us.' She smiled as she said it, then leaned forward and kissed his cheek. 'Am I not a good diplomat, Henry?'

'That is clearly where I went wrong,' he said, joking to cover the effect the sensation of soft lips pressed to his cheek was having on him. 'I should have kissed more diplomats in Vienna. The Congress would have been over in half the time.'

Chapter Twelve

They found no trace of the runaways in Banbury, but caught them in the village of Kineton beyond it. The Swan Inn stood on a corner where the main road swept around to the left and the postilions, knowing the route, slowed and drew up just before the entrance to the yard.

Henry jumped down and one of the boys twisted in the saddle. 'Do you want to stop here, sir?'

He had left the door open and, even inside the post-chaise, Melissa could hear the raised voices from the yard.

'If you would,' Henry said. 'If you can block the entrance, so much the better.'

He came back to help Melissa out and the post-chaise moved forward a few feet across the mouth of the inn yard. 'If I am not much mistaken, we have them.'

Four horses stood, sweating and still harnessed to the post-chaise. Both postilions were on the ground, both with their hands fisted belligerently on hips.

Facing them, with his back to the entrance, was Charles Harlby. Melissa could not see his face, but his neck was red and his voice raised. 'I tell you I'll pay you when we get to the Grange. Damn it, you've come this far.'

'And we'll see the colour of your money before we go another furlong,' the older of the men said. He was as small and wiry as a jockey and looked as tough as the harness leather on his team. 'You paid for Chipping Norton at the beginning, then you goes changing your mind.'

'Hoping to confuse anyone following,' Henry murmured in her ear. 'Fortunately we didn't locate their starting point and get given the false information.'

'Your pockets are to let, I'm thinking,' the man said, well into his stride now. 'I've been watching—you hardly tip, you've skimped on refreshments. We don't move until we get paid. I'll wager this is an elopement—'

'It is no such thing!' Letitia, her walking dress rumpled, her hair coming down, looked exhausted as she climbed down from the post-chaise. 'This is my husband.'

'But that's the thing,' Henry said as he walked forward. 'He isn't, I am afraid.'

'You again!' For a moment Melissa thought the other woman might faint, but she took hold of the door frame and took a visibly deep breath. 'We were married yesterday morning.'

'You took part in a ceremony performed by Horace Cartwright, who used to be a Church of England clergyman until the Archbishop of Canterbury removed his licence to minister or preach. He is, in the popular phrase, unfrocked,' Melissa said. 'The ceremony was invalid and you are no more married to Mr Harlby here than you are to the gentleman in front of you.'

'I don't believe you.'

She was defiant, but Melissa could see the uncertainty in her eyes.

'I am truly sorry, but you have been cruelly deceived. Henry, can't we go inside? Surely they have a private parlour. We cannot discuss this out here.'

'Private parlour, ma'am? That we do.' The raised voices had brought the landlord out into the yard. He wiped his hands on his vast apron and looked at the group in front of him. 'Nice private room, all snug and some refreshments?'

'That would be ideal,' Melissa said brightly, as though Henry and Harlby were not facing each other, fists clenched, and Letitia was not on the verge of either tears or strong hysterics. 'Come along, Letitia.'

'You stay here,' Harlby ordered her.

'I think we could all do with a nice cup of tea and something to eat, don't you, Letitia?' She took the other woman's arm and began to steer her towards the inn.

'I said stay here, damn you, woman!'

Letitia flinched, gasped and stared, wide-eyed, at Harlby.

It must be the first time he has let the mask slip in front of her, Melissa thought, and kept walking, half supporting the trembling girl.

'Do not swear in front of ladies,' Henry said mildly. So mildly that Melissa glanced back, surprised, and caught a perfect view of Henry landing a solid punch to Harlby's chin. He stood looking down at him as he sprawled on the cobbles, dazedly shaking his head, and turned to the postilions.

'Here.' As Letitia sagged against her, Melissa saw a banknote changing hands. 'That is for your trouble and your discretion. This person will not require your further services. I'd be obliged if you would tell your colleagues outside that they may come in and make themselves comfortable. I suspect we may be a while.'

Both men touched their caps and the younger ran out to the street.

'Come on,' Melissa said firmly and dragged Letitia with her into the inn where a highly interested group of staff had gathered to watch the excitement. A maid came forward to show her to the parlour and, with a sigh of relief, and without taking too much trouble to be gentle, Melissa dumped her burden into the nearest chair and checked around for weapons. There was not as much as a poker in the fireplace, so it was probably safe enough.

Henry came in a minute later with a groom, lugging the slumped figure of Harlby between them. 'This chair will do.' They let him fall into a deep wing chair that kept him upright. A coin changed hands and the man grinned and went out.

'Henry, could you leave us for a moment? I don't think Harlby's going to be a problem for a minute or two.'

Henry raised an eyebrow but stepped outside, pulling the door almost closed behind him.

'Right. Letitia, listen to me. Are you still a virgin?'

Miss Houghton blushed violently. 'I… I… You have

no right to ask such a thing,' she said, looking like nothing more than a cornered field mouse.

Melissa hardened her heart—she was going to have to bully the girl to get the truth out of her. 'I need to know whether you might be with child. Harlby would be delighted if you were because that would further entrap you.'

'But he has reformed. He swore to me,' Letitia said, indignant now.

'No, he hasn't. Just answer my question or I'll send for a doctor to tell me if you are a virgin or not.' She wouldn't dream of doing such a thing, but it did produce a reply.

'No. I mean, yes, I am. Last night… I was so tired and upset about you and that man attacking us and I couldn't stop crying and Charles said… Charles said he would sleep in another room.'

'Thank goodness for that. Henry! You can come in now.'

He raised an eyebrow and she smiled. 'The worst has not happened. You are very fortunate that you are such a watering pot, Letitia.'

Harlby stirred and dragged himself upright in the chair. 'What the—?' He got two unpleasant words out before Henry cuffed him sharply.

'There are ladies present. You can mind your language or I will break your jaw. Your choice.'

'You have no right to interfere. This lady is my wife.'

'No, she is not. You were seen with Cartwright and his identity has been confirmed by a church official,' Henry snapped. 'You lured this lady into a false marriage, knowing that her conscience would never permit her to go with you as anything but your wife.'

'I cannot believe it.' Letitia seemed to have rallied. 'I trust Charles. His past mistakes are just that. They are behind him now.' She looked at Harlby as though imploring him to reassure her.

'The love of a good woman was all that I needed to see the error of my ways,' he said sanctimoniously.

Melissa resisted the urge to box his ears. 'Letitia, don't you think it would be best to return to London and make enquiries? If we are telling you the truth, then you will be safe there. If we are lying to you, then you are no less married. What can you lose by it other than some time travelling?'

'It is a trick,' Harlby protested. 'They will take you back to your aunt and uncle.'

'Then shall we call upon the local vicar?' Melissa said, suddenly having a brainwave. 'He is sure to have a clerical directory, even if it is a year or so out of date. The verger who told me about him said it is almost ten years since Cartwright lost his licence.'

'There, a perfect solution,' Henry said. 'Miss Houghton, all it will mean is a delay of perhaps an hour or so. There is no need to tell the vicar that you are concerned in the matter, only that we fear a relative has been deceived.'

Letitia visibly wavered. 'It might be best. You are mistaken, of course, but if it means you will no longer trouble us…'

'I'll ask for directions to the vicarage,' Melissa said, reaching for the bell pull.

'You bitch.' Harlby was on his feet. 'Just because

that chit of a friend of yours has told tales, you have a grudge against me. What does it matter to her? I didn't want her afterwards and she's landed herself a marquis, hasn't she?'

Letitia looked too confused and shocked to put two and two together, but Melissa saw understanding dawn on Henry's face. He knew she was friends with only one marchioness—Prudence—and now he also knew what Prue's own husband did not: that Harlby was the man who had seduced and abandoned her.

There was no point in denying it. 'Do you desire to find yourself in a nightmare?' she enquired. 'You know who her husband is and, therefore, you know his reputation. I asked Lord Henry not to call you out and he agreed. My friend's husband will not duel either. Like Lord Henry, he would only fight a gentleman and you are scum. That means he will deal with you in some other manner. He was raised in a slum and made his fortune as a privateer. Just imagine the friends he could hand you over to. Death would be far too good for you— he would make your life a living hell.'

'Charles?' Letitia's whisper fell into a crackling silence. 'Is this true? That you seduced a lady and abandoned her?'

'What does it matter?' he said with a shrug. 'I have got you now—and I am not abandoning you.'

'No, he'll not let you go in a hurry, Miss Houghton, because you have a fortune,' Henry pointed out.

'And now you've run off with me and spent a night with me it makes no matter whether we are wed already or not,' Harlby said with a grin. 'Your uncle will insist we marry or you are utterly ruined.'

Now what do we do? Melissa looked at Henry and could see the same calculations running through his mind. *Use force? Drag Letitia kicking and screaming away from Harlby?*

Outside the window there was a clatter of hooves, the sound of a horn and running footsteps. Either a stage or the Mail had arrived.

Letitia, who had been slumped against the table, straightened up and pulled a handkerchief from her reticule. She blew her nose, sniffed and glared at Harlby. 'I do not care. You would not speak to me like that if you were the person you pretended to be. You are a horrible man and I was a fool to fall for your lies. I would not marry you again for any reason on earth.' She glared at Melissa as though expecting opposition. 'I don't care if I am ruined and I have to spend the rest of my life as a spinster—that would be better than being married to him.'

'Oh, well said, Letitia.' Melissa gave her a hug. 'He is on the verge of ruin himself—financial ruin. He needed an heiress desperately. You have a kind and loving heart and it is no fault of yours that his is made of stone.'

'We will ensure that all your creditors know that you are in the basket, Harlby,' Henry said. 'Debtors' prison is a most unpleasant place and I cannot imagine you have any friends willing to buy you out of it. I'd make a run for the Continent with what you can scrape together if I were you. There's no need to worry about Miss Houghton—after all, she has been with us the entire time, lending her countenance to Miss Taverner, who has had to make an urgent journey to Birmingham.

'Here,' he added, taking some coins from his pocket

and sending one spinning towards the other man. 'That should hire you a horse for a few miles. Or you could take the stage for a while. The walk the rest of the way will do you good.'

Harlby snatched it out of the air, spun on his heel and was out of the door before any of them could react.

'Good riddance,' Henry said as it slammed shut. 'He'll keep his mouth shut because he needs to gather as much money as he can to get abroad before his creditors discover he is utterly ruined.'

'I think I heard the key,' Melissa said, puzzled. She tried the door. 'I thought so—he has locked us in. Why on earth would he bother to do that? We only have to ring and someone will let us out.'

'Or climb out of the—'

'My jewel case!' Letitia gasped. 'It is still in the carriage.'

'Window,' Henry finished saying, struggling to get it open. 'The confounded thing hasn't been opened in years.'

There was the sound of the horn again, suddenly loud as he forced the pane open and swung a leg over the sill.

'I am so sorry,' Melissa said and she and Letitia sat down in unison at the table. She felt as though all the strength had gone out of her legs. Goodness knew what the other woman felt like.

'It could have been worse,' Letitia said with a sniff. She blew her nose again. 'You stopped him before it got even worse. Did he really harm a friend of yours? A marchioness?'

'Letitia, if you feel any gratitude for what Lord

Henry and I have done, then I beg you to forget you ever heard him say that.'

Letitia blinked at her. 'I— Oh, yes, I see. I did hear him say something about another lady, but I was so upset I didn't hear properly. In fact, I didn't really understand what he was talking about. I certainly will not repeat it.'

'Thank you.'

There was the sound of the key turning and Henry came in. 'That was the London Mail just gone through. Harlby's on it with his own bags and your jewellery case, I fear, Miss Houghton.'

'I do not care,' Letitia said. 'It will give him enough money to leave the country and that is all I want now.' She looked, and sounded, exhausted.

'I could give chase,' Henry offered.

'No. Most of my jewels are in safe storage with Rundell, Bridge & Rundell, the jewellers. Charles did not realise that until this morning when he asked me to open the box for something to pawn. That was when I first saw him lose his temper,' she added drearily. 'I thought for a second he might hit me.'

'He is certainly capable of hitting a woman,' Melissa said, touching her own cheek where a thick coat of powder had failed to cover the bruise. 'Goodness, I know it is a very prosaic thought to have, but I am so hungry.'

'Then we will order luncheon and set out for London after we have eaten. If you could see to that, Miss Taverner, I will tell the postilions that we require a post-chaise with two horses. I will hire a mount and ride until I can pick up the phaeton again.'

'Very well, Lord Henry.' Melissa noticed his formality when addressing her. That distance had to be observed carefully now. Just as they were shielding Letitia, she was offering Melissa protection should anyone see them together so far from home.

Letitia washed her tear-stained face, collected herself enough to apologise profusely to Henry for hitting him with the breadboard, then they ate a substantial luncheon and set out again in the post-chaise with Henry riding alongside. They changed horses in Banbury, then Brackley and finally arrived back at Winslow. They spent the night there, with Melissa explaining to the landlady that her friend was nervous of sleeping in strange places and they would therefore share a room, leaving her 'husband' to sleep alone.

The next morning they made their first change at Aylesbury, choosing The George, just in case anyone should recall their questions on the outward journey and put two and two together.

Blushing, Letitia excused herself and went inside, leaving Melissa and Henry leaning against the post-chaise.

'Letitia is much calmer now,' she reported. Herself, she was feeling tired. Her face still throbbed and she was aching with long hours in a swaying vehicle. Now they had achieved their aim it was as though all the energy had drained from her. Or perhaps it was because she was alone with Letitia, working to buoy up her spirits and without Henry's company to stimulate her.

'She is angry, I think. Furious with him and possibly even more so with herself for being taken in. I suspect her aunt and uncle are going to find they are dealing with a very different young woman when she gets home.'

'She has you to thank for that,' Henry said.

'No, she has *you*. I would never have been able to set out in pursuit alone and by the time I had found one of my friends and their husband to help me we would have been too late. You saved her, Henry.' She smiled up at him as he leaned against the yellow and black panels of the post-chaise. His shave that morning had been rushed, there were dark shadows under his eyes and she felt a warm rush of affection and, perhaps, just a tingle of something else.

'My hero,' Melissa said and, as she had a few times before, kissed his cheek.

'No, I'm not—' Henry shook his head in denial and their lips met, clung. His arms came round her as hers went around his neck and they stood there in the shadow of the post-chaise for a long, aching moment.

Then Henry lifted his head and they stared at each other, wordless until a horse snorted and stamped its foot and Melissa stepped back, turning. The vehicle had shielded them from the rest of the yard and the arch-way to the street and she breathed a sigh of…of relief, she supposed. Relief and frustration. She wanted still to be kissing Henry, still to be in his arms.

Something moved behind one of the ground-floor windows and she stiffened, but she could see no face staring out at them. Someone had simply passed by.

'What is it?'

Other than the fact we have just kissed?

'I thought I saw someone at the window, but I must have been mistaken. There is no one looking out.'

'Good,' Henry said. He sounded quite calm.

Perhaps the adventurous life of a diplomat made him capable of dealing with such situations.

Whatever this situation is...

'We are tired and there has been a great deal of tension and drama. Emotions become a trifle high under those circumstances,' Henry said, as though referring to a momentary loss of temper or a mild case of hysterics, not a kiss that was still doing remarkably disturbing things to her interior. 'Here comes Miss Houghton.'

And that is that, Melissa thought rather blankly.

In fact, she was not aware of thinking of anything very much on the rest of the long, weary journey back to London. They arrived at Paddington at nine in the evening and drove straight to Brook Street, stopping only for Henry to return the phaeton and pick up a hackney carriage.

Henry helped both women down. 'Well,' he said, gesturing towards the front door. 'Shall we see what our reception is going to be?'

Chapter Thirteen

'That went better than I could have hoped,' Henry said as they stood on the pavement and watched the post-chaise trot away. He hailed a hackney carriage and sank back against the squabs with a sigh of relief. He did not want to have to live through a scene like that again.

'I am just thankful that Letitia had so much time to compose herself. She was very firm, I thought,' Melissa said. 'Just imagine what would have happened if her uncle had found them together—he would have insisted she marry Harlby without any thought for what kind of life she would lead after that.'

'It is what any parent or guardian would have done,' he said.

'It is barbaric.' Melissa banged a fist down on to the seat beside her, raising dust that made her cough. 'It is a crude statement that the only thing that matters is a woman's role to produce children that are the undoubted offspring of her husband. Now, if this became known she would be ruined. Ruined for what?' she demanded.

Henry knew better than to protest that he didn't make the rules.

'Even if he had taken her virginity then, provided she was not with child by that horrible man, how is she not perfectly marriageable?'

'It is the way of the world,' Henry said, realising as he did so that he must be even more tired than he had thought to utter something so provocative.

'You do not believe it is right, do you?'

'No. No, of course not.' It was not something he had ever considered, he realised, although he did not say so—honesty at that moment seemed distinctly perilous.

'It is very respectable prostitution,' Melissa said. 'Young women are sold to the bidder with the most money or the best lineage or the most convenient political connections.'

He found he was shocked and that was not something that happened very often. 'Prostitution?' She had told him before that she did not want to be married, but she had not been so outspoken, so...*shocking.*

'Think about it,' she said fiercely. 'Think how you would feel if you were a woman forced to marry a man who would own everything that was yours before. A man who could beat you or ignore you, who could force himself on you whenever he wanted, keep you pregnant while he dallied with mistresses and prostitutes. Young ladies are meek and sweet and obedient because they have been trained to be, like horses broken to the bridle.'

Even though in the dark he could not see her face, he realised she was more than angry, perhaps even weeping.

'Surely things are not so bad?' he asked. 'Obviously there are bad husbands, neglectful or even cruel ones.

But on the whole a woman receives protection, shelter, status, companionship and children.'

Silence.

He had a suspicion he was digging himself deeper into a hole. He had not taken her seriously before, he realised. What did he know with the only example he had ever observed closely being his own parents? His father had been cold, distant and, yes, he had mistresses. His mother had fought back with anger and equal coldness. His imagination skidded away from the fact that they had four sons. It had never occurred to him to wonder what it must have been like for his mother when she found herself married to the Duke of Walton, a man who had trouble distinguishing between his own offspring and for whom the word *selfish* might have been coined.

'You must know of some successful marriages? Look at your four friends—you told me they are deeply in love.'

'Yes, it is possible. Our vicar at home and his wife seem supremely well suited. But my own parents... I have never heard Papa be actively unkind to Mama, but he treats her as if she has no ideas of her own, no intellect to work things out, to form opinions. And she allows it. If I fell in love with someone who loved me, then... But it is so rare, such a risk. I have seen what happens when it is...wrong.'

The carriage stopped with a jolt before he could respond. 'Home and the drawing room lamps are lit, so Cousin Almeria is awake and waiting for me. Thank you for your help, Henry. No, don't get down.'

He got out anyway, but didn't come too close—he suspected she didn't want him to see her face. But a gentleman did not leave a lady standing on a doorstep alone while she found her latch key.

Then she was inside. 'Goodnight. Thank you, Henry' floated out before the door closed.

Time to go home. He gave his direction to the driver and sat in the dark, thinking about Melissa. Trying not to think about that kiss in the stable yard, the one they had carefully not spoken of.

Or perhaps it had meant nothing to her and was easily dismissed. Yes, that would be the best thing to hope.

The clock on the face of St James's Palace struck twelve the next day as Henry walked into the sitting room he shared with James.

'What's wrong?' His friend looked up from the dictionary he was consulting and peered at him.

He might seem to be lost in a world of mathematics, linguistics and cyphers, Henry thought, but he had a sharp eye for other people's moods.

'I've just been down to Whitehall, thought I'd better report that I was back in town. Apparently the French embassy professes itself most interested and concerned to hear about Laverne's exploits and he has disappeared from the scene. We are not so tactless as to enquire what has happened to him, but I assume he is now out of the country.

'My friend the Graf von Arten, however, made himself scarce and was then spotted in Oxford the other day, which has caused a certain stir in the hen coop. The place, as you know all too well, is stuffed with foreign scholars of all varieties, so it is anyone's guess whom he was there to see. I am living in dread of being dis-

patched to find out and, frankly, I had more than enough
of the place in my student days.'

'Lord, yes,' James agreed, head in the dictionary
again. 'My memories are of debt, too much bad drink,
dusty dons and draughty rooms. Ah, got it!' He scribbled a note, then shut the book with a thump.

'How are things with your intriguing lady friend?'
he asked after Henry had fidgeted about the room for
a few minutes.

'I do not know, if I am to be honest,' he admitted.
The armchair looked too inviting. If he sat in that, he
wouldn't move for the rest of the afternoon. To describe
his sleep the night before as inadequate was understat-
ing the case.

He leaned against the table and avoided meeting
James's gaze. Talking things through with someone
was tempting, but you did not discuss a lady with another man and you most certainly did not admit that
you had spent a night, however chastely, in bed with
her, or that you had found yourselves kissing with unexpected passion in public. And very much wanted to
do it again.

'What took you out of town?' James asked, eyes
down on the complicated table he was drawing.

'Can't say, I'm afraid.'

'Oh, right. At least it wasn't Oxford, eh?'

'No,' Henry agreed. 'Not Oxford.' And not some secret mission for his superiors either.

He stood up. He would write a note to Melissa, enquire if she was recovered from their travels, see how
she replied. He was worried about her, although he
could not put his finger on precisely why.

* * *

Melissa opened the letter from Henry, sitting at her desk. She had been trying to write and had spent the time alternately gazing into space and jotting down sentences that, on second reading, were either totally insipid or completely melodramatic. She seemed to have lost the will to write.

I am tired and concerned about Letitia, that is all.

The message from Henry could hardly be called a letter, more of a note. It said that he hoped she was recovered from their journeying and he stood ready to escort her anywhere the fancy took her, should she require it. A person of their acquaintance had mentioned a circumstance which might lead someone to jump to conclusions about a certain lady's identity. She could be assured that he had no idea who that might be. He was, he signed himself, her friend *H. de V.B.K.C.*

She had known he would be discreet about Prue and Harlby, but it was kind of him to reassure her.

What on earth did all those initials stand for? She roused herself to find the *Peerage* and looked up the Duke of Walton. Henry, it appeared, had been blessed with the name of Henry de Vere Broderick Knight Cary. She would tease him about the Broderick—so pompous—she thought, just as soon as she found the energy.

She put the note in a drawer, her writing into a portfolio and went to find a book to read. An idle afternoon and an early night was what she needed.

'Miss Taverner.'

'What? What time is it?' She peered up at Gertrude,

who was in her wrapper, her hair in curl papers, a candlestick in one hand.

'Midnight, miss. I was just going to bed, seeing as you didn't need me, and Miss Staines has been in her room this half-hour past. It is Her Grace—downstairs with Lady Cranford.'

Something was very wrong—they would not be dragging her from her bed at this hour to give her good news. 'Give me my robe.'

She pushed her feet into the slippers, belted the robe and hurried down to find that neither Verity nor Prue were sitting down. They stood either side of the cold hearth in full evening dress, glinting with jewels, and neither was smiling.

'What is wrong? Is someone hurt?'

'No,' Verity said quickly. 'Nothing like that. Nothing physical.'

'We have been at Lady Troughton's ball,' Prue explained. 'And we started hearing whispers and comments and—'

'We thought we had best come and speak with you immediately. We need to decide what to do.'

'About what? Oh, do sit down, you are making me feel dizzy. Whispers about what?'

'That you and Lord Henry are lovers. That you and he have been staying in one of his father's country manors.'

'*What?* That's ridiculous. I have never been anywhere near a country house with him. Where is it supposed to be?'

'Somewhere near Daventry, apparently, but that's not important. You were seen, in his arms, in an inn yard in Aylesbury, which is a likely enough place for you to have been changing horses on your way back from there.'

'But I was only out of London for three days. Why would I have gone to this house, wherever it is, misbehaved with Henry and then come back again, when we could perfectly well have done whatever it is we are supposed to have done here, in London?'

'No one is counting the days precisely,' Prue said. 'There are so many parties, guests move from one to another.'

'It is enough that the rumour starts,' Verity added and she looked so serious that Melissa found herself fully awake and very alarmed. Verity was always so positive that to hear her sound so grim was ominous.

'I cannot prove where I was without involving Letitia Houghton,' she said.

'But what is this tale of you being seen embracing in an inn courtyard? That is so ridiculous, we might be able to do something with that,' Prue said thoughtfully.

'That is the part that is true,' Melissa admitted. 'Don't look at me like that! We were tired and relieved and dizzy with travelling and I meant to kiss Henry on the cheek in a friendly way—to thank him—and he moved and… And I am not quite sure what happened next.'

'I think it is quite clear what happened,' Verity said, with a flicker of grim amusement. 'Is there anything else inexplicable that might rear its head and complicate matters even further?'

'We did spend the night together.'

'Two nights.'

'Yes, but the second one I shared a bed with Letitia. The first one…'

'You didn't! My goodness,' Prue said. 'Was it very enjoyable?'

'No, it was not,' Melissa replied sharply. 'He had been hit over the head with a breadboard by Letitia and I had been hit in the face by Harlby and we had to keep waking each other up at hourly intervals to make sure we did not have concussion and my face hurt and I was very tired and just wanted to sleep.'

'Oh, dear,' Prue said, almost, but not quite, keeping her lips from twitching. 'How disappointing—he is rather handsome.'

Melissa glared at her. 'Who saw us?'

'That is the problem, we do not know. Obviously someone in society, because they recognised Lord Henry and are in a position to spread the rumour widely, but beyond that we have no idea.'

Melissa told herself to stop panicking. 'Henry is not courting anyone at the moment, so there is no one to be hurt by this. He's a man—men are expected to have affairs. Therefore I am the only one affected and I really do not care about balls and parties and what people say.' That was not true, but she had to be positive. 'It will all blow over in time if Henry and I simply ignore it.'

Verity looked dubious. 'It might be unpleasant for a while, but we will all stand by you, that goes without saying, and I am not certain how many people wish to offend a duchess, a marchioness and two countesses.'

'Thank you.' She felt sick. Who could have been so spiteful? Then she remembered that glimpse of someone at a window in the inn. Was that the person who had gossiped? But she had not even been certain they had looked out or whether they were male or female. 'I must warn Henry.'

'I imagine he knows already, unless he has stayed at home with a good book,' Verity said. She stood up. 'We must go and I am sorry to leave you facing an uncomfortable night, but we did not want you to wake up and discover what was happening with no warning.'

'Scandal sheets,' Prue said, wrinkling her nose in distaste. 'Or someone cutting you when you are out shopping.'

'Oh.' Yes, this was going to be very unpleasant for a while.

'There is Lady Oswestry's reception tomorrow. We had all accepted invitations to that, had we not?' Verity said. 'What would be best to do? If you do not go, that will add fuel to the flames because it will seem you are admitting it and if you go it will probably be most uncomfortable.'

'I will think about it and let you know.' Melissa walked with them to the front door, kissed and was kissed in return, then walked blankly into the sitting room and sat down at her desk.

She must write to Henry, whether or not he had already found out what was happening.

Henry slapped his hand of cards down on the table and swivelled in his chair. Through the smoky gloom of the card room he could see faces at each table as players looked up in curiosity or annoyance at the disturbance.

'Say that again, Carruthers.'

'Don't take me up so, Cary.' The fussily dressed

man at the next table shifted uncomfortably, but managed a titter. 'All I said was that you have rather strange tastes in lady friends. But I expect this one enjoys a little travel. Aylesbury is a most historic town and she's quite the bluestocking, so they say. Miss Ta—'

'If you repeat a lady's name, Carruthers, I will be asking you to name a man—your second,' Henry said. Carruthers was an inveterate gossip, an irritating gadfly of a man who relished stirring up trouble, then skipping out of the way of the consequences. He was long overdue for an appointment with some cold steel, or hot lead, on Hampstead Heath.

Henry ignored the knot in his gut, the worry about Melissa, and concentrated on making Carruthers shut up. Then he could discover what the hell this was about. It certainly was not caused by him squiring Melissa around London—not with the mention of Aylesbury. *That kiss.*

'My dear chap, I do apologise. See me utterly contrite.' Carruthers fluttered be-ringed fingers. 'I was quite mistaken. Do rest assured, not another word will escape me on the subject.'

Henry turned his back on him. To make any more of it, to take Carruthers by his lace-trimmed neckcloth and shake the origins of the story out of him, would only serve to underline its importance.

'The man's a complete commoner,' James said. 'Ignore him. I'll raise you ten.'

Play began again, but in the eyes of the other men around the table Henry could read an amused interest. He must warn Melissa.

Chapter Fourteen

Henry was on the doorstep of the Half Moon Street house at ten the next morning. Melissa answered his knock. She looked heavy-eyed and on edge.

'Oh. Henry. Gertrude has just gone out with a note for you. The most ridiculous thing has happened.'

'I know.' He followed her into the hallway and closed the door behind them. 'Someone appears to have seen us at The George in Aylesbury and is spreading the story all around town. How did you find out?'

'Verity and Prue came to see me late last night. They had heard the whispers at Lady Troughton's ball.'

'Damn.' Henry followed her through into the drawing room and they sank down on the sofa. 'I heard it at a gaming club off St James's Street and hoped I'd stopped the mouth of the rumour-monger who was sniggering about it, but if it has reached the society matrons, then we have a problem.'

'Verity says the story is that we were at your father's house near Daventry, which is ridiculous. I mean, why would we go all that way for a couple of nights when we could perfectly well misbehave ourselves in London?'

'Quite. But logic doesn't enter into it. It's a good story, so why spoil it with the facts?'

'That's what the others said. And that kiss at Aylesbury—that is true. I thought I saw someone at the window.' The look she sent him was puzzled, hurt. 'Who would be so unkind? Who have either of us so injured that they would want to make such unpleasantness for us? The only person I can think of is Charles Harlby, but surely he would have gone straight to London, to sell Letitia's jewellery.'

Henry moved along the sofa and put his arm around her. It was painful to see the look on her face and he wanted to make it go away, protect her. And he could not. 'I do not know, but as you say, it seems unlikely to be Harlby. There must have been someone there—it is a busy town with several routes converging on it. We were recognised and some people like to make trouble, just for the sake of it. Having a story to tell, some gossip to spread, makes them feel powerful.'

'It gives me a powerful urge to box their ears,' she said, with a flicker of her usual spirit. 'I shall not regard it.'

'Things could be quite unpleasant at social events,' Henry warned. 'But you may be right—if we do not react, then it may well simply fizzle out, like a damp fuse.'

'I will kiss everyone, all my friends and especially the men,' Melissa said suddenly. 'I have seen other ladies do it—they drift around, gushing and kissing cheeks and calling everyone *daahling*. I shall do the same—to you, to Will and Ross and Max and all the ladies, of course. And if anyone says anything about us

I shall look blank and confused and demand to know what they are talking about.'

'It might work,' Henry said, rather dubious. 'Certainly if any gentlemen make remarks I will demand an apology or—'

'Don't you dare fight duels, Henry Cary!'

'Not much choice,' he said lightly. 'Not to would be to acknowledge that you are my mistress, not a lady.'

'Oh. Could you not simply hit them?'

'I will try to avoid any such situation arising,' he said, crossing his fingers behind his back. Not that he actually wanted to fight a duel, but if honour demanded it, he most certainly would. 'Have you any invitations for this evening?'

'There is a reception being held by Lady Oswestry to welcome home her brother who has been on a scientific expedition to the South Seas. He is going to display some of the items he collected and there will be music, I expect, and a supper. It will be easier to go about talking to people than it will at a dance.'

Her chin was up and her smile was fixed and he had to fight down the urge to take her in his arms and tell her to stop being brave and sensible and he would make it all go away. Which of course, he could not, unless…

'Melissa, you have been compromised, quite innocently, obviously, but that is neither here nor there. There is a perfectly straightforward remedy in this situation: we should get married.'

If he had stuck a pin in her, she could not have recoiled more violently. 'Don't be ridiculous,' she said fiercely from the other end of the sofa where she had come to rest, trapped against the arm. 'You do not want to get married, do you? No, don't answer that. If you wanted to marry someone else you would probably have told me, because we are friends. And if you wanted to marry me you would have asked me. And you would not have done so because you know I do not wish to marry anyone. So this is simply a pointless, gallant, gesture to convention. I thought you had more sense.'

'Confound it, Melissa! I am only trying to make things better for you.'

They sat at either end of the seat, glaring at each other until he suddenly found himself laughing. 'Oh, for goodness sake, look at us—like a pair of glowering bookends on a shelf. Very well, I promise not to make any more *gallant* gestures unless you want me to, although I deny that such things are pointless.'

'Thank you.' She visibly relaxed, reminding him of nothing more than a flustered hen settling back on her nest and smoothing her ruffled plumage. The fact that she was wearing a rather charming morning dress in shades of brown and russet only added to the fantasy. 'I am surprised you can find anything to smile about, though.'

'I am merely enjoying your company,' he said mildly, finding that it was true, even under these circumstances.

'Really?'

She sounded so weary that he moved along until he was sitting beside her again and put his arm around her shoulders. Some instinct told him that a hug might be welcome, but Melissa turned towards him, burrowed up against him and rested her head on his shoulder.

'That is so comfortable and everything is so horrid. I hate that people can be so unkind.'

'Shh.' He held her close and felt her curve against him and then, with a little sigh, she was asleep.

Of course, she had probably had a sleepless night after her friends had called. It said something for her courage that he had not found her packing her bags when he arrived.

She was fast asleep now, snuggled firmly into the crook of his arm and making rather endearing soft whiffling sounds.

Henry settled himself more comfortably, rested his cheek against the top of her head and found himself drifting off, too. He did not fight it. They had a difficult evening ahead of them and he had not exactly spent a tranquil night either, once he had finally got to his bed.

A sudden unpleasant thought had him opening his eyes. Gentlemen of the diplomatic corps, those of junior rank, at any rate, were not expected to make themselves the subject of gossip and speculation. He foresaw a rather difficult interview ahead of him.

To hell with it. This feels good.

He closed his eyes again, thought of nothing but the feel of warm, soft woman against his body, of the scent of her, subtle and fresh, of a bubble of peace before it all became very, very difficult.

Something unpleasant was waiting for her, but if she did not open her eyes, then she did not have to remember what it was.

And wherever she was, it felt so good. Warm, safe, firm. There was silk under her cheek and the smell of clean linen and starch, something citrusy, the subtle undertone that said Henry.

'You are awake.' Yes, that was Henry.

'How do you know?' She stayed where she was.

'Your breathing changed.'

A clock struck with silvery, familiar notes. The overmantel clock. She counted… Ten, eleven.

'Have I been asleep?'

'We both have. Neither of us had a very good night.'

His voice sounded extra-deep with her ear pressed against his waistcoat. Comforting. Then she remembered what it was that was lying in wait when she opened her eyes.

'It was no dream, then?'

'No.'

She felt his sigh and opened her eyes, twisted round so she could look up into his and, without conscious thought, lifted her face for his kiss.

There was no hesitation. His mouth was firm and warm on hers, then hot as he parted his lips and she did the same, gasping softly as his tongue touched hers. It should have felt strange, but somehow she knew what to do in response. Or her body did. She stroked her own tongue against his, exploring, letting him explore in turn.

The urgency, the sudden fire, that had sprung up between them in the inn yard was there again, but controlled now, waiting to be unleashed. In its place was a warm wash of sensation, the wonder of discovery.

And this is only a kiss. Only…

Henry lifted his head, sat back, steadying her as she swayed. 'Not a good idea,' he said with a lightness belied by his breathing.

'No.' Melissa tugged her rumpled gown into some

kind of order. 'It must not look as though we have ever exchanged more than a peck on the cheek in our lives.' She was surprised at how calm she sounded to her own ears when, in reality, she was feeling anything but composed.

She wanted Henry in a thoroughly carnal way and suspected that he felt the same. Although, she cautioned herself, men did appear to feel like that about almost any female. And Henry had reacted strongly when she had carelessly mentioned taking a lover and had then never mentioned it again, so it seemed unlikely that he had any thought of doing more than kiss her.

Which was all to the good, given the situation they found themselves in. The last thing she wanted was Henry talking himself into offering for her again. That would be disastrous. For a moment she struggled to recall just why that should be, before common sense reasserted itself.

'I had better go,' he said and stood up. 'Practise your gushing, Melissa.'

A note arrived mid-afternoon from Verity in answer to hers. Her four friends had consulted and agreed hers was a good plan to try. Their husbands were briefed and they would arrive at the reception at half past nine, allowing her to sweep in a few minutes later with a wide field of men—and women—to embrace in a light-hearted manner.

Melissa scribbled a note to Henry to warn him to be there and ready at the same time and then devoted the remainder of the afternoon to soothing Cousin Almeria, who had heard the rumours in the unlikely setting of the Royal Institution and was berating herself for her careless approach to chaperonage.

She got changed far too early, could not find the slightest appetite for her dinner and finally sent Gertrude out to hail a hackney carriage at a few minutes to half past nine.

Her cousin, resplendent in a purple toque and grey satin and emanating respectability, insisted on accompanying her. 'Shutting the stable door after the horse has bolted,' she said, 'but I will do what I can.'

'Do not forget that I was out of London at the time, visiting my old governess who is very sick in Birmingham, and accompanied by a friend who I refuse to name in case any of this nonsense rubs off on her.'

'If only I had not met so many people while you were away,' Almeria lamented. 'There was that afternoon lecture and then I attended Mrs Lamprey's At Home and I saw quite a few of my acquaintance when I was shopping. I should have mentioned in a casual manner that you were out of town. Now it will seem strange that I did not.'

'You weren't to know. If I could name Miss Houghton, I would, but we cannot risk it. We are here.'

They shed their cloaks into the hands of waiting maids in the foyer, then climbed the sweep of stairs to where Lady Oswestry stood with her husband and recently returned brother.

To do her credit, Her Ladyship did not as much as blink when she saw Melissa, although her very lack of reaction was telling. Melissa shook hands, was introduced to the very tanned Lord Algernon Black and, head up, sailed into the ballroom, the location of the reception.

She saw Ross Vincent, the Marquis of Cranford, first. The tall, scarred and powerful ex-privateer was not someone she had ever imagined herself kissing, but she could not pick and choose now.

'Ross!' She rushed up and kissed him on the cheek. She had to stand on tiptoe, but that made the whole thing more obvious. 'Dear man. It has been ages!'

Heads turned as Ross bent to kiss her cheek in return. 'At least a week. I swear you look lovelier than ever.'

'Flatterer.' She dealt him a light blow on the arm with her fan. 'Where is darling Prue?'

'Over there, I think.' He gestured and she swept off, feeling curious eyes boring into her back as she went.

'Prue, darling. I'm so glad to see you.' There was quite a large group near Prue, who was talking to a rather imposing matron whose toque was a rival to Cousin Almeria's. 'Oh, good evening, Lady Spratt. Honestly, I did not think I would come this evening— I was so exhausted after that journey, but I told myself not to be feeble and make the effort.'

'What journey might that be?' Lady Spratt had clearly heard the gossip. She raised an eyeglass and regarded Melissa critically.

'Oh, Birmingham. My poor old governess. Sick and pitifully short of funds.' She lowered her voice a little. 'Spends all her pension on good causes, which is all very well, but no help when she herself is ill. But I think she will be all right now—I found her new lodgings and a most respectable maid.'

'It must have been very wearying,' Prue said, full of sympathy.

'Three days travelling, and one day rushing around house and servant agencies! I swear that I can still feel that post-chaise swaying.'

'One had heard that you had been out of town,' Lady Spratt said, her gaze avid.

'Really? I wonder how.' Melissa smiled vaguely, her hands tight on her fan to stop them trembling.

'You were seen in an inn yard in Aylesbury,' the older woman said.

'Was that The White Hart or The George?' Melissa mused. 'I stopped at one going north and the other coming home.'

'I have no idea.'

'I thought you were fully informed about my movements,' Melissa said, feeling her self-control slipping. *The nosy old vulture.* Then she saw Henry. This was the moment. She had to carry this off and then, at least, they would have muddied the waters.

'Lord Henry! How lovely to see you again.' He took her hand as she reached him and bent his head so she could kiss him on the cheek. 'My saviour from Aylesbury.'

Now there was no doubt about it: everyone around them had abandoned all pretence and were watching and listening. 'It is infuriating how people will try to take advantage of ladies travelling alone. If it had not been for Lord Henry's intervention, I would have probably still been on the road back behind a pair of complete slugs,' she informed Will, the Duke of Aylsham, who had strolled up with Verity on his arm. She blew him a kiss, just so he did not feel left out.

'Yes, we were so grateful when we heard of it,' someone standing behind her said. Mrs Grainger, she realised as she turned. 'I was dubious about allowing dear Letitia to accompany Miss Taverner, but you know what these girls are, always wanting to rush off and help their friends. But there,' she added comfortably to Lady Spratt, 'it all turned out well, thanks to Lord Henry.'

'Oh, good evening, Mrs Grainger.' Melissa beamed at her. 'It was so kind of you to allow Letitia to come with me.'

'I could hardly refuse, my dear.' She turned away with a smile, leaving Melissa trying not to look too relieved.

Henry had strolled away, chatting to an army officer in full dress uniform, she was glad to see, and none of her friends crowded too close in a way that might have suggested that she needed supporting.

'How very fast of you, Miss Taverner,' a honey-sweet voice said next to her.

She looked around, eyebrows raised, to find a slender blonde woman beside her. 'I do not believe I have had the pleasure of an introduction,' she said coolly.

'Isobel Duncombe. But then, judging by your behaviour, you hardly need an invitation to become most intimate, do you?'

'Lady Duncombe.' She had no idea who she was or why she should be so very hostile. 'You quite mistake me. I can assure you, I only become affectionate towards those who have shown themselves to be my friends and I do not believe that you are, are you?'

Lady Duncombe's smile was thin. 'No, I do not think I can be counted as such.' She turned away, still smiling, and strolled across to a small group of ladies. They leaned towards her as if she was telling them something of great interest.

Melissa shivered. Perhaps her efforts at averting suspicion were not as effective as she thought, although what on earth had Lady Duncombe against her?

She began to circulate, taking care to greet all her acquaintances effusively and, when she encountered Jane with Ivo, her husband, she kissed them both on the cheek.

'How goes it?' Ivo, Lord Kendall, asked.

'It has been partly successful. Mrs Grainger was a great help, but then, she is hardly a figure in society and her word may not carry much weight. I have just had a most prickly encounter with a Lady Duncombe. I cannot imagine what I may have done to offend her, but she is no friend.'

Jane frowned in thought. 'I don't know her, but we met her husband last week, did we not, Ivo? A prosy bore, I thought,' she added in a whisper.

'Well, he is a diplomat and I suppose he is employed to calm down heated discussions by smothering them,' Ivo suggested.

A diplomat? Perhaps Henry knows her.

For some reason that made her feel uneasy. In fact, now that the energy she had expended to will herself up that staircase and into this reception was ebbing away, she was feeling decidedly fragile. Perhaps now was the time to retreat and go home.

She looked around for Almeria, hoping to locate her

by her purple toque, and instead saw Henry emerging
from a side room. For a moment she wondered at the
grim expression on his face, then he was smiling, bow-
ing slightly to a Roman-nosed matron. Melissa drifted
towards him and they met in front of an unoccupied
table and chairs. She did not make the mistake of sitting down with him.

'Do you know a Lady Duncombe?'

Henry became very still and the social smile froze.
He was relaxed and smiling again so rapidly that she
thought she had imagined it. Then, when he spoke, she
knew she had not.

'Why?' he said bluntly. 'What have you had to do
with her?'

'Nothing, except that she spoke to me just now and
in no pleasant manner either. I cannot imagine what I
have done to make her dislike me.'

'I suggest you go home now,' Henry said. Then, as
some other guests came closer, 'I can assure you, Miss
Taverner, it was no trouble at all.' He bowed slightly
and walked off leaving her even more confused and,
somehow, more apprehensive.

'Whatever is the matter, Melissa? You are standing there like Lot's wife, petrified into a pillar of salt.'

'Oh. Almeria. Do you mind if we leave now? I
think… I feel we have done all we can for the moment.'

'Yes, I agree. I had a most interesting discussion
with Lord Black, Lady Oswestry's brother, you know.
Apparently the moths on the South Sea islands that he
visited are of great size. He was most helpful in describing them…'

She talked on relentlessly, pausing while they thanked

their hostess and took their leave, and persisting until they were in a hackney carriage and trotting home.

'I think we have had some success,' she said. 'It helps that you are not prominent in society and that Lord Henry is merely a younger son. Mrs Grainger's intervention was welcome, although she can hardly be said to have any influence with the arch gossips, and I did hear one spiteful soul say that the wife of a man who was virtually a cit would do anything to get in the good graces of the friend of a duchess.'

'It is not easy killing gossip, is it?' Melissa said with a sigh.

'About as easy as killing cockroaches,' Almeria said grimly. 'Nothing works with them except a heavy weight. I suspect the only thing to do with this is to allow it to calm down and wait for someone with much higher social standing than you to commit an indiscretion.'

'Or give up and move,' Melissa said. She was weary, she was hurt and she was angry and London no longer felt the same place that it had when she'd arrived, full of excitement and hope, just a few weeks before.

Chapter Fifteen

Nothing ever looked quite as bad in the morning when the sun was shining, Melissa told herself. It did not matter that her sleep, such as it was, had been full of nightmares where she found herself in the middle of a grand ball, stark naked, or that her appetite for breakfast had quite deserted her.

She had come to London to be independent, to make her own living by her writing. That was what was important, not enjoying a social whirl, mixing with the cream of the *ton*. Not being able to go to parties would limit what she could write for the newspapers, of course, but she could question her friends, ask them to be on the lookout for fashionable new ensembles. The weather was improving now, so she could walk in the parks at the time when everyone who was anyone was taking the air, talk to the modistes who would be happy to share descriptions of their latest creations once their clients had worn the outfit once. And she should make an effort and finish the book she was writing, then sell that.

'Melissa, dear? You have been sitting with the butter knife in mid-air for minutes.'

'I'm sorry, Almeria.' She put the knife down, picked up her coffee and took a sip. 'I was resolving not to scurry back to Dorset as though I have done something wrong, something to be ashamed of.'

'Of course you haven't,' Almeria said stoutly. 'You are quite right to stay here. It will all blow over in a week or so.'

'I will have to see what Henry and Verity and the others say after last night. Should I make the effort to keep attending parties or would it be best now to stay away, I wonder?'

The door knocker sounded and Gertrude came in a moment later. 'The post, Miss Taverner. And yours, Miss Staines.'

'No invitations. Not one. That is a bill from the haberdasher.' She flipped over the rest. 'More bills, an advertisement for a show at a gallery, a letter from Mama.'

She read the letter, full of news of the everyday happenings in the village. Georgie Parsons had broken his leg. Mrs Whitely had been safely delivered of twins. The Rector's sermon last Sunday had caused controversy, because nobody felt inclined to forgive their enemies if that included the French, and could Melissa please send two yards of pale green twill ribbon to contrast with the enclosed scrap of silk? Was she retiring to bed at a sensible hour every night and eating properly?

And so on and so forth…

Life in Dorset sounded remarkably unchanged.

No, I am not going home.

Another knock at the door. 'A note, Miss Taverner.'

'It is from Henry.' She broke the seal and read the

few lines. 'He suggests we meet tomorrow afternoon in the Abbey, of all places.'

'That sounds a very sensible choice to me,' Almeria said. 'Today, being Sunday, it will be crowded, but in the week it is hardly the place that the *ton* would frequent as sightseers. However, if you were to be seen, it is somewhere you could be expected to visit as someone new to London.'

'I suppose so. I had best take Gertrude with me.' She wanted to see Henry, she wanted to be held by him, but that was hardly possible in Westminster Abbey. Hushed conversation was the most she could hope for.

Melissa decided to walk to the Abbey along the Queen's Walk at the side of Green Park, then across St James's Park. Gertrude strode along a pace behind, silent and clutching an umbrella, radiating disapproval. Whether she was put out at the length of the walk, or opposed to her mistress meeting a man in this way, was not clear and Melissa had no intention of asking.

At least she arrived at the North door feeling warm, if windswept, and she thought she probably had colour in her cheeks, which could only be an improvement on her wan complexion that morning.

A verger asked her if she required a guide, but she refused, asking instead for directions to the cloisters, although she did purchase a rather closely printed pamphlet of historical and architectural information.

There were a few visitors, some led around by a verger who was pointing out various tombs and memorials, others wandering unaccompanied, guidebook in hand, but the vast, soaring space seemed almost empty.

She must come back another time, armed with more information, she thought, slowing her pace as she made her way from the North transept to the South and looking around her, so as to seem to be just another sightseer.

At first the cloister appeared to be empty. 'Why do you not sit there?' she suggested to Gertrude, pointing to a stone bench which lay in a shaft of sunlight.

The maid nodded and went to sit primly upright, umbrella clasped in front of her, as Melissa made her way along the stone quadrangle, her footsteps echoing from the ornate ceiling. As she turned the corner Henry stood up.

'You found it.'

'The Abbey is rather hard to miss.' She glanced around. 'And a good place to meet. We will be able to hear anyone coming in.'

'I know who saw us,' Henry said flatly. 'It was von Arten. He had been in Oxford, apparently, giving my superiors some cause for thought, and by some devilish bad luck stopped to eat at The George.'

'How do you know?'

'He was there last night and he spoke to me after you had left. I suspect he was looking for me and struck lucky with the reception. He wanted to gloat, in a most light-hearted and elegant manner, of course. He knows we were responsible for exposing Laverne and he saw his chance for revenge. He is aware he is being watched now and that he is going to have to leave the country and we handed him a farewell gift for us on a plate.'

'What did you do?' She was not certain whether she was relieved that the person who had spread the tale was not someone she might meet face to face, or frightened for what more the Graf might do.

'Nothing.' Henry shrugged. 'He is leaving. What could I do? If I hit him, as I was very much inclined to do, it would cause even more of a stir. I can hardly call him out without, again, causing more talk. At least we know who it was.'

'Yes.' Melissa stared rather blankly at an ornate memorial plaque to some worthy of the previous century who was depicted on his way up to heaven, accompanied by a bevy of very fat cherubs. 'You did not tell me about Lady Duncombe.'

Henry went very still. 'Did I not?'

'You know perfectly well that you didn't. When she spoke to me last night she was acid, positively waspish, in fact, and remarked that I was fast. She seemed so hostile under a very light and airy manner, but I have no idea why she should dislike me so. She clearly did not believe for a moment that I had just given you a kiss on the cheek because we had met by chance.'

'No, she wouldn't,' Henry said.

'You do know her, then.'

'Yes.' His face showed as much expression as the stone effigies in the Abbey.

'*Henry.* Stop being mysterious. How do you know her and why doesn't she like me?'

'She is the wife of Lord Duncombe, a diplomat who neglects her, so she says, for pretty young men. But despite that, she likes the life and from the moment she arrived at the Congress she was ready to enjoy herself.'

'That explains why you know who she is. It doesn't explain anything else.' She was beginning to wish that they had met at the Tower—at least there might be some thumbscrews or a spare rack to hand.

'Neglected wives—attractive, wealthy, titled ones—find themselves with remarkable freedom.'

'You mean she took lovers?' She was being very slow, Melissa realised as an unpleasant, sickly feeling took possession of her stomach. 'You mean you were her lover?'

'Briefly.' Henry grimaced. 'I thought her charming and, heaven help me, alluring. I discovered that she is as hard as nails and utterly self-centred. I attempted to end the liaison as tactfully as possible, but one does not leave Isobel, she dismisses you when she has finished with you. I made her angry and she likes to pay debts.'

'And she thinks that we are—that you grew tired of her, but that you are now with a very ordinary female of no great looks, no status, no influence. She is furious with both of us.'

She tried to sound objective. *Do not let him see that you care.* Somehow that had become very important.

Henry snorted. 'You are *not* ordinary and to say you have no great looks is, if you'll forgive me, arrant nonsense. Isobel is merely resentful that I am not pining away for her, I imagine.'

'Does she know von Arten?'

That's right, a calm, thoughtful tone. Not jealous. Never that.

'She knew him in Vienna. I had forgotten that they were often together. I did wonder at one time whether they had been lovers and then clean forgot about it.' Henry ran his hand through his hair. 'Fool that I am, I should have realised that nobody influential is going to take a great deal of interest in the gossip of a foreigner hanging around on the fringes of society. But they are going to listen to Isobel Duncombe. Of course he would have told her, and the fact that they are close enough for him to know she is angry with me, and predict how she would react to the knowledge that I am apparently carrying on a liaison with you, makes me wonder…'

'You think your superiors would be interested to learn of a connection between them?'

'Very interested,' Henry agreed. He clearly had no idea that she had been affected in any way by the revelation that he and Lady Duncombe had been intimate.

Melissa found that she had run out of anything remotely coherent to say and was saved by the sound of footsteps ringing on the stone slabs around the corner of the cloister.

Henry got to his feet and in a few long strides was into the next wing of the square and out of sight. Melissa opened her pamphlet and tried to focus on a paragraph about the coronation chair as a cleric appeared, black cassock flapping around his ankles, his arms full of a pile of ledgers.

'Good morning,' he said, halting in front of a small door in the wall. He began to juggle the books in order to reach the handle.

'Good morning. Allow me.' Melissa ducked past and opened it for him.

'So kind. God bless you.' He disappeared inside.

I very much doubt it, not with me thinking the decidedly uncharitable thoughts that I am.

Melissa sat down again. This was jealousy, she realised, although she had never felt it before. Envy, of course, sometimes, but never this raw, painful anger at another person for having something that she wanted, that should belong to her.

She doesn't have him any longer, she thought and with it came the realisation that she was in love. With Henry.

It had to be that. If she simply loved him as a friend, then she would be angry with Isobel Duncombe for the way she had behaved, then and now. But she wasn't— she was bitterly envious because Isobel and Henry had shared something that she wanted.

It felt dreadful, as though she had swallowed something corrosive. It did not matter that their affair had happened before she had met him, that he clearly disliked Isobel and had been disillusioned about her long before this act of spite.

Melissa swallowed and looked out over the scythed grass in the centre of the cloisters.

Breathe. Be calm. Do not let him see...anything.

Footsteps. Henry was coming back. She smiled and was quite pleased that it felt natural. 'What will happen now? To von Arten and Lady Duncombe, I mean?'

'He has already found he is no longer welcome, or even tolerated. If he has any sense, he is packing his bags and will make for Ramsgate or Dover and the next ship across the Channel. If he doesn't, then he will find himself on one, like it or not—' He broke off and looked at her, then took her hand.

Don't do that. Don't touch me. Don't look as though you care, because I cannot bear it.

'Now,' Henry said, pressing on as though she was not sitting there like one of the automata from Merlin's

Mechanical Museum, 'where does this leave us? I think your performance last night as a slightly dizzy, somewhat over-affectionate young lady went some way to helping. With von Arten's imminent departure and, I would hope, with Isobel Duncombe being persuaded that London is not a very congenial place to be for the foreseeable future, this should all die down. I would suggest that you continue to attend whatever entertainments you are invited to and continue to kiss your friends. I will encounter you from time to time in a casual manner, and someone will do something outrageous and divert attention from us.'

'That sounds very sensible,' Melissa said, extracting her hand from his strong, warm grasp.

Those fingers had held her, that casually elegant body next to her had been pressed to hers with passion, those lips that were now laying out a sensible, coherent strategy had been anything but coherent when they had met hers.

But that was simply male desire, not friendship, and he had clearly recognised it for the mistake that it was.

What a fool she was to fall in love. She had been happy as Henry's friend. Amused, excited and entertained by their small adventures, soothed by finding another mind that understood her fears and accepted her opinions and her ability to think for herself. Now she had to step back from that friendship, become distant, before he guessed her true feelings.

And if he did realise, what would he do? Feel sorry for her, obviously. Propose out of kindness? No, surely not. Henry had made it clear he had no intention of marrying yet and when he did it would be to someone suitable to be a diplomatic wife. Which she, quite clearly, was not.

Might he suggest an affair? No, not if he knew how she felt, he was too sensitive for that. And it would be worse, far worse, to have him and then lose him than to never have been his at all.

'You are very quiet.'

'Just thinking. This has been unpleasant and it has distracted me from my work.'

'I am sorry von Arten crossed your path.'

'If you had not helped me with Letitia's elopement, then this would not have happened. It is futile to say *What if?* or to feel guilty about other people's unpleasant natures.' Melissa stood up, suddenly resolute. 'I must go home now and work.'

'I'll walk with you and find a hackney carriage.'

'No. Best not run the risk of being seen alone together just now. Gertrude is waiting for me. Goodbye, Henry.'

He was not quite fast enough to hide his surprise at her abrupt tone. 'Yes, of course. You are quite right. I will see you soon, I am sure.'

She walked away, her heels clicking on the worn old stone, and did not look back when she reached the corner and turned. After a moment she heard the patter of Gertrude's feet as the maid followed her.

The choir had begun to practise while they had been in the cloisters and the pure notes soared up into the shadowed heights of the Abbey to be lost in centuries-old stonework as she walked briskly across from one transept to the other and out of the high-arched door into the churchyard.

The weather had turned grey and breezy while they had been inside and Melissa waved at the nearest hackney carriage, eager to be gone.

Running away, she told herself. *But what else can I do?*

Henry shifted into a more comfortable position, not easy on the unyielding stone, and listened to the echo of Melissa's retreating footsteps as they died away.

Retreating. That was the correct word, because he had the distinct impression that she was running away from him. That hurt, he realised. Both the fact that she felt she must hurry from him and the conviction that something was wrong that she had not told him about.

This whole mess with von Arten and Isobel's nasty attempt at revenge—obviously that was troubling her, but she had spoken of it quite freely. No, he realised, it was after he had admitted to the affair with Isobel that something had changed.

Had he shocked her? He didn't think so. After all, she had discussed taking a lover without blushing and listened to his advice on the subject without any sign of prudishness. Did she despise him for his bad judgement, or blame him because Isobel was bearing a grudge? That did not seem like Melissa.

He got up to go, still puzzled, even more uneasy. That *'Goodbye, Henry'* had had a distinct feeling of a final farewell about it. He walked around the cloister slowly, giving her plenty of time to leave the area, then walked out of the Abbey, across St Margaret's churchyard, up King Street and into Whitehall.

He must tell Mr Philps, his immediate superior, about

the talk and he rather thought he was going to have to admit to his past affair with Isobel. Unless the old fox knew about it already. He probably did, Henry realised, as he strode past the entrance to Downing Street. That was embarrassing and wouldn't look good on his record, unless, of course, it was considered useful.

It occurred to him that he was going to have to explain about the journey with Melissa, too. At least Philps would keep his mouth shut about that and all he needed to know was that he and Melissa had been in pursuit of an eloping couple. No names needed to be mentioned and none of the details of the journey, such as who spent what time in whose bed, either.

His stride slowed to a stroll as he neared the glossy black door that led to Mr Philps's domain. His work on von Arten and Laverne had attracted praise, but he was not at all sure of the reception of this latest instalment of the story involving gossip, the widow of a prominent member of the House of Lords and the admission that he had been away from London for some time without informing the office. Henry walked past the door and into the nearest coffee house. He needed to think this through very carefully, because the last thing he wanted to do was to compromise Melissa any more than she was already.

She was too important for that, he admitted as he paid for a pot of coffee and waved aside an offer of the latest newspapers. Just when had that happened?

Chapter Sixteen

Melissa looked at her diary as soon as she reached home and found, as she had hoped, there was nothing in it for that evening. Cousin Almeria was bustling about getting ready for a visit to an old friend in Hampstead and seemed too concerned about where she had put a particular journal to notice anything wrong with Melissa's manner.

'Oh, there it is, under the cushions. I do swear these things have a life of their own. Now, dear, do you mind that I will be staying overnight?'

'No, of course not. You haven't seen Miss Haviland for over a year and Gertrude will be here. I intend catching up with my work.'

Melissa smiled and listened and helped locate Almeria's reticule—under yet another cushion—and waved her goodbye with a sigh of relief. Now she did not have to pretend to be cheerful in front of her.

'Luncheon, Miss Taverner?'

She had no appetite, but Gertrude would fuss if she didn't eat. 'Some cold meat and bread and butter, please.'

For some reason all she wanted to do was to write and the novel that she had struggled with was what she wanted to work on. Perhaps she would not have to brood about Henry while she did so, she thought, putting some cold chicken between slices of bread and butter and taking it to her desk.

The story had begun as a rather mannered tale of small-town society, then it had turned into a dramatic tale of villains, lovers and mystery. Now Melissa pulled a fresh sheet of paper towards her and began afresh. Her heroine was the same, but now she was alone.

> *Orphaned?*
> *Fleeing a lecherous former employer?*

She scribbled in the margin.

> *In the small town and fighting to make a respectable living?*
> *A milliner perhaps?*
> *Or a piano teacher?*
> *Governess?*

She left question marks and pushed on. She was in love with a good man, but he was... Married? Lost at sea? No, betrothed to another. Honour meant that she could not show the slightest partiality for him, let alone her true feelings.

Her pen moved over the paper, the words flowing as easily as the ink. There were brackets and question marks, crossings-out and footnotes, but they were just details. The centre of the story would be the heroine's heartbreak and her battle to overcome it and carry on alone.

Melissa stopped when she realised that she could hardly see the paper in front of her. It was six o'clock, the rain was pouring down and the room was in deep shadow. She rang for Gertrude to light the lamps and set the fire, then stood up to stretch and walk up and down to ease her stiff back.

Why was this novel coming so easily when the subject matter was so difficult? Because, she realised, the 'horrid' novels she had sold so readily to the Minerva Press had been enormous fun to write. They had needed skill to construct and imagination but, she could see now, they hadn't touched her heart, they were not about feelings.

I hadn't lived. I hadn't experienced anything. And now I have I am feeling for my heroine and the book is better for it.

Suddenly panicking that it might not be coherent, or even any good at all, she went back to her desk and began to read through what she had written as Gertrude bustled about with the coal scuttle and lighted tapers.

There were inconsistencies, some clumsy phrasing, gaps, but her heroine was real, she thought, her circumstances believable, her heartbreak all too familiar.

It was not Melissa's heartbreak and this was a different woman, she was very clear in her mind about that, but the release of writing about real feelings was unexpectedly soothing. Then she realised why: she could solve this problem, find happiness for the woman on the page, even if she must learn to live with her own sadness.

'At what hour would you like dinner, Miss Taverner?'

She was not hungry. 'I do not…' No, not eating, pining, was not going to help. She would make herself ill, her friends would descend and find out what was wrong and even they could not solve this problem. So they would feel sorry for her and try to cheer her up and she could not bear that…

'Miss Taverner?'

'I am sorry. The usual time, please, Gertrude.'

She had left home to be an independent lady and, if hard work and sheer willpower could make her that, then she would achieve her ambition. The gossip would die down, Lady Duncombe and the Graf von Arten would leave London and she could enjoy a social life again.

Love had never been something she had expected. All she had to do was to remind herself of that whenever she began to feel sorry self-pity. All would be well, just as long as she did not have to talk to Henry again until she had this under control.

The good resolutions worked for a week, although Melissa found that she could sleep only if she worked late into the night. She ate properly, went for brisk walks at the right times to glean enough fashion notes to keep the newspapers content and told her friends and Almeria that the book was going so well that she had no time for socialising.

It was partly true. The book was growing, developing, becoming more complex. Was it publishable? She had no idea, it was so unlike anything else she had ever written. And it generated more ideas that she would jot down in a notebook. Ideas for more stories that might please the Minerva Press, but focused on romance more than on wildly improbable adventure. She would come back to those, she promised herself.

Meanwhile, if she focused on the heartbreak of her heroine, Camilla, she found she could push aside her feelings for Henry. No, not push aside, she corrected herself, as she paused at the entry to Green Park, looking at the trees where he had waited for her that first morning, sleepy and slightly tipsy. She could close the door on thoughts of him for a while, but they came back with the dull ache of missing his company and the disturbing, sharper jabs of desire, of longing for the sensation of his lips on hers again.

She should have realised that a week was all the grace her friends would allow her. They cared for her, as they cared for each other, and they would not allow her to dip below the horizon and quietly vanish into her own little bubble of solitude.

The week after her meeting with Henry in the Abbey she and Almeria were indulging in a lengthy breakfast. Rain had prevented them taking an early walk and shopping in the drizzle held no appeal either.

'I promised Professor Winkler that I would read through his draft speech to the Entomological Society,' Almeria said, reaching for the marmalade. 'I must confess that I have been putting it off because he does ramble on so. I will just have another slice of toast before I start it.'

'And I am not happy with the chapter I wrote yesterday.' Melissa stared moodily at the tea leaves in the bottom of her cup. 'I don't want to re-read it and discover that it is as bad as I imagine, but I suppose I have no choice in the matter.' She took the remaining piece of toast.

The door knocker rattled and they both glanced at the clock.

'Goodness, ten already. I wonder who that can be.' Almeria dabbed her lips with her napkin and prepared to rise.

'Verity, by the sound of it. No—it is all four of them.'

'I expect they have come to see why you have become a hermit all of a sudden,' her cousin said. 'I will leave them to see if they can extract the truth and go and apply myself to the Professor's maunderings.'

So, Almeria was suspicious of her retreat into her work as well, Melissa thought as Gertrude opened the breakfast room door.

'Her Grace the Duchess of—'

'It is all right, Gertrude, you do not need to announce us,' Verity said, sweeping in with the others on her heels.

'Please bring more tea and coffee through to the drawing room, Gertrude.' Even if they did not want it, Melissa felt she would probably need it. 'How lovely to see you all.'

'Yes, isn't it?' Jane agreed as they sat in a row on the sofa and regarded her with the air of connoisseurs at a Royal Academy exhibition.

Gertrude came in with a tray, set it down and left.

'You are all out and about early.'

'Because we are worried about you,' Lucy said, with

no attempt to lead around to it. 'You have been shut away for a week, we haven't heard a word from you and Lord Henry does not look well.'

'He is ill?'

'I do not think so,' Verity said. She got up and poured herself a cup of coffee and then sat again, stirring it thoughtfully. 'We have only seen him on few occasions. He was at a Drawing Room at the Palace, Jane saw him at an ambassadorial reception—that sort of thing. He isn't going to parties or balls. And he looks thinner to me.'

'I expect he has a great deal of work to do. Perhaps he is to be sent on a foreign posting and is studying the language.' She shrugged. 'Who can tell?'

Thinner? Perhaps he was ill, whatever Verity thought. She tried to look interested but unconcerned and felt she was probably simply appearing shifty.

'If anyone can tell, you can,' Prue said with uncharacteristic sharpness. 'You are his friend, are you not? What is wrong? The gossip has virtually died away, faster than we dared hope. And yet you are shut up here and Lord Henry looks grim.'

'I am writing and the story is going very well. I do not want to stop and be distracted from it. And Henry has his own work. He seems light-hearted sometimes, but his duties are really very serious.'

'So you have not fallen out with him?' Prue asked.

'No. Certainly not.'

The expressions on the four faces opposite reflected doubt, disbelief and concern. Melissa stared stubbornly back.

'That kiss in the inn yard you told us about—there

was more to it than a peck on the cheek, wasn't there? He hasn't taken advantage of you, has he, Melissa?' Jane blurted out, ignoring a hiss of waning from Verity.

'No, it wasn't a peck and, no, he hasn't—whatever you mean by *taken advantage*. I am quite capable of making up my own mind about these matters.'

'You are lovers?' Lucy was wide-eyed. 'I know you always said you meant to take a lover, but we thought you were in jest.'

'No, we are *not* lovers. Goodness, may I not kiss a man without you turning it into a full-scale love affair?'

'Well, no. Not if you do it in public,' Verity said with infuriating reasonableness.

'It was an accident.' Melissa ignored the raised eyebrows and pressed on. 'I haven't slept with him. I mean, I have, but we haven't… He had been hit on the head, I had been punched in the face and we had to pretend to be married. So we were in the same bed. But neither of us was in any fit state to do more than take it in turns to stay awake to make certain the other did not expire in the night of a concussion. Even if we had wanted to. There. Satisfied?'

And then, shockingly, surprising herself, she burst into tears.

'Darling!' Verity went down on her knees in front of Melissa's chair and gathered her up in her arms. 'I am so sorry. We did not mean to badger you, but we are so worried about you. It isn't like you to shut yourself away like this. But if you are working and you haven't quarrelled with Lord Henry, then we quite understand and we will go away and stop pestering you.'

Melissa tried to stop weeping, managed only to give

herself hiccups and finally subsided back in her chair, Verity's handkerchief clutched in her hand.

'You are not,' she managed to say, 'pestering, I mean. And everything is—' She couldn't finish.

'We will go,' Jane said, standing up. 'We are upsetting you. I expect you have been working too long and are exhausted.'

'Yes. No. No, I am not tired. And probably I should make the effort to go out more.'

'Come to call on me tomorrow,' Jane said. 'I am At Home on Tuesdays, as you know. It will make a change from your writing and you will be showing your face in society again. Anyone who calls is likely to be sympathetic. I do not encourage the gossips to feel comfortable, I can assure you.'

'Yes. I will do that.' It would do her good to socialise again and there would be no risk of Henry being there, she told herself. Sooner or later she was going to have to meet him again, but not yet. 'Thank you.'

Perhaps she should write to him. He must be wondering what had happened to her. Or perhaps he had forgotten her… No, she would write, a chatty, friendly note to reassure him all was well and that she knew the gossip had died down.

'Can you tell us about the new book?' Lucy asked. 'Is it another tale of suspense and blood-chilling mystery? Or have you begun on your book for Mr Murray?'

'Neither. I suddenly found myself with the beginning of a story and I have no idea how it is going to end.'

'Happily, I hope,' said Jane. 'With the villain defeated.'

'There is no villain. At least, if there is, he has not

yet appeared. It is certainly not a comedy and I am hoping it will not be a tragedy. It certainly appears to be a three-volume work!'

'How exciting. No wonder you are reluctant to leave your desk,' Verity said. 'We will not keep you from it. Until tomorrow afternoon at Jane's, then.'

Melissa saw her friends to the door and waited while they crowded into Verity's smart town carriage.

She felt better for the tears, she realised, hoping that they seemed to be due to the stress of the unpleasant rumours and not anything more...*painful? Personal?* They began to well up again and she turned around resolutely, went to her desk and found a sheet of letter paper.

Dear Henry,

I thought I would send a note in case you'd wondered whether I had vanished from the face of the earth or was hiding away out of embarrassment after the gossip about our adventures on the road to Birmingham.

The truth is that I have been seized with a story and it is going so very smoothly that I dare not stop lest I lose the thread.

I do hope that the rumours have not compromised your position in any way, although I am sure the intelligence that you have been able to transmit regarding certain people has raised your credit high enough to overcome any amount of dalliance on the King's highway!

I have to confess to missing our adventures, and still smile when I think of the encounter in

the Queen's Temple, but a certain amount of dis-
cretion is the wise course for the moment, I know.
With my best wishes,
M.

Was that too friendly? She read it again and decided that, no, it was not and that to send something stiff and starchy would be hurtful. Besides, no one else would see it and Henry, who regarded her as a friend and nothing else, would read it as simply a note to keep in touch.

She sealed it, wrote the address and, before she could change her mind, rang for Gertrude to have it delivered by one of the lads who hung about in the street hoping for odd jobs.

There, that should keep Henry at a safe distance without offending him and purchase her time to find the courage to face him again without revealing how she felt. Tuesday's At Home at Jane's house would be a pleasant way of easing herself back into society. Something to look forward to, she told herself firmly.

'France,' Henry announced as he met James Herbert on the landing of their apartment on Tuesday afternoon.

'What about it?' James peered at him over the top of a pile of dictionaries. 'Are you going to the sitting room? Because, if so, you can take the German grammar off the top before I drop the lot.'

'Yes.' Henry retrieved the book, straightened the perilously sliding pile and opened the door. 'France is where I am being sent next. Second Secretary at the Embassy.'

'Oh, well done. That's a very good posting and a

promotion into the bargain. Your espionage work has paid dividends.'

'It looks like that. And not a word was said about that wretched gossip.'

James grinned. 'No doubt they either thought it was just that, rumour, or it was true and you are just the man to seduce secrets from French politicians' wives.' He put the books down with a grunt of relief and picked up a letter. 'This came for you yesterday and must have got lost under the papers.'

'Thank you.' He took it and glanced at the address. Not writing that he recognised, but when he broke the seal and opened the single sheet he smiled. Melissa. So that was why he had seen nothing of her: she was writing. That was good to hear and the cheerful tone of the note reassured him. He had missed her company and the way it was so easy to talk to her, the way she appeared to understand him without explanations.

He had missed those sudden, impulsive kisses, too. Missed those too much for comfort, if he was to be honest with himself. At night they had been giving him dreams that were uncomfortably arousing and he kept waking in a hot tangle of sheets with the fading tendrils of torrid reveries. In fact, it was probably a very good thing that he had not seen Melissa recently, because he imagined his face would betray thoughts that were utterly inappropriate in a friend.

The sound of the door knocker echoed up the stairs, then the sound of Mrs Logan, their landlord's wife, answering it.

'Not visitors, I hope,' James said, glancing up. 'I wanted a quiet afternoon working on this.'

But, from the sound of voices below, the callers had been admitted. Surely that voice was familiar? Henry got up and opened the door.

'Hell's teeth, that's my father.'

Chapter Seventeen

'**D**amn.' James gathered up his papers and two of the books and made for the door. 'I'm off.'

He went out and Henry heard him say, 'Good afternoon, Your Grace…sir, madam. Pray excuse me. Lord Henry is in the sitting room here.'

Thank you, James!

Henry could hardly pretend he had not heard that, so he opened the door, resisting the instinctive movement of his hand to straighten his neckcloth.

'Sir. Won't you come in? And your companions? I will ring for Mrs Logan to bring tea.'

'No time for that. This is not a social visit.' His father marched past him as he held the door, followed by a middle-aged lady in a slightly dated ensemble and a stony-faced gentleman with the air of a prosperous country squire about him.

'Will you sit? This armchair here is the most comfortable, ma'am.'

She sat down without a word or a smile.

'To what do I owe the pleasure—?' Henry began

asking, only to be cut off by an abrupt gesture from his father.

'This is Mr and Mrs Taverner, from Dorset,' the Duke said. 'They came to me two days ago with a story that I would have found hard to credit if I had not already heard rumours. Rumours which, at the time, I dismissed as impossible to relate to any son of mine.'

'But which you now find credible?' Henry was not certain how he was holding on to his temper. 'I would be interested to know what fault of character you have observed in me in the past to cause you to believe that I would debauch an innocent lady. That is, I assume, the crime of which I am accused?'

'Miss Taverner is not your mistress?'

'No, Your Grace. Not now, not ever. Miss Taverner is an acquaintance. A friend.' As soon as he said it he knew it was a mistake.

'Friend?' Mr Taverner spluttered. 'Young ladies do not make *friends* of men.'

'Not normally, no, sir.' That earned him a frustrated glower.

'I met Miss Taverner in the company of her friends, among whom is the Duchess of Aylsham, the Countess of Kendall, the Marchioness of—'

'Yes, yes,' Mr Taverner interrupted him. 'All ladies who, while of the utmost respectability, naturally, are somewhat, that is to say, are inclined—' He broke off, having worked himself into a tangle.

'Are inclined to be somewhat independent in their thoughts and actions?' Henry suggested.

'Exactly.' Melissa's father did not seem best pleased at having to agree with him. 'What is suitable for a married lady of high rank is not fit for a single girl of modest estate.'

'Then I am surprised that you permit Miss Taverner to reside in London in her own household,' Henry said coolly. 'Oh, but of course—she is of age and in possession of independent means and is, therefore, her own... mistress. Is she not?'

Mrs Taverner gave a low moan and groped in her reticule. The sharp scent of sal volatile filled the room.

'That does not mean she is without the protection of her family,' his father snapped. 'Mr Taverner is fully within his rights to exercise his parental prerogatives.'

'As Miss Taverner and I are not, nor have ever been, involved in an unseemly relationship, I feel the point is irrelevant, sir.'

'Your name has been linked with that of my daughter,' Mr Taverner stated.

'It has. Ill-natured gossips linked it, not our own actions.' He was skidding on thin ice now and he knew it, but he was not going to allow her father to label Melissa as some kind of fallen woman, or even the victim of seduction. She was blameless and innocent of anything except wanting to help others and of generous affection to her friends.

'So you deny that you and my daughter kissed in some squalid alehouse in Aylesbury where you had lured my innocent child?'

'I deny ever luring anyone to a squalid alehouse anywhere. The establishment to which I believe you refer is a most respectable posting inn. I had been of some small service to Miss Taverner and she was so grateful that, in all innocence, she kissed my cheek. This took place not in some private chamber, but in the public inn yard which, I would have thought, demonstrates just how innocent it was.'

'And what, pray, was she doing in a posting house in Aylesbury?'

'Rendering assistance to a female acquaintance. That is not my story to tell and I must direct you to Miss Taverner for details of the matter.'

'Are you denying intimacy with my daughter?'

'I am, sir, upon my honour.' His conscience felt entirely clear on that point. They had been intimate in that they had shared a bed, a few kisses, some deeply personal thoughts, but that was not what Mr Taverner meant. *Have you taken my daughter's virginity?* was his meaning and the honest answer was, *No, but I would like to.*

'Are you a Roman Catholic?' Mrs Taverner asked suddenly.

'No, ma'am, I am not.'

Hell, how did they find out about that?

'So you deny taking Miss Taverner not only to a Roman Catholic church, but to an actual service?' His father was an unpleasant shade of red. Henry assumed the man was a staunch Whig supporter who regarded the exiled Catholic Stuart pretenders to the throne with deep loathing and fully supported all the restrictions on Roman Catholics in the country.

'No and no. I did both. Or, rather, Miss Taverner accompanied me to a service. This was to assist me in observing the activities of a man believed not to have the best interests of the country at heart. As a humble tradesman accompanied by his sister I was less conspicuous. I can assure you, our adherence to the Established Church of England has not been shaken in any way by the experience.'

'Then you refuse to marry my daughter?'

'I have not been asked my intentions, sir, although the answer is, yes. And besides, Miss Taverner is, I believe, resolute in wishing to remain unwed. As nothing has occurred to make it necessary for her to reconsider, I have no intention of asking her. Perhaps you did not hear my assertion just now, made upon my honour.' He made no attempt to hide his anger. One could not call out a man old enough to be one's father, but a refusal to take a gentleman's word was a deep insult.

Mr Taverner's complexion began to resemble the Duke's and Mrs Taverner was fanning herself with her handkerchief.

'I believe, Mr Taverner, that it would be prudent at this juncture to discuss the matter with your daughter, who, one hopes, can set your mind at rest.' His father was looking grim, but at least had calmed down enough to speak in a conciliatory manner.

'Yes. Yes, I suppose so, Your Grace.' Mr Taverner looked around the room as though half expecting to see some signs of Henry's supposedly rakish lifestyle, then, as his gaze met Henry's, he looked away, down at the table.

'What is this?' He snatched up a single, folded sheet of paper.

'My private correspondence.'

'My daughter's handwriting!' Before Henry could reach out for it Mr Taverner spread open the letter and read it. He thrust it at the Duke. 'Look at this! Dalli-

ance on the King's highway—encounters in temples—
adventures. My poor innocent child corrupted by this…
this rakehell.'

'Every word in that letter has a perfectly innocent
explanation, if you were not so set and determined on
believing the worst, sir. Or, perhaps, so set and determined on securing a title for your daughter, whether
she wants one or not.'

The older man turned pale. 'You have not heard
the last of this.' Taverner crushed the letter in his fist.
'Come, Mrs Taverner, we will see what our daughter
has to say on the matter.' He almost hauled his wife to
her feet and through the door.

Henry found no inclination to see them out. He
turned to his father. 'Is it necessary for me to repeat
that Miss Taverner is a friend, that I have not seduced
her, ravished her or otherwise deprived her of her virginity—or do you accept my word?'

The Duke narrowed his eyes at him. 'Damn it,
Henry, of course I do. You are my son and a Cary. You
would not dishonour your word.'

'How gratifying that you believe that when, after all,
you hardly know me.' He said it lightly, but heard the
echo of bitterness in his voice and despised himself for
the weakness of caring what his father thought of him.

The Duke showed his familiar ability to ignore anything he did not wish to hear. 'Why not marry the girl
and be done with all this fuss?' He waved a hand as
though to dismiss the minor irritations of furious country gentlemen and slurs on his son's good name. 'I had
Nicholls check on them. The man's a blustering idiot,

but they are perfectly respectable, local squires for generations back. It is not as though you are the heir, is it?'

Or the spare, or even the spare to the spare.

'As I reminded her father, Miss Taverner does not wish to marry anyone,' he said, holding on to his temper. 'She is an intelligent woman, in possession of an adequate income to support herself and a respectable chaperon in London.'

'*Pshaw.* What's the matter with her? Plain? Lame? Frigid? Some kind of religious fanatic?'

'Sir, with the greatest respect, I cannot allow you to insult Miss Taverner. If you persist, I must ask you to leave.'

He expected an explosion of temper, but his father narrowed his eyes and, for the first time in many years, Henry had the feeling that the Duke was actually looking at him and seeing a person. 'Quite right, my boy. Even so, you'd do better to bite the bullet and marry the chit, put a stop to all this fuss.'

'What I had best do is go and make certain her father is not bullying her,' Henry said grimly. It occurred to him suddenly that Mr Taverner owned the house in Half Moon Street. If her father refused her permission to live there, locked her out, then Melissa had nowhere to go. He could hardly believe that her funds would permit the rental of a house in such a respectable area and she would not wish to hang on her friends' coat-tails for more than a brief stay.

If he offered marriage with no strings attached, simply his name, would Melissa accept? Then he recalled her angry tears that evening in the carriage when she had poured out her feelings about marriage. What sort of friend would he be if he added to the pressure on her to do the conventional thing?

Instinct told him to go to her now, common sense pointed out that his presence would probably only add to her father's conviction that they were intimate. He would wait.

'I am staying in town for the next few days,' his father said. 'Come and see me when you have resolved this. It should not take long.' The slight softening had only lasted so long, it seemed.

Henry saw him out and sat down to watch the clock.

Melissa sank down on the sofa with knees that had suddenly become too weak to support her.

She heard Gertrude close the front door, then the maid looked around the door. 'Can I get you anything, Miss Taverner?'

'No. Thank you. Has my cousin come home?'

'No, Miss Staines said she'd probably take dinner with friends this evening and not to expect her back until late. Are you all right, miss?' Even in the basement, Gertrude could not have failed to hear the raised voices.

'Yes. My father is always rather…forthright in an argument. Everything is perfectly…fine.'

Everything was a complete disaster, in fact, she thought as the maid closed the door. She had been shocked to see her parents, but pleased with the resolute way she had stood up to them. Even when her father had threatened to evict her from the house she had stayed calm and retorted that she would take lodgings somewhere much cheaper and if that was in a far less respectable area, then that was his fault.

Was Lord Henry's word not good enough for him? she had demanded. He should be ashamed to doubt not only his daughter, but the son of a duke.

'Very well,' her father had said, suddenly ominously calm. 'The rumours may be exaggerated, but there is no smoke without fire, young lady. Your reputation is damaged and that young man is going to make it good. I have his father's support in this. The Duke was deeply shocked.'

She had shaken her head.

'Then we will see what his employers think about that. Does the Diplomatic Service want members who cannot be trusted not to create a scandal? I do not think so.' He had smiled and she had felt afraid for the first time. 'Tomorrow I shall go and tell them just who they are employing. Presumably Lord Henry thinks himself above marriage to a mere gentlewoman. He will find that there are worse things that could befall him.'

As she sat and stared blankly at the closed door, she knew exactly why Henry had refused to marry her: he was being a true friend and honouring the feelings she had expressed so strongly to him. He was respecting her wishes, respecting *her*—and it was going to cost him his good name.

No wonder I love him.

But what could she do? She had no doubt her father would carry out exactly what he threatened and she could hardly arrive on his heels to plead with Henry's superiors to ignore him—their attitude to all this would be even more rigid than her father's. No doubt any number of discreet liaisons would be acceptable, but a diplomat who attracted scandal, fuss and attention would be of no use to them.

Could she appeal to her friends—or, probably more effectively, their husbands? No. That would cause even more upset and Henry would be lucky to escape with any employment whatsoever after that. And it was all because he was honourable enough to be a good friend to her.

The solution, when it came, surprised her so much that she gasped out loud. What would Henry have done if she had not told him how vehemently she did not want to get married? He would have offered for her, of course. His reputation would have been secure, Whitehall would have been unmoved. There might have been a few wry smiles at the expense of yet another man caught in the net of female wiles, but nobody would think the worse of him.

What if I ask him to marry me?

Henry did not want to marry yet, of course. He certainly had no idea of marrying *her*, but would he care so very much? They got on well together, they were friends. That was more than most married couples began with.

No, she could not do it and Henry would not agree.

It grew darker as she sat there, struggling with her conscience, her desires, her fears. As the clock struck six there was a knock at the front door.

Papa and Mama had come back. She did not know how she was going to find the strength to deal with them now.

'Lord Henry, Miss Taverner.'

'Henry! Oh, I am so sorry about all of this.' She found she was in his arms where she must have hurled herself and, blushing, backed away. 'Sorry.'

'Don't apologise, Melissa.' He was smiling, but she knew him well enough to hear the weariness in his voice and also the iron. He was bracing himself for something.

'Henry, I—'

'Melissa, don't—'

'You first,' she said, feeling a coward.

'This is unpleasant at the moment, I know, but please do not worry, I have no intention of offering marriage.'

He was watching her and she knew he was concerned that he had guessed her wishes correctly.

'Thank you.' She bit her lip. *Now what to say, to do?* 'You look exhausted.'

'It has been a long day.' He took a couple of paces across the room, then came back. 'And it started out so well.'

'Come and sit down and tell me. Some good news would be welcome.'

'I went to see Mr Philps this morning and was told that I have a new posting.'

'Where? Is it a good position?'

'Far better than what I feared, which was Constantinople and having to learn Turkish, of which I speak not a word. And certainly very much better than going back to being an under-employed younger son with nothing to do but lounge around town.'

'Henry, do not tease. Tell me.'

'Second Secretary at the Paris Embassy.'

'That is very good, isn't it? I am so proud of you.'

He smiled. 'Thank you. Yes, it is an excellent posting.'

'And now your day has been ruined.'

There was no doubt in her mind now about what she must do. Paris was a prestigious post, which meant it must also be a sensitive one, with a newly restored king on the throne and all the undercurrents that Henry had mentioned when they had been on the heels of von Arten.

At least she did not have to pretend to be anxious and fearful, because she was. Melissa stood up, hesitated and then took the armchair opposite and regarded him from what suddenly felt a rather unsafe distance. How was he going to react?

'Henry, I know what I said before and I meant it, but everything has changed and I feel so… Henry, I think we should get married.'

She had said it and now it could never be unsaid, although by the look on his face he appeared to believe that he was hearing things.

Chapter Eighteen

'Did you just say that we should marry?' When Melissa nodded wordlessly Henry sank back in the chair and stared at her. 'You said that you do not want to marry anyone, ever.'

'I know I did. But circumstances change. We are in a wretched situation now, but if we simply get married—'

Am I doing this because I love him? Yes. But I cannot tell him that. Not ever. Or he will think that is the only reason that I want to marry.

'Simply?'

'You know what I mean. Obviously I am not the kind of wife you would have chosen as suitable for a diplomat, but I can learn. And I promise not to try to have any scandalous books published under my own name. And I wouldn't… I am not your choice and I cannot complain if you want to take a mistress, although I don't exactly repel you, do I? I mean, we kissed and you seemed to like it.'

'Words fail me.' She saw him take a deep breath. 'To get one thing out of the way—if I was married, I would not take a mistress. Secondly, you are not going to compromise your principles simply because our fathers are none too pleased with me at the moment and there is some talk. It will blow over in time. This is not your problem, it is mine and I will deal with it by being firm with both of them.'

Oh, Henry, I do love you and you have forgotten that I was only ever against a loveless marriage...

Somehow she had to convince him that she wanted to marry him and, at the same time, not reveal her feelings for him or that she thought he needed help with his own position. If he saw that she loved him, he would marry her out of pity. If he realised that she was intent on saving his career, then he would refuse out of pride.

'It is just that... I am so scared, Henry.' She put a quaver into her voice, hating how feeble it made her seem. 'I find my principles—if they were ever anything that grand—do not stand up very well to being frightened.'

Henry was protective, she knew that. If he did not realise that she was frightened for him, not herself, that might be enough to win him over.

'Frightened? Melissa, are your parents bullying you?' He came and knelt in front of her and took both her hands in his. Warm, strong hands that she wanted to hold on to tightly.

'Papa has refused to allow me to stay here and I do not have enough money to find respectable lodgings, so I will have to go back with them and I can't bear it and Cousin Almeria will be without a home again.'

'I will help you with rent,' he offered immediately. 'We can find somewhere you and Miss Staines can be comfortable. It might not be a whole house as good as this, I fear, but we will find somewhere decent.'

'I cannot be a charity case, Henry. And besides, if anyone found out, they would say I was a kept woman.' She saw that strike home. It was her turn to take a steadying breath. 'This would save my good name and independence.' She paused, and added as though as an afterthought, 'I would not interfere with your life, I promise. I could ask Papa to give us this house as a wedding present, but you could keep your lodgings in St James's. You needn't accompany me to things, because I've noticed fashionable people don't and they smile at my friends because they do go everywhere with their husbands. And anyway, you will be going to Paris.'

Henry sat back on his heels, released her hands and stood up in one fluid movement that made something deep inside her flutter and, at the same time, unsettled her conscience. Was she doing this because she desired him? Was that distorting her judgement?

No. They were like two wild animals entangled in a hunter's net and the only way out was to cut themselves free, take their enemies by surprise and make a success of whatever this new, unexpected, life would give them.

'If we do this,' Henry said, 'then I swear you will lose nothing that you feared marriage would imperil. Believe me, I sacrifice nothing by this marriage and I gain a great deal. You will live where you wish, you will write what you wish and I will make your money over to you when it passes to me by marriage. What do you wish to do about your cousin?'

He was agreeing? Melissa blinked away sudden tears. 'I believe she would wish for respectable lodgings near the centre of London. Her own finances are just enough for her to live comfortably, provided she does not have the expense of rent as well, but I must ask her. I should not presume to organise her life for her.'

'Very well. You discover her wishes. I shall go to see my father. I am sorry if you do not care for it, but this is going to be a ducal wedding to gladden the hearts of every society matron in London.'

'It is?' she murmured faintly. Somehow she had forgotten the Duke.

'Oh, yes,' he said, eyes narrowed as he worked it out. 'A special licence, an extravagant trousseau, a wedding at the family town house in Grosvenor Square, a large but exclusive guest list, a lavish wedding breakfast and every evidence of the Duke of Walton's entire approval of his new daughter-in-law. Would you hate that very much?' he asked, apparently noticing her parted lips and total silence for the first time.

'You take my breath away. One moment we are cautiously discussing provision for Cousin Almeria, the next you have planned the entire wedding. It sounds wonderful. Terrifying, but you are right, of course, we must give no indication that we have been forced into this by the gossip. That has simply precipitated matters. Our consciences are entirely clear.'

'Well, they are,' Henry pointed out. He smiled suddenly and it was as though a weight had been lifted from her heart. 'That makes a nice change.'

'My conscience is always clear,' Melissa said, teasing. Fifteen minutes ago she had thought she could never tease Henry again.

He held out his hand and, when she took it, pulled

her to her feet, raised it to his lips and kissed it. 'Does a month give you long enough to prepare?'

'Yes. Yes, I am sure it does.' She had no idea, she realised as she said it. All sensible recollections of what had been involved in her friends' weddings seemed to have fled. 'What about Paris? May I come with you?'

'Of course you may. Philps will be delighted at the thought of another diplomatic wife to share the entertaining—if you do not object to the thought?'

I am terrified at the thought! But if Mr Philps is pleased, then he is less likely to listen to the gossip. And surely Papa cannot find out who to complain to about Henry and secure an appointment until tomorrow? But Paris?

She could hardly believe it. Paris with Henry.

'I think I would enjoy it,' she said, trying to sound moderate and thoughtful. 'Why not go and see your Mr Philps now, as well as your father? I will write to Verity and the others because they will know all the things I need to do. Should we go and see Mama and Papa in the morning? Only I have no idea where they are staying.'

Henry, halfway to the door, turned. 'You do not need to go anywhere near them unless you want to. They are at the Bath Hotel in Arlington Street. I will call first thing after breakfast tomorrow morning and inform your father that you have done me the honour of agreeing to marry me. He will want to discuss settlements, of course.'

That would be perfect timing, she thought with relief. 'I will go and see them, but only after you have broken the news, otherwise I may lose my temper and that will not help. And as for settlements, I will employ my own solicitor for that,' Melissa said firmly. 'It is my money, after all.'

'That *will* go down well! I shall come and see you tomorrow as soon as I have broken the good news to your parents.' The smile was back and he took two strides across the room, kissed her firmly on the lips and then walked out before she could do more than gasp.

What had she done? The right thing, she could only hope. Henry seemed to be more than resigned, almost cheerful, in fact. But he was a diplomat, she reminded herself. He had probably been trained to smile and be agreeable under all circumstances, up to and including a declaration of war. And he was a gentleman—she had, in effect, proposed to him. The only thing she could think of that would lead him to refuse her was a prior engagement to another woman.

Would she ever know what he really thought? Perhaps not. He would not lie to her, she hoped, but neither would he say anything he thought would hurt her. She must be careful never to put him in a position where he needed to do either.

Melissa went to her desk, picked up her pen, put it down again. She needed her friends and she needed them now. It was only seven o'clock and she might catch one of them at home. She would begin with Verity.

She found the Duke and Duchess of Aylsham having a rare evening by their own fireside. Young Thomas was teething again and they were both, they announced as all three of them sank into the exceedingly comfortable chairs in the Duchess's small sitting room, exhausted.

'It is all very well, these mothers who tell me just

to leave him to his nanny and the nursery maids, poor little chap. How can they be so heartless?' Verity said. 'But he is sleeping now. So what brings you at this hour? Not that we are not delighted to see you. Can you stay for dinner?'

'Yes, I can, thank you.' Melissa swallowed and then just blurted out her news. 'I am getting married.'

'What?' Verity leapt to her feet. 'Oh, that is marvellous. Let me kiss you. Lord Henry, of course? I knew the protestations of *We are just good friends* must be a smokescreen. Will, send a carriage to Jane, Prue and Lucy, see if they can join us—oh, and the husbands as well because you will need someone to talk to while we plan. Goodness, but this is wonderful. Was it a very romantic proposal? Did he go down on one knee? What did he say? Do you have a ring yet?'

She whirled back to her seat and then her smile faded. 'What is it? What is wrong?'

'It is not at all romantic. We had no choice. Mama and Papa arrived and they had been to complain to the Duke of Walton. Henry refused to marry me because he knew I was opposed to it and so Papa said he would go and blacken Henry's name with the Diplomatic Corps.'

'Oh, no!' Verity looked around for her husband, but he had already gone to summon their friends. 'Perhaps Will and the others can do something.'

'I think that might leave the impression that Henry had done something discreditable and needs defending,' Melissa said carefully. 'He has no idea that Papa was making those threats, but as soon as I heard that his next posting is an excellent promotion, and to the

Paris Embassy, I knew I could not risk Papa damaging that. So I proposed.'

'*You* proposed?' It was rare to see Verity absolutely at a loss, but now she was positively gaping.

'And he could hardly refuse, being a gentleman,' Melissa said, keeping talking because the alternative was to indulge in hysterical laughter. 'Henry has gone to speak to his superior now—apparently they like diplomats to have wives—and will see my father in the morning. There will be no problem, I am certain. But Henry thinks we are marrying because I am afraid Papa will drag me back to Dorset. He knows Papa has told me I cannot stay in the Half Moon Street house. I pretended I was afraid of Papa's bullying,' she admitted.

'So Henry does not know you fear for his career and he agreed to protect you?'

'Exactly. Just imagine how he would react if he realised—please, do not say anything that might make him suspicious.'

'No, of course not. But are you certain about this?'

'I am. And we are both quite content with the match. We have no intention of… It is like most society marriages, only with the advantage that we are friends. It will be perfectly amicable, I have no doubt.'

'But you are— No, I will say nothing until the others arrive. I do not think anyone had any plans for this evening that could not be broken.'

They spoke of trivialities and of young Thomas's teeth and the problem with the new stove in the kitchens that was driving Verity's cook—and, by extension, Verity—to distraction and gradually Melissa felt calmer.

This was the reality of married life, even for a duchess—fractious babies and harassed cooks. She and Henry could achieve the comfortable domestic harmony that Verity and Will had, she was certain of it.

And then Will came in and she saw the intense look that passed between the two of them and knew that here was something quite different. A love match, full of passion that simmered below the calm surface. The thing she could never have.

Jane, Lucy and Prue came in with Will, their husbands behind them.

'What is it?' Jane said. 'What is wrong, Melissa?'

'Nothing at all,' Verity said brightly. 'Melissa and Lord Henry are to marry.'

Melissa saw the looks that passed between her friends. They knew something was not right with that announcement, but they also knew that this was something to be discussed in the absence of the men. They gasped obligingly and came and kissed her and announced how delighted they were.

'Henry wishes to marry in a month,' Melissa told them. 'And I need your help, all of you, if I am to be ready in time. I have so many questions.' All the men looked uneasy. 'But after dinner,' she promised.

Chapter Nineteen

Gertrude answered the door to Henry's knock the next morning and beamed at him. 'Miss Taverner is in the drawing room, my lord.'

'Thank you, Gertrude.' He surrendered hat and cane and wondered just why he was feeling so much on edge.

The interview with Mr Taverner had gone as well as he had expected—in other words, it had been an exercise in biting his tongue and being civil to the man.

I'll make ambassadorial rank after all, if I am this good at keeping my temper, he had thought, then cheered himself up somewhat by informing his future father-in-law that his superiors knew all about the match and were delighted for him. He also broke the news that Miss Taverner planned to employ her own solicitor to negotiate the settlements.

'I'll have you know that the house in Half Moon Street does not belong to my daughter.'

'I am aware of that, sir. Melissa thought it likely that you would wish to give it to us as a wedding present,' Henry said smoothly. 'She likes the neighbourhood.'

'Hah! I suppose your father declined to make you a present of anything.'

'On the contrary, sir. A very neat little estate in Hert-fordshire will be mine on marriage.'

If I were keeping score, that would be game to me, he'd thought as he walked away along Piccadilly.

'Henry.' Melissa jumped to her feet as he entered, scattering papers around her. 'I am so glad you are here.'

He had half expected one of her impetuous kisses, to find her in his arms. More than half expected it, he realised. Anticipated it with some pleasure, if he was honest.

'And I am glad to be here.' He walked to her, bent and kissed her cheek and captured the hand that lifted to touch his face. It brought them close together, so close that Melissa had to tip her head back to look up at him. Her fingers curled within his, smaller, warmer, trusting, and, when he sought her lips, her other hand came round his neck and stroked into the short hair at his nape.

And then she stiffened, pulled away. 'Sit down here on the sofa and tell me what has happened.'

What had *happened* was that she had recoiled just now from his kiss and he knew he could not let that go unmentioned. 'I apologise for kissing you just now. I should not wish you to think that I will take liberties simply because we are betrothed.'

Now she was blushing. He had never seen Melissa blush and look self-conscious before. 'Goodness, no, that is not what I thought at all. It was a very nice... I mean, it is merely that I am so agog to hear what happened yesterday after you left me. And this morning.'

'There was no problem with Philps at the office. He merely congratulated me and said he could recommend a lady who gave private lessons if you needed to improve your spoken French. My father—'

'So I may go Paris? I did not really believe it last night.'

'You need not if you dislike the idea,' he said before the breath was knocked out of him by Melissa hugging him.

The kiss that landed on his lips was anything but restrained, but she pulled back a moment later and beamed at him. 'Not go? To *Paris*? With you? Of course I want to go.'

'Excellent. It will not be until at least a month after the wedding. My father was pleased and surprised me not a little by informing me that a small estate in Hertfordshire would be mine on marriage. I have been there once and I think you will like it. The house is hardly a mansion—seven or eight bedchambers, if I recall—but it is light and airy and the situation is pleasant.'

'It sounds delightful,' Melissa said faintly. Seven or eight bedchambers? How large a staff? 'And Papa?'

'He huffed and puffed and almost burst a blood vessel when I told him about you employing your own lawyer. In fact, when I suggested that this house would make an acceptable wedding present I think he may have popped several buttons on his waistcoat. You can expect a visit this afternoon. I will stay if you wish, but I think it might be less inflammatory if you see him without me on this occasion.' He found her hand and squeezed it.

Again that blush, but she did not pull away this time. 'I agree. I have no desire to be on bad terms with my parents, however it might seem from what I have said.'

'I know. They simply do not understand you.' He gave a gentle tug and smiled as she curled up against his side, her head on his shoulder.

'Tell me what the Duke said,' she demanded.

'As I said, he seems pleased. More at the thought of killing the gossip than anything, I suspect. He fully approves of my plans for the wedding and will send a team of staff down to Lockleys Manor—that is our new country home—to prepare it so we can use it for our honeymoon.'

Was it his imagination, or did she stiffen at the mention of the honeymoon? It did not seem like Melissa to be shy—this was the young woman who had spoken lightly about taking a lover, after all. Perhaps it was simply the reality of the situation that was making her nervous. At least she had that quartet of thoroughly outspoken friends who would make certain she did not come to the marriage ignorant.

'It will give us the opportunity to get used to our new life before we are plunged into another novel experience—Paris.' He hesitated, but he had promised himself that he would be honest with her. 'I have no idea how a normal marriage works, Melissa. I told you that my parents were distant, but we were all distant in a way, scattered through a house larger than some villages.'

'You must have been so lonely.' She wriggled closer, as though to comfort him.

'I had tutors and various instructors. Riding, fencing, shooting and so forth. But I do not want to bring up children that way.' They were so close he felt her stiffen. 'Not that we have discussed such a thing and, of course, if you do not—'

He broke off, realising suddenly that if Melissa did not want children, then things became very difficult indeed. He should have discussed it with her, but there were so many things to decide, things they had never mentioned at all before.

'I think I should like children. I had always assumed that I would not have any, because of not being married, and I did feel that it was no great loss because I never felt much at ease with babies. But Verity and Will's little Thomas is a sweetheart and Ross's Jon, Prue's stepson, is adorable.' She laughed a little, the warmth of her huff of breath just tickling his neck. 'I will probably be a terrible mother, forgetting the baby while I write. I expect they will chew the blotting paper and drink the ink and I will never notice.'

Henry felt himself relax. If Melissa welcomed the idea of motherhood, then, presumably, she was not averse to the physical side of marriage to him, which had not been something that had occurred to him until she had pulled away from his embrace a few minutes before.

'So, we have to learn to be a family of two in plenty of time before the first child arrives,' she said, sounding disconcertingly brisk about it. 'We are both used to sharing our accommodation, which is a beginning.'

'I hardly think that two bachelors sharing an apartment, with no responsibilities other than to pay the rent and throw our dirty linen in the hamper, could be said to be trained for matrimony.'

'I suppose we have to learn to compromise,' Melissa said, sounding doubtful. 'I propose that we try to be completely honest about the things we do not like or which irritate us about the other. Then we can have a civilised discussion and not fall out.'

'That sounds an admirable idea. After all, it might not occur to me that my habit of smoking cheroots in bed could annoy you and your refusal to allow coffee in the house will certainly concern me.'

'Oh!' Melissa sat up straight. 'How ever did you guess that?' she asked.

'What?' Henry twisted around on the sofa in horror and realised that she was teasing him, her face solemn, her eyes sparkling. 'You wretch, Melissa.' He lunged for her, tickling her ribs, and she collapsed against him, laughing and batting at his hands, then, as she recovered her balance, tickling back.

Quite when it turned from horseplay into something quite different he was not sure, but one moment they were tussling and laughing and the next Melissa was lying back against the cushions, his body over her, one hand thrusting into the tumbling mass of her hair, the other braced on the side of the sofa to support his weight.

She looked up at him, lips parted, eyes wide so that he could see his own reflection in them. She was soft under him and he was hard, aching.

Mine, a voice in his head said clearly.

'Melissa.' Question or statement?

She seemed in no doubt which it was. 'Yes, Henry.'

Her eyes widened, the pupils dilated. 'Oh, yes. Please kiss me.'

He found he was not embracing some shrinking, shy girl, but an eager, demanding woman. Her legs parted to bring him closer, her arms were around him and her lips opened under his, her tongue answering his own's every move.

But she is a virgin, the voice of conscience warned him, even as his senses reeled with the warmth of her, the scent of her, the supple body yielding and demanding at the same time. It was a contortionist's feat to get up from their tangle of limbs without hurting her, but he managed it somehow and slid inelegantly to the floor with a thud to sit with his back to the sofa.

He twisted his head to look at Melissa.

She stared back, hair tumbled, lips swollen. 'Oh, Henry. I think we had better practise this on a bed, don't you?'

At noon the day before he had felt as though he would never find anything amusing again. Now, looking into her eyes sparkling with fun, he found himself laughing helplessly and she joined in, curling around so that her arms encircled his shoulders and they rocked together in mirth that was only slightly hysterical.

He sobered up eventually, hauled himself to his feet and, recalling that this was the drawing room in the middle of the morning and that anyone might come in at any moment, sat down in an armchair.

'You do not find yourself shocked by it?' he asked carefully.

'Did I not say I had thought about taking a lover?' She seemed surprised he had even thought to ask.

'The reality is sometimes rather different from what we imagine.'

'For better or worse?' Melissa asked and the sparkle was back in her eyes.

'Better, I sincerely hope.' Henry remembered something that had kept him awake in the night, something he knew they should discuss and which was likely to wipe that smile from her lips.

'Melissa, seriously now, there is something we should speak of.'

She uncurled herself and sat up straight. 'Yes?' she said, wary now.

'We have had no courtship and we have come to this point in a most unconventional manner. Usually a man and a woman finding themselves compromised are already attached—lovers, or in love. Or their engagement is the result of a formal courtship with a clear understanding that theirs is a suitable, convenient marriage and that mutual affection may develop over time. Or, rarely I suspect, couples who are considered suitable matches for each other fall in love and marry. But we have come to this as friends.'

He broke off, searching for the right words to convey his thoughts. 'I suppose our emotional state is closer to the couple who have experienced a formal courtship and found they are able to contemplate life together.'

'Henry, are you attempting to warn me that you are not in love with me and do not expect to be?' Melissa asked with an abruptness that took him aback.

'Yes, I suppose I am. And that I do not have such expectations of you either. I want to be honest because we are friends and perhaps the one thing that will ruin that is if we are less than truthful with each other,' he said, gaining confidence with his explanation as she nodded. 'As you said when we first spoke about your friends, marriages founded on true love are very scarce. Pretence or delusion would only end in hurt.'

'Oh, I quite agree,' Melissa said. For some reason he had a flash of recollection, of the way she had looked as she was separating Harlby from Miss Forrest in that garden the first time they had met: resolved to see something difficult through. 'Have you ever been in love, Henry?'

He shook his head. 'No. I am not certain I know what it is or that I have ever observed it. Have you? Been in love, I mean.'

Melissa blinked and he realised that was probably an exceedingly tactless thing to ask because, if she had, she was not about to marry the object of her affections.

'Yes, I have,' she said after a moment. 'You are aware of the person even when they are not with you. You want their happiness more than you desire your own. They become a part of your soul.'

It was as though the house had gone silent. She did not look sad and yet he felt as though he had caused her pain he could not understand. 'Do you still love him?' he said, because he had to know.

'Yes,' she said simply. 'But he does not love me.'

'Do I know him?' Henry asked, even as every instinct screamed at him to be silent.

'No, I do not think you know him at all,' Melissa said, her smile rueful. 'There is absolutely no need to be jealous, Henry, or concerned. Loving someone does not make one's friends any less important and I swear

I will always be faithful to you.' The smile flickered. 'In thought and deed.'

'Did he hurt you?'

'No. He had no idea how I felt.' She said it quite simply, clearly not asking for sympathy.

His mind was buzzing with questions and he knew he had asked all he could and more than he should. To press her would be stretching friendship too far and he tried, and failed, to imagine himself being as open and honest if the shoe had been on the other foot. The kindest thing would be to forget the subject had ever been mentioned.

They spoke for a while longer about the wedding date, about French lessons, which Melissa decided she did not need because at least two of her friends were very fluent and would help her, and about how long they would have for their honeymoon before they must return to London and prepare to move to Paris.

Melissa got up and fetched a notebook and began to jot down lists and Henry, watching her concentration and enjoying their occasional verbal tussles when they did not agree on something, thought how very lucky he was to be marrying a friend.

He did not have to edge around subjects, he did not have to coax and, in turn, Melissa listened and contributed, argued and was prepared to compromise.

'What about your work?' he asked when they had exhausted every topic on his list.

'Oh, I can write anywhere,' she said airily. 'I wonder if any of the journals would like a column on life in Paris? Quite anonymous, of course. Would the Embassy object, do you think?'

'I suspect they would if you could be identified,' he said. 'So you will simply need to ensure that you cannot be.'

They exchanged conspiratorial smiles and Henry got to his feet. 'I must go. I cannot believe the work that has landed on my desk suddenly. All the briefing papers for Paris, all the French newspapers to wade through and the Duke's estate manager at Lockleys Manor has despatched a positive mountain of documents and maps that he is certain I am agog to read. They are accompanied by a list of questions to which he solicits the favour of my response. I do not suppose that you know anything about land drains, woodland leases or roof repairs?'

'Nothing whatsoever,' Melissa replied firmly. 'And I have a mountain of work as well—you would not believe what is involved in getting married to a duke's son!'

'I am thankful I do not, my lady.' He raised her hand to his lips in a mock-formal farewell. 'I suppose you realise that you will be Lady Henry?'

'I do and I am resigned. After all, imagine if your name was Algernon.'

The sound of her laughter followed him out of the door and sent him off towards Green Park and the footpath to Whitehall with a smile on his lips.

He was happy, he realised. Happy and relieved, which was peculiar, because the last thing he would have thought he wanted was to be married. But this was Melissa, his friend who he also desired. Which, when he came to think of it, should have felt wrong, but didn't. A strange thing, this marriage business. The only thing that lurked uncomfortably in his mind was her admission that she loved another man. He told himself that, as a friend, it ill became him to be jealous of someone, when he would have what the other man could never possess.

Chapter Twenty

Where had the past month gone? In a confused whirl, it seemed to Melissa now, looking back and finding nothing to hold on to. Dress fittings, shopping, endless lists, decisions that seemed trivial one moment—a string quartet to play at the ceremony or a portable organ?—and important the next—exactly how should the settlements be worded?

There had been no time to write and no inclination either. Where ideas had once filled her thoughts, characters had spoken to her and plots had tangled themselves, was now simply a blank.

And most of all, she had missed Henry, who, apparently obeying some peculiar instinct for propriety and tradition that bridegrooms possessed, became distant and formal. More often than not he sent his father's assistant secretary, Mr Nicholls, with messages.

Had she a particular colour in mind for her bedchamber at Lockleys Manor? Was she retaining Gertrude as her personal maid or was she going with Miss Staines, who had announced her intention of moving in with her friend, the widowed Mrs Lethbridge, whose professor husband had just died? In which case should Mr Nicholls send a selection for her to interview?

She had been conscious all the time of Henry thinking of her and what she might need, and she was grateful, of course she was. Only she wanted *him*. It was ridiculous to be brooding about that now when she was standing on the landing of the great staircase of the Duke's house in Grosvenor Square, waiting to walk down and be married to the man. But what if he had changed? What if he was regretting agreeing to marry her?

'Perfect,' Jane said, making her jump as she pushed in a slipping hairpin. 'You are looking lovely. All ready to go, Mr Taverner.'

Her father cleared his throat and offered his arm. Her four matrons of honour—as Verity had pointed out, they hardly qualified as maids any longer—took their places behind, and down in the hallway an alert footman made a sign to the string ensemble to change from the vaguely twiddly music they had been playing to something more purposeful.

For once, mercifully, her father was silent, as he had been ever since they had arrived that morning at the Duke's residence. Her mother had coped much better with the magnificent decoration, the quantities of very superior servants and the ponderous hospitality of the Duke himself, although she at least had been able to occupy herself with supervising her daughter's dressing.

Prue, who had declared herself in charge of hair, had listened meekly to a flow of instructions and then done exactly what she and Melissa had agreed, arranging her coiffure into a simple style to support the truly magnificent tiara the Duke had lent her.

Now Mama would be down with the rest of the guests, accompanied by Almeria, who had secreted a large number of handkerchiefs and two bottles of smelling salts about her person.

Thinking about that got her down the stairs and almost across the hallway towards the open double doors. Then she was inside the great salon and there was Henry.

'What is it?' her father muttered urgently. 'You cannot have an attack of the vapours now, for goodness sake, Melissa!'

She started walking again towards the man who did not look at all like *her* Henry. This Henry had his hair in a ruthlessly fashionable crop and he was dressed in an immaculate suit of deepest midnight blue, his linen a startling white in contrast. That was not new, she had seen him often enough now dressed for formal balls, but then the formality had been offset by Henry's air of relaxed energy, of being on the verge of movement, of laughter and of action.

This Henry stood stock-still, almost rigid, hands clasped behind his back, his face unsmiling as he watched her walk towards him.

Melissa almost turned and ran. She had been relying on Henry's smile, the warmth in his eyes, to give her the courage to make this endless walk and now… And now he was as nervous as she was, she realised as she got closer. He was pale and she guessed that he was clasping his hands behind him to conceal any tremors.

Suddenly she felt better. She lifted back her veil,

ignoring her father's *tut* of disapproval and smiled—
a small, secret, just-between-friends smile—and saw
Henry's shoulders relax, his eyes crinkle as he smiled
back. It would be all right, this was her Henry after
all, his father had not waved some ducal magic wand
and turned him into a pattern book of aristocratic respectability.

After that it was easy to take his hand, to repeat the
vows she had never thought she would say, promising
to love, honour and obey the man beside her.

She had not even noticed the guests as she had entered, she had been so stricken with nerves. Now, on
Henry's arm, she turned and blinked at a sea of faces,
most of them unknown or familiar only from balls and
receptions.

They were probably thinking that she was a non-
entity to be marrying the son of a duke. *Not even very
pretty*, she imagined them whispering. She would show
them, if only because she could not let Henry down.
She put up her chin, smiled her most dazzling smile
and, assuming her best deportment, paced slowly down
the aisle between the rows of chairs, reminding herself
who she was.

*Lady Henry Cary. I rank immediately after Jane
and Lucy and above viscountesses. My goodness, this
is real*, she thought as they reached the door and the
Duke, her new father-in-law, came forward and kissed
her cheek. Then she was surrounded by her friends and
Henry was being slapped on the back by James Herbert, his best man, and Mama was weeping on Papa's
shoulder while Cousin Almeria cast her gaze upwards
and visibly sighed.

I am married to Henry.

He was having to fight to stay at her side as they were swept towards the reception room where the tables had been laid out for the wedding breakfast, so she clung to his arm and found herself whisked sideways, though a door and into a small room. Henry locked the door. 'I have not had the opportunity to say that you look lovely and I could not be more delighted that you are my wife.'

Not as delighted as you would be if you loved me, she thought with a pang, but he was already taking her in his arms and kissing her.

After a moment Melissa wriggled free. 'My hair!'

'Sorry,' Henry apologised, not looking at all regretful.

'We should go out,' she said severely while her willpower lasted. 'Oh, I am so glad we are escaping to Hertfordshire after the breakfast!'

Melissa was still sleeping, her head on his shoulder, as she had been ever since the carriage had left Watford. Henry checked that the rug was still tucked around her and went back to his own disturbing thoughts, the ones that had been circling ever since she had yawned, closed her eyes and given in to weariness, excitement and too much rich food and drink in the middle of the day.

He had made an effort to go and spend some time talking to his in-laws, aware that they had hardly exchanged any conversation since he had informed Mr Taverner that he and Melissa intended to marry. It was not as though he had been avoiding them, exactly, but they had been down to Dorset twice and when they returned had made no effort to socialise. Henry was aware

that he had been relieved by that and that he should
make an effort to build bridges, but the suspicion that
they were keeping well clear so as not to provoke any
upsets that might jeopardise this advantageous marriage annoyed him.

While they were all waiting for Melissa to change
into her travelling outfit he had strolled across and given
Mr Taverner his most diplomatic smile. 'A happy day,
sir.'

'Indeed. I am delighted that the pair of you saw
sense, although I imagine Melissa's powers of persua-
sion were what won out in the end. Her concern for your
career is laudable.'

'What—?'

But his bride was coming down the staircase, surrounded by her friends, her mother weeping happily behind. The surge of guests carried Mr Taverner forward,
away from Henry, who could hardly abandon Melissa
at the foot of the stairs in order to drag her father aside
to demand to know what he was talking about.

The unease was lost in the excitement and bustle of
departure, in the pleasure of being alone with Melissa
to talk about the day and in watching her pleasure at the
passing scene, laughing at her sharp observations on
the people and places they could see from the carriage.

But when she had fallen silent the unease returned.
Melissa had admitted to being frightened by the prospect of the life in front of her if she lost the house and
she was clearly feeling battered by her father's bullying insistence that they wed. That was nothing new,
but that last remark about his career—what was that
supposed to mean?

He shifted his wife slightly as she stirred in her sleep. If Melissa had been worried about the effect the gossip might have on his work, then, surely, she would have mentioned it? He shook his head as though that would help dislodge the circling thoughts. There was one thing he was certain of: he could trust Melissa to be honest with him. Which meant that her irritating father was merely taking the opportunity to dig at him now he was certain that the knot was tied.

The man was not going to get under his skin or into his mind, Henry resolved as the carriage slowed and then turned sharply to the left. He saw a lodge cottage, gates set wide, and then they were passing through a patch of light woodland.

'Melissa, wake up. We are about to arrive.'

She opened her eyes, blinked up at him in the gloom and smiled. Something inside him gave a strange lurch, as though he had experienced a shock.

'What is it, Henry? Have I got a terrible crease down my cheek from sleeping squashed up against you? Or is my hair coming down?'

'Neither. I was just…just enjoying looking at you.'

'That is very gallant when I know I look a fright.' She patted at her hair, then reached for her bonnet. 'I am sorry I slept like that. You must have been bored, especially once it got dark.'

'I had a lot to think about,' Henry said, pushing back at the tendrils of disquiet that still seemed to curl around his mind like mist. For Melissa to have admitted that she was frightened, that her anxiety about the future overrode those strongly held views on marriage, that had taken courage and honesty and he should feel ashamed for puzzling over her motives. She had been his friend and his duty was to protect her, but now she was his wife as well and something more. Something he did not understand.

The carriage came to a halt in front of the house he vaguely recalled, its pleasantly undistinguished exterior illuminated by lights in many of the windows.

'Either we are expected or the staff are having a marvellous party,' Melissa said, just as the front door opened and black-clad figures began to spill out and down the steps. The staff had been watching for them.

'That is Bailey, our butler, and Mrs Dawkins, the housekeeper. You recall I told you that she is a Belgian refugee and the widow of an English sergeant? Four footmen, four housemaids and there's the kitchen staff bringing up the rear with what I assume is the boot boy.'

'Goodness, I hope they have not prepared a vast supper, I am still recovering from the breakfast.'

'I wrote and warned them that a cold supper upstairs would be all that was required,' Henry said. The carriage door swung open and he jumped down before the groom had a chance to fix the step. 'Now, my lady.'

Melissa was tall, but slender, and he caught her so much by surprise that when he reached in, lifted her out and then up into his arms, she could do no more than give a faint gasp.

'Thank you, everyone,' he said as he climbed the steps past the startled faces of their new staff. 'We will meet you all in the morning, but for now, after a very long day, I believe that our supper awaits.'

'Yes, my lord. All is as you directed,' Bailey said.

'My lady's woman arrived some time ago and is up-stairs.'

'Thank you.' Henry carried on walking over the threshold to the applause of the staff, and straight through the hall and up the stairs.

'Henry! Put me down.'

'Are you suggesting that I am too feeble to carry you, my lady?' If truth be known, he was regretting setting such a brisk pace, but it was only one flight of stairs. He grinned at himself—it would be ironic if a ridiculously romantic gesture resulted in him straining a muscle on his wedding night.

'Not at all, but I do not want you to put your back out,' Melissa said primly, with her disconcerting habit of echoing his thoughts. There was a thread of laughter under the words.

He reached the landing and walked towards the only door that stood open. 'Here we are. This should be the shared sitting room between our bedchambers.'

Gertrude, Melissa's maid, came out of one of the connecting doors as he set his wife on her feet. Henry suppressed a groan.

'Good evening, Gertrude. Are you comfortable in your new quarters?' Melissa was already shedding bonnet, pelisse and gloves into the maid's hands.

'Very, thank you, my lady.'

'I shall not require you further tonight,' Melissa said.

'Your nightgown is laid out, my lady and there is hot water—'

'Thank you, Gertrude,' Melissa said firmly. 'That will be all.' Her ears, he saw, were rather pink, although her voice was perfectly composed.

'My lady.' Gertrude bobbed a curtsy. 'My lord.' The door shut behind her with a solid click.

Melissa was not certain which of them moved first, but hardly had the door closed than she had her back to it, her arms were entwined about Henry's neck and he was kissing her like a man who has found water in a desert.

She had thought herself weary after a long, emotional day, but now she had never felt so awake, so alive. Now she could show Henry that she loved him, even if she could not say the words.

There had been moments when she had allowed herself to imagine what this might be like. Embarrassing, tentative, slow, she had assumed. This was none of those things. Clothes were being pushed and tugged, buttons popped, something tore, but they were coming off. Henry's coat had gone, she realised as her hands encountered the softness of linen shirt sleeves. There was a sudden draught on her shoulders as her bodice slipped from them, then on her legs as her skirts crumpled to the floor.

Henry's neckcloth came away in her hands. He tossed aside his waistcoat and began to drag his shirt over his head. He emerged tousled, wild, urgent and they stilled, staring at each other until Henry took her hand and began to back towards one of the bedchamber doors. Candlelight flickered in his eyes and made the bare skin of his shoulders and chest gleam.

'I had meant to take this slowly. Very slowly. Carefully.'

'I would much rather that you did not.' What was she

wearing? Melissa could not drag her gaze from his, but she thought all that was left were her corset, her chemise and her stockings. Far too much.

They were through the door now. The candles were lit here, too, and the big bed loomed behind Henry, very old, very masculine, with its crimson hangings and carved oak posts, but he kept going until his back was to one of the posts.

'Shall I snuff the candles?'

Melissa shook her head, suddenly too shy to say *I want to look at you*, even though it meant that Henry would also be looking at her at any moment. She pulled her hands free and turned, presenting him with the tightly knotted laces at her back, half expecting him to take a knife to them.

Everything slowed. She felt him working on the knot, his breath warm on her nape, the sudden relaxation as he freed it, then the hiss as the laces were pulled through the eyelets and the corset fell away over her hips. She breathed out, a long, luxurious exhalation, then caught her breath as his hands slid round and cupped her breasts through the filmy chemise, his thumbs fretting at her nipples.

'So sweet,' he murmured against her neck, 'so eager to be free.'

Instinct made her arch her back, thrusting against his palms as the fire of his touch burned down through her belly, down to where the ache was building. 'Henry.' She twisted round and he released her, his fingers working at the fastening of his breeches. Then he was kicking them away and she had only a fleeting, fascinated glimpse of him as he lifted her again, carried her to the bed and laid her down.

'I think you may have the right of it,' he murmured as he knelt beside her, bent to kiss her. 'Fast may be best. We can always slow down later.'

Nothing was making any sense and yet, deep down inside, it was all just as it should be. Her thighs parted and somehow that was perfect as his weight came over her. She curled up to meet the exciting hardness of him, then gasped as he touched her intimately, stroked and murmured encouragement as she gasped and yearned beneath him.

That hardness again, a discomfort that made her gasp and almost recoil, then sudden fullness, rightness and the end of any coherent thought as they became one, found a rhythm and fought together to ride the twisting, tightening sensation that was lifting them.

Henry's hand slipped between them and, as his caress pushed the building pleasure inside her beyond the point of bearing, she cried out and heard his answering shout as she was falling, falling, into pure sensation.

Chapter Twenty-One

Henry drifted back into awareness, eyes closed, his body blissfully relaxed as he sprawled over gently moving softness. Something was stroking his back, gliding up and down, feather-light, deeply comforting.

He inhaled a long appreciative breath of warm female, rose scent, the musk of lovemaking and realised where he was.

'Melissa?' He opened his eyes and found himself almost nose to nose with her.

'Mmm…?' Her eyes were closed as her hand continued its slow caress. 'Henry?'

'Who else might it be?'

He stiffened, suddenly remembering that she might have had a vision in her head of that other man, the one she loved. Then she chuckled, making her body move tantalisingly under his, and opened her eyes and the look in them was for him, only for him.

'That was…surprising.'

'I am squashing you.' He rolled to one side and then gathered her in against his body.

'I don't mind. I liked it. You feel interesting.'

'Interesting *and* surprising?'

'Aren't I supposed to say things like that?'

'You can say anything you like to me.' Her eyes flickered and then her gaze was steady on him again. 'Are you all right, Melissa? I understand it is painful the first time.'

'There was so much happening, so much to feel,' she said, wriggling back a little, apparently to see him better. 'It did hurt, I think, but not for long.' Her lips curved into a small, secret smile. 'It was worth it. May we do it again?'

Yes. Oh, yes. 'Not that, exactly. Not tonight,' he said regretfully. 'It is too soon, you will be sore. We will wash, have some supper, a little wine, come back to bed. If you are not too tired, then there are other things.'

Her eyes, midnight-dark, opened wide. 'That sounds intriguing.'

'Oh, I hope so,' he said as he slid off the bed and went in search of his dressing room.

Marriage, Melissa concluded after a week, was not at all what she had expected. What happened in the bed-chamber was far better than she had dared to hope and certainly much more interesting—the word that made Henry snort with amusement whenever she used it—than she had imagined.

She had thought she would be shy with him when they were not in bed, but miraculously, he was her friend Henry again except for a fleeting touch, a lingering look and those long silences when he seemed to be brooding over something.

She told herself that he had a great deal on his mind. There was Paris to prepare for and the novelty of this estate with its eager steward, Mr Gregory, a man bursting with questions and explanations. It was no wonder that Henry was preoccupied and it was not as though she did not have a great deal to do herself.

There was the novelty of managing a household of more than two servants, although it was clear that Mrs Dawkins could run everything blindfolded. She did an excellent job of pretending that she needed Melissa's decisions on numerous matters and obliged by carrying out all their conversations in French. Whether this was going to leave her with a Belgian accent Melissa did not know or care; fluency was her chief concern.

Then there was a long list of messages of thanks for gifts to be sent and letters to be dispatched to Cousin Almeria and her friends in London and in Dorset. Over breakfast on the first morning Henry had told her not to expect calls from their new neighbours for at least ten days because it would be known that they were on their honeymoon.

Melissa had nodded and murmured something about tact and understanding and filled up his coffee cup in what she hoped was a suitably wifely manner. She hoped she had hidden her disappointment, because meeting some new people, and perhaps making friends, would have been a welcome distraction from the hollow feeling inside her.

Whatever had made her think that marrying a man she loved, but who did not love her, would be a good idea? When they made love she had constantly to worry that she might say something, do something, that would reveal how she felt about Henry. For the rest of the time she had to resist her need to touch him, to look at him, to tell him that she loved him.

When she tried to write, things became even worse. She found she had lost the thread that was guiding her through her new story, the one she had been so pleased with. Writing about a woman who was in love with a man she could not, in honour, be with, had somehow been an outlet for her heartbreak over Henry. Now, married to a man who, if he had been able to exercise choice, would never have wed her, she found herself lost as she tried to put herself into her heroine's shoes.

Putting it to one side and picking up *The Rogue Lord of Castle Darke* again felt equally impossible. Writing melodrama and exaggerated emotions had been fun, now she simply could not focus on constructing the plot. For the first time that she could remember Melissa closed her notebooks and pushed them into a drawer.

Henry came in as she stood up from the desk and lifted her right hand, innocent of ink stains, in his. 'Not writing? Does it not go well?'

'It does not go at all at the moment,' she admitted because she had promised herself to be as honest with him as she could. 'Too much change too quickly, I expect.'

'I would have thought that you could write on the deck of a ship in a hurricane,' Henry said, his frown at odds with his bantering tone. 'I have seen you scribbling in your notebook as we lurched along the highway in pursuit of Harlby and jotting notes on the edge of your dance programme at balls—and do not tell me those were fashion observations, because I will not believe you.'

'Everything has changed,' she said. 'I will find my inspiration again soon, I am certain.'

'I hope so,' Henry said and frowned. 'It is not like unicorns, is it?'

'Whatever can you mean?' she asked, half laughing, half puzzled.

'You know—they can only be captured by virgins.'

'If virginity is essential for inspiration in novel writing, then I would not like to speculate on the married life of Sir Walter Scott, for example. That would be most improper.'

'True,' Henry said, pretending to recover from deep anxiety. 'I would hate to think I was responsible for stopping you writing.'

'Of course not,' Melissa said and laughed. It didn't sound quite right, but Henry did not appear to notice. 'Now I must go and find Mrs Dawkins. We are surveying all the kitchen equipment with Cook—in French. At diplomatic dinners in Paris I may not be able to contribute much on international relations, but I will be able to inform everyone about the latest styles of coal-fired ranges.'

'That will be an enormous help,' Henry said lightly and took her in his arms. 'Tell me,' he added, suddenly serious. 'Are you happy, Melissa?'

'Yes, of course I am,' she said and smiled against his lips as he kissed her.

Something was wrong. Henry watched Melissa as she left the room, giving a sudden backwards glance over her shoulder as she left.

She admitted to not being able to write and now she

was lying to him. She was *not* content and he knew her well enough now to be able to tell. Was she unable to write because she was unhappy? And what was at the root of it? Did she realise now that she had made a mistake in putting aside all her strongly held arguments against marriage? Or was it simply that she yearned for the man she loved but could not ever have?

He sat down at her desk and studied the perfectly clean blotter, the neat stacks of paper, the dry pen nib. Melissa had told him she wished to marry because she was frightened. Now he no longer believed that. Her father, although naturally a blusterer, had no real power over her, he could see that now. And if her nerve had been severely shaken by that first encounter, she had had plenty of opportunity to change her mind. Men could not withdraw from an engagement, but ladies could, and Melissa had the nerve to say what she thought, how she felt.

But she had not. She had not wed him for ambition—he knew perfectly well she cared nothing for her new title and status. Nor for gain—he had never once heard her bemoan her financial situation or express envy of her well-off friends.

Mr Taverner's disturbing words at the wedding breakfast came back to nag at him again. *'Her concern for your career is laudable.'*

Had Melissa thought his position was somehow jeopardised? Surely he had said nothing to make her believe it might be. Mr Philps had made no comment when the rumours had begun to swirl and he was never reluctant to send a sharp note and a demand for an interview if one of his young men displeased him. Clearly he ignored gossip.

But what if someone told him that the rumours were true and that Henry had seduced a well-bred virgin and was then refusing to marry her? What if a furious father presented himself at Philps's office, threatening to make a scandal? The diplomatic situation in Paris was still delicate. The King was only recently restored and his court was touchy about his status, still smarting from the various unkind, although in Henry's opinion well-deserved, slurs on his intelligence, character and general ability to rule. Send them a diplomat trailing scandal and accusations of a loss of honour in his wake and they might well see that as a slight. Would Philps risk that? Probably not. But how would Melissa know that?

Henry pushed back from the desk. Minutes later he found himself on his front steps, hatless and with no very clear idea of how he had arrived there. It was raining. It always seemed to be raining that year, except on a certain sunny Saturday in April. Somehow, with Melissa, that sunshine had never left him, however dank the weather. Now, careless of mud and puddles, he strode off across the carriage drive and towards the small park, conscious of nothing but the need to get away and to think.

'Henry! There you are, I was becoming concerned.' Melissa jumped up from her seat at the table in the dining room and came towards him, shaking her head in reproof. 'You are soaked—goodness knows what Yarrow is going to say.'

He had no interest in his new valet's opinion and that must have shown on his face, because Melissa's smile faded.

'It is only a cold luncheon. Shall I send down for some soup to warm you?'

'No.' He realised they were not alone. 'Thank you.'

A jerk of his head was enough to send the one footman in the room out.

Melissa narrowed her eyes at him, but stayed silent until the door was closed. 'What is wrong?'

'I had thought that you would never lie to me. It seems I was mistaken.'

She did not ask him what he meant, thank heavens. He was not going to have to deal with excuses and more lies. Melissa remained where she was, one hand resting on the back of a chair, her eyes fixed on him.

'You knew that, if you asked me to marry you, that I would without hesitation, didn't you?'

'Yes. I knew I could rely on your honour, the fact that you would always protect me.' Her chin was up, but it was not defiance she was showing, he realised, it was a stubborn refusal to break down.

'You can stand up to your father, whatever he threatens you with. You refused to be cowed when you decided to move to London, because you knew he would bluster and bully and then give in when he got nowhere. You knew that, with your cousin and the advice of your friends, you had sufficient resources to find good lodgings, even if they were not as excellent as the Half Moon Street house.' He waited and Melissa nodded, a jerk of her head.

'So why did you tell me you were frightened? Why

did you pretend that you could not stand firm, all of a sudden?'

Her lips tightened to a thin line and he saw her knuckles whiten, but she did not speak.

'It was because your father threatened to go to Whitehall, to blacken my name with my employers, was it not?'

'Yes.' She was so pale now that he thought she might faint. 'And, yes, I lied to you.'

'You thought I needed to hide behind a woman's skirts?' He found himself so angry that he was shaking.

'No. I thought that it was due to me that my friend would have his career ruined through no fault of his own and that I was in a position to prevent that.' She swayed where she stood and Henry took a step forward, but she made an impatient gesture, twisted and sat down on the nearest chair.

'You could have talked to me, told me what he was threatening, and I would have dealt with it.'

'That would have brought the potential scandal to the notice of your Mr Philps, would it not? And you thought I was strongly opposed to marriage, so you would still have refused to offer for me and things would only have become worse.'

'So you sacrificed yourself? Did you think I would want that?'

'I knew you would not. I knew you would hate it.' She was on her feet again, vehement, fierce.

'Then why the hell did you do it? Because your heart had been broken over this man you say you love?'

She went white. 'Because it is what people do when they— When a friend is in trouble.'

'You have put me in an impossible position.' There was a ringing in his ears and an almost irresistible urge to fling out of the room, get away from her. Or from himself.

'When you, a man, go against your own best interests for the sake of honour, that is the right thing?' she demanded. 'But when I do it, I am putting you in an impossible position? That, Henry, is sheer hypocrisy.'

'It is my duty to protect you,' he said flatly.

'Such cold things, male duty and honour. Things of the head. It is not like that for women. For us it comes from the heart.' She turned away. 'I made a decision that I thought was for the best. It is too late now to change anything.'

Too late. That was the truest thing she had said. He had lost his friend and had a wife in her place. A wife who did not want to be married. A wife who saw what mattered most to him as something cold and hard. He walked out without another word.

For better or worse...until death do us part. There was nothing left but to make the best of things.

He wasn't hungry. The footman came past bearing a tureen, but he ignored him and kept going into his study. It was dark, cool and its desk was stacked with work in preparation for Paris. Melissa had considered that posting more important than their friendship, so he supposed he had better get on with it. Get on with the rest of his life.

There was no point in crying over it. But willpower somehow did not appear to stop her eyes burning and her handkerchief becoming sodden. She had too much sense to weep because of a decision she had made for the best, one that she knew might rebound on her, Melissa told herself and blew her nose. She was not weeping, she had caught the under-housemaid's cold, that was all.

Henry was angry, she understood that. And he felt betrayed and she could sympathise. But that did not help her see a way forward to any hope of happiness. Their marriage would be like that of his parents: distant, without trust or understanding, two people legally locked together.

Drearily, she went up to her room.

When she went down again, much later, Bailey was in the hall.

'Have you seen Lord Henry recently?' she asked, hoping her voice did not give her away.

Vain hope—the servants always know what is afoot.

'His Lordship is in his study, my lady. I believe he has been there all afternoon. I did venture to enquire if he would care for some tea and he intimated that he did not.' The butler stared fixedly at a point over her right shoulder.

'And what exactly did His Lordship say?'

'He suggested that I remove myself and invoked… that is to say…'

'He told you to go to the devil?'

'Yes, my lady.'

'Thank you, Bailey.'

That was not like Henry, to shut himself away and

sulk. Or was it? They had not been married much more than a week. She eyed the closed study door warily, approached and, with a rapid glance to make certain that Bailey had gone, put her ear to the panel. Silence. But the doors were so well made he could be holding an orgy in there and she wouldn't hear.

Melissa raised her hand to knock, then changed her mind, eased the handle, cracked open the door and looked in.

Her husband was asleep, slumped over his desk, his head on his folded arms. And she realised, peering through the shadows, he was still wearing the same clothes that he had been that morning.

She cleared her throat. There was no response so she walked in and put her hand on his shoulder. 'Henry.'

He woke, jerking upright. 'What the—?'

'No, you will not wish me to the devil,' she said briskly. 'If you have caught the under-housemaid's cold, made worse by getting thoroughly soaked and chilled and then not changing, then it is entirely your own fault. I will tell Yarrow to have a bath prepared.'

'I am perfectly—'

'If you do not wish me to lie to you, Henry, then you will not lie to me. You are tired and damp. You might wish to catch pneumonia, but it would make a great deal of trouble if you do.'

Whatever he had expected—wifely fussing, perhaps—it was not this. Henry stood up, gave an abrupt nod and walked out.

Melissa pulled the bell and, when Bailey appeared, asked him to see that hot water for a bath was sent up immediately and Yarrow despatched to his master's dressing room. Then she went to consult with Mrs Dawkins on the subject of cold remedies.

Best to be prepared, because the man she loved was not going to be a good patient, she was sure of it.

Chapter Twenty-Two

He was damned if he was ill, Henry thought as he soaked in the steaming tub and listened to the unmistakable sounds of female fussing going on in his bedchamber beyond. He had become chilled, that was all, and even if it were not, a cold in the head was no reason to take to his bed.

If Melissa thought she could prove that she was a good wife by overreacting like this, then she was wrong.

Yarrow came in and dropped a muslin bag of something into the bath. Herbal aromas rose from the steaming water. 'Coltsfoot and mint, my lord.'

Old wives' remedies, Henry thought mutinously, although the scented steam was curiously soothing. He would give it a few minutes more.

When he got out it was to find that Yarrow had warmed the towels and that distracted him enough for a nightshirt to be over his head before he could bat it away. It would give those confounded women something to think about, he thought, waving aside the proffered robe and walking into the bedchamber. The fire was lit, there were the visible humps of hot bricks in the bed, but no females.

'Time I was dressing for dinner, Yarrow.'

'Her Ladyship said you would be eating in your chamber, my lord.' The valet indicated the table set by the fireplace. 'She intimated that she would also be dining alone as she did not wish to catch the cold.'

'Give me my robe.' Confound the woman. He had not got a cold. Yes, it would have been sensible to have changed and bathed soon after he had got so wet... Ah, of course, this was an excellent excuse for eating separately while they both recovered from that scene in the dining room.

He shrugged into the robe, sat by the fire and realised just how bleak he felt, although he was no longer chilled and he was certain he was not unwell.

No, it was Melissa. He was angry with her and he hated that. His pride was dented, he could admit it. But he did not understand why she had not just told him what her father had planned. And he did not comprehend why he felt so bereft now.

The flames in the hearth twisted and flickered and he fell into a half-doze, half-trance, watching them. Things could never be the same again now he had thrown her gesture back in her face, however justified he felt himself. He had ended their friendship. How could that be so painful when they had only known each other for little more than two months?

'They do say there is such a thing as love at first sight,' she had said in the course of that first walk on that misty morning in Green Park. *'But I do not know about friendship,'* she had added dubiously. But she had

been wrong about that and he had been right to say that one had an instinct for a friend.

There was more than friendship between them, of course, he told himself. There was the physical attraction, the wonder of finding how compatible they were in bed and the constant warmth of desiring her. How were they to find that again?

There was a pain in his chest and he rubbed his clenched fist over it, but it did not ease. *Heartsick, that's what you are*, he jeered at himself. *Broken-hearted.*

The implications of the thought brought him fully awake, staring open-eyed at the flames.

You love her, you fool. You are in love with Melissa. In love with your wife. That is why this breach hurts so much, that is why making love with her is different from anyone else before.

Henry sat and let the knowledge wash over him, work through him, until he found he was smiling. Then he laughed and fell back in the chair sobered again. He loved Melissa, which was unexpected and wonderful. But now what?

Did he go and tell her? What did he say? *I love you, so it doesn't matter what you did?* But it still did, because he could not understand her. *I love you and I desire you and let's go to bed and make up?*

Oh, yes, the voice of reason jeered in his head. *It is likely that she would forgive the things you hurled at her, rejecting her sacrifice in marrying you.*

How about, *I love you, so forget that other man?*

Yarrow came in followed by a footman with a tray and made up the fire while the footman set out the food. The kitchen staff, knowing that he had missed eating luncheon, had sent up a substantial meal. There was a bottle of claret, a good rich soup, a chicken fricassee with rice and a dessert under a cover.

He stared at the spread without appetite, but ate most of it, knowing that starving himself was not going to help. Then he lifted the lid on the dessert and found a lemon tart. It was small, elaborate, perfect and decorated with shavings of chocolate. Someone had laboured over this.

He recalled a conversation over luncheon one day. What would they each want for their last meal if the hangman was waiting outside the door? Melissa had decided upon peaches, ripe, warm and juicy. But he had named a chocolate and lemon tart, something she had never heard of, she said. Sweet and bitter, dark and sharp and delicious, he told her. And she had remembered.

Peace offering or reproach? Neither, Henry realised. Melissa did not think like that. She was concerned that he had made himself unwell, so she had chosen a dinner for him with care and had added something she knew would tempt him.

She still cared for him, he realised.

And I love her. So how do I discover whether she might possibly feel more for me than a somewhat strained friendship?

'Lord Henry rang for Yarrow at seven, my lady,' Gertrude reported the next morning. 'And Yarrow says His Lordship intends coming down for breakfast. He does not think he has caught the cold,' she added as she slid the final pin into Melissa's hair.

'He deserves to,' Melissa said, making a joke of it. It would not do for the servants to know just how deep the sudden rift was between herself and Henry. 'Men think they are indestructible.' In the mirror she saw Gertrude's brisk nod of agreement.

Henry was in the breakfast room, inspecting the dishes laid out on the sideboard, when she came down a few minutes later.

'Good morning. I understand you have escaped the cold.'

'It would seem so. May I bring you a plate?'

'Some eggs and a slice of bacon, please.' Melissa sat down, shook out her napkin and smiled her thanks at the footman when he put a teapot beside her. 'Thank you, Peter. We will serve ourselves.'

Henry sat down as the footman left. 'That was a very pleasant dinner you sent up last night.'

'Yes, we are lucky in our cook.' His tone had been neutral, but she felt uneasily as though Henry was leading up to something.

He buttered some toast and cut into the sausage on his plate, sending appetising odours wafting towards her. 'I appreciated the lemon tart.'

'I noticed that morning that Cook had a big bowl of lemons and when I was wondering what dessert you might like if you had lost your appetite a little, I ordered that. We found a recipe and I believe she was quite pleased with it when it was finished.'

'That was thoughtful.' He carried on eating and so did she, puzzled and a little apprehensive.

She had woken that morning with an uneasy sensation of dread and then remembered what had happened. She had lost Henry's friendship and perhaps all hope of real happiness in their marriage. Now she sensed he was on the verge of making some announcement. That he no longer wanted her to come to Paris with him? Could that be it? And if it was, would she protest or give way? She pushed her plate away, her appetite gone.

Henry put down his cutlery and said abruptly, 'Yesterday, that was my pride talking. I resented having a woman come to my rescue. I did not think why you did it, only that it was my duty to protect you, not yours to sacrifice so much for my sake. For friendship. I was wrong.'

'It was not a sacrifice,' Melissa said softly, hope struggling to the surface. This was not forgiveness, this was an acknowledgment that he had been wrong. 'It was not for friendship,' she added, almost in a whisper.

He did not appear to have heard her. 'I spent a difficult evening and a worse night trying to understand myself, thinking with my heart, not my head. It hurt that I thought I had lost your friendship. It still hurt when I thought how I might repair that because, by then, I had realised that if I could not hold your friendship then I had no hope of you ever coming to love me.'

'Love you?' Was she still asleep and dreaming? Had she caught something worse than a cold and was hallucinating? 'You wish that I loved you?'

'I love you,' he said simply. 'I never realised it, until I thought I had lost your affection and any hope you might come to love me some day. I know you love someone else, I know you may never be able to forget him, but I had to tell you how I felt.'

'Oh. Henry.' She found she was on her feet, stumbling around the table towards him. And he was standing, too, holding out his arms, and she fell into them even as her hip caught the edge of the table and dragged off the cloth, sending everything crashing to the floor around them.

'Henry, I never can forget him and I will always love him because he is *you*. There was never anyone else. Ever.' She looked up, lifted her hands to caress his face as he stared at her, shock and hope chasing incredulity away. 'Only you, my love and my husband. I thought it was hopeless, that you saw me as a friend and nothing else, and I was too much of a coward to risk losing your friendship by letting you guess.' She managed a smile, although she felt her lips tremble. 'I thought you would pity me.'

He gasped. 'Pity you? When I was desperate for you to take pity on me and love me just a little?' Then he was holding her so tight that she could hardly breathe, saying, 'I love you, I love you,' into her hair. Then, 'I was so blind.'

Melissa was aware of the door opening behind them, a sharply indrawn breath, then it closed again. 'Henry.'

'Yes?'

'I can't breathe.'

'Sorry.' He released her, then seemed to notice the wreckage of the breakfast table. 'What on earth?'

'I think the earth shook,' she said, torn between laughter and tears of joy. 'Someone came in, but then they fled again. We cannot leave this for the staff, it isn't fair.'

They picked up the unbroken things, scraped spilt sugar and splatters of preserves on to plates, made a heap of what was broken and gathered the rest up into the tablecloth. There was a tentative tap on the door and when they called, 'Come in!' John, the footman, appeared, rather red about the ears.

'I'm so sorry,' Melissa said. 'I tripped. Please apologise to the staff for me.'

'Um… My lady, you have marmalade on your skirts. And, my lord, your left leg. It looks like the mustard.'

'Oh, dear,' Henry said, so brightly that she almost dissolved into laughter again. 'I think we had both better go upstairs and change. Thank you, John.'

'I think we need more privacy for this discussion,' Henry said as they reached his bedchamber door. 'Ah, Yarrow. That will be all for now. Take the morning off.'

'My lord?' He glanced between them. 'Thank you, my lord.'

When he had gone Henry turned the key in the lock and just looked at her. Melissa looked right back and what she saw made her heart stutter in her breast.

'I realised that I loved you in the cloisters at the Abbey,' she told him. 'I was so jealous of Isobel Duncombe and I realised, all of a sudden, why. I couldn't tell you, dare not let you guess.'

He nodded. Made no move to come closer. 'I can imagine. What if I had been kind about it, pitying? Unbearable.'

'But you did not know I loved you when you told me just now,' Melissa said. 'You are braver than I was.'

Henry closed the space between them and took her hands. 'I told you that I did a great deal of thinking last night. I realised that you must have made that decision to marry me very rapidly in the time between your father leaving you and my arrival. A friend would have warned me and tried to help me find a way around the situation, but you were thinking with your heart, weren't you? I hoped I was right, that you had forgotten that other man and that you loved me and so you made a sacrifice unhesitatingly.'

'Loving you, it was not much of a sacrifice,' she said, threading her fingers through his.

'Yes, it was,' Henry said, gathering her in close. 'I would never have realised it until I knew myself in love and realised what it is like. You were faced with marrying someone you loved, but who did not love you in return. That must be hurtful every hour, every day.'

'It was better when we were in bed,' she murmured against his chest and felt him catch his breath.

'I should have realised then that we loved each other.' He lifted her and carried her towards the big four-poster. 'It was never like that for me before.'

'Were there many *befores*?' she asked.

'Not so very many. Enough to tell the difference with you.' Henry stripped off his clothes and she followed suit, grimacing as her fingers encountered the marmalade on her skirts.

'I am all sticky—' was as far as she got before he was beside her on the bed, bending to take her fingers between his lips, sucking off the sweetness with unmistakeably lascivious intent.

But when she twisted beneath him so she could look up into his face he released her hand, his expression softening into a tenderness that spoke directly to her heart. 'I love you, Melissa.'

She had always been greedy for his touch, eager for his possession. Too eager, she realised now as Henry began his slow, sensual wooing of her body, his hands lingering, his focus intent, it seemed, on exploring every inch of her skin. She let her own hands travel over him, scratching smooth skin, tangling in coarse hair, delighting in finding new places that made him close his eyes when she caressed them.

'Too much,' he gasped as her fingers closed around him. 'Now, Melissa. Take me.'

And she opened to him, arched up as he surged within her, kept her eyes wide, her gaze locked with his as they drove towards the peak and then, finally, fell with him into the light and the dark and the whirlpool.

Perhaps three hours later they lay in each other's arms, quiet and still at last, listening to the rain hammering against the window panes.

'I used to envy my friends, although I would have died rather than admit it,' Melissa said, turning to wrap her free arm over Henry's chest. 'I wanted love and thought I would never have it, so I told myself not to care.'

'And I believed it was some kind of foolish romantic dream, not reality. Not something that could ever happen to me or that I would know how to deal with if it did.' Henry reached out and pulled across a coverlet, the softness of silk settling around them. 'Marriage stopped you writing, didn't it?'

'Marriage, when I believed I was not loved, stopped me,' she admitted. 'Anything with deep feeling was too painful and anything frivolous was just that—frivolity I was in no mood for. I can write again now, I know I can and I will finish the book for Mr Murray, *and* I will continue to write my Gothic tales.'

'Good, because I want to read everything you have written, or will write. We can find the laughter again.' Henry trailed his fingertips over the most sensitive, ticklish part of her ribs, making her giggle.

'And the friendship.'

'Love and laughter and friendship. That sounds perfect to me,' Henry said. 'Oh, and chocolate tart on a regular basis. And making love at every opportunity.'

'I think you may have worked out the flawless recipe for marriage.' Melissa sat up so she could kiss him better.

'It will need work and practice,' Henry said thoughtfully. 'I propose that we apply ourselves to it for the next sixty or so years and then we may be perfect.' His smile twisted, became something altogether more vulnerable, more serious. 'Is it possible to love anyone more than I love you?'

'Or I you? We will find out, my love. My friend. My heart.'

* * * * *

If you enjoyed this story, be sure to read the first four books in Louise Allen's Liberated Ladies miniseries

Least Likely to Marry a Duke
The Earl's Marriage Bargain
A Marquis in Want of a Wife
The Earl's Reluctant Proposal

Afterword

Henry's Favourite Chocolate and Lemon Tart

Chocolate was more often used for drinking than in recipes at this time, so I thought this tart—a variation on lemon meringue pie—was unusual enough to have appealed to Henry.

It comes from *The New London Family Cook: Or, Town and Country Housekeeper's Guide* by Duncan MacDonald, who was head cook at the Bedford Tavern and Hotel, Covent Garden, in 1812.

> Rasp a quarter of a pound of chocolate, and a stick of cinnamon; add to them fresh lemon-peel grated, salt, and sugar. Take two spoons-ful of fine flour, and the yolks of six eggs well beaten and mixed with milk. Put these into a stewpan and let them be a little time over the fire. Then take it off, put in the lemon-peel cut small, and let it stand till cold. Put it into a puff paste, beat up enough of the whites of

eggs to cover it. When baked, sift sugar over, and glaze it with a salamander.

A salamander is a very hot circular grill.